Hood Consigliere 2

Lock Down Publications and Ca$h
Presents

Hood Consigliere 2

A Novel by *Keese*

Lock Down Publications
Po Box 944
Stockbridge, Ga 30281

Visit our website @
www.lockdownpublications.com

Copyright 2022 by Keese
Hood Consigliere 2

First Edition October 2022
Printed in the United States of America

This is a work of fiction. Names, characters, places, and incidents either are products of the author's imagination or are used fictitiously. Any similarity to actual events or locales or persons, living or dead, is entirely coincidental.

Lock Down Publications
Like our page on Facebook: Lock Down Publications @
www.facebook.com/lockdownpublications.ldp
Book interior design by: **Shawn Walker**
Edited by: **Tamira Butler**

Stay Connected with Us!

Text **LOCKDOWN** to 22828 to stay up-to-date with new releases, sneak peaks, contests and more…
Thank you.

Submission Guideline.

Submit the first three chapters of your completed manuscript to ldpsubmissions@gmail.com, subject line: Your book's title. The manuscript must be in a .doc file and sent as an attachment. Document should be in Times New Roman, double spaced and in size 12 font. Also, provide your synopsis and full contact information. If sending multiple submissions, they must each be in a separate email.

Have a story but no way to send it electronically? You can still submit to LDP/Ca$h Presents. Send in the first three chapters, written or typed, of your completed manuscript to:

LDP: Submissions Dept
Po Box 944
Stockbridge, Ga 30281

DO NOT send original manuscript. Must be a duplicate.

Provide your synopsis and a cover letter containing your full contact information.

Thanks for considering LDP and Ca$h Presents.

Keese

Prologue

The inflatable motor boat was untied from the fairly large, dark-colored yacht. Two of the three occupants shoved the small steering wheel and throttle with the key in the ignition. With the instructions, the boat's motor coughed and sputtered to life. The captain of the small boat steered away from the yacht, on which all lights and engines were turned off, and toward the shore that was less than five hundred yards away.

As planned, the three of them rode in complete silence, watching the sea around them, as well as the land ahead, with the high-tech infrared goggles they had been given. The boat moved at a pace that would not draw attention to the sound of the motor. While one occupant navigated the boat, the other two checked their silenced weapons.

There was a job to be done!

The three of them all dressed alike. Dark-colored, rubber scuba gear, in case one or all had to swim back. Their heads were covered with rubber hoods, not so much as to keep their hair from getting wet, but to keep from leaving any forensic evidence at the place where they were to engage the target. Their shoes were waterproof, and the only accessories they wore were holster clips that were strapped around their waist bands. One of the occupants checked the time on a waterproof glow watch: 2:43 a.m., western time. So far, everything was going as planned. The task at hand should be an easy hundred grand in each of their pockets.

And though the occupant with the watch wondered why the price for such easy work had been so high, he never expressed his curiosity. Besides, his mama didn't raise a fool! Easy money was the best money.

Twenty-two minutes later the boat hit dry, packed white sand, and the two passenger occupants raised the boat's motor out of the water. The captain checked a handheld GPS locator and looked to the left, up the beach. All the houses were widely spaced out, some with private decks, and huge in size. Malibu, California. The home of wealth and pampering! Just as predetermined by the captain of the big yacht, they had beached the motor boat a quarter of a mile away from the intended target. Again, without words, the three occupants checked their weapons before taking off, at a slow jog, west. It was time to earn their keep!

***

Such a privilege it is to watch an angel sleep, Sunami was thinking to himself. He sat in cozy armchair, watching his daughter as she slept in a crib/small bed. Her stringy but curly black hair lay perfectly, bright caramel skin as soft as, if not softer than, the finest silk. Rain was the spitting image of her mother, except for the nose she had inherited from her father. Sunami could do nothing but adore her.

Rain was quite an elegant little lady, Sunami reflected as he traced her frame with loving eyes. At just over a year old, she already had plenty to say!

Well, most of it was gibberish, but it was entertaining all the same. She could already perfectly pronounce "daddy" as well as "da-da." Sunami had insisted to everyone who was surprised that it was because she was a daddy's girl, by nature. She could also say mommy, mama, gan-ma (which stood for grandma), car, and baby.

A smile curled Sunami's lips as he thought of his daughter's birth and how she had gotten her name. He had been in Chicago on business when his wife Hypnotic's water had broken. Luckily, Sunami's mom had been hanging close to her in the final stages of the pregnancy. By the time Sunami had gotten the call and had a plane ready, Hypnotic had gone into labor.

At the hospital, in Los Angeles, Sunami changed into scrubs and was led into the room where Hypnotic had been pushing with all her might! She had looked crazy as hell, Sunami remembered fondly. An hour and a half after he arrived, his newborn baby girl came into the world. The doctors and nurses allowed them a little time after the baby had been cleaned. Then came the conflict.

"What are you going to name her?" Sunami had asked.

"I thought we agreed that you were going to name our first? Don't you remember?" Hypnotic asked sweetly.

"Yeah. But I think you should do it. You've just gone through hours of labor bringing her into the world, you deserve to name her."

"Baby, don't start. I didn't even pick out names because you were supposed to do it!

"Bae, it ain't that fucking hard to come up with a name. Just name her!" Sunami said, irritated.

Before Hypnotic could really show her ass, the lead doctor came into the room. He noticed the strained faces and the father's mother holding the baby.

"So...who's going to name this beautiful young lady?" he asked cheerfully.

Sunami and Hypnotic both looked at each other, giving the other the eye to speak up. There was a moment of strained silence before the three of them spoke at once.

"Me, dang!"

"Me, dang!"

"Me, damn!" they said simultaneously. Laughter filled the room as they tried to ease the tension. The doctor wrote on the notebook he had in his hands. He looked up, then, inquiringly.

"Will that be McKnight or Wright? And how do you want it spelled?" he asked business like.

"What?" Sunami asked.

He realized that the doctor had taken their answer to his question as the name for his daughter. Then he realized that the name would, indeed, fit. So, before the rest of them caught on to the doctor's mistake, he answered, "That'll be Rain. And her last name will be Wright. It sounds a lot better than Rain McKnight. What you think, baby?"

***

The memory had Tsunami smiling as his heavy eyelids began to close. The past five nights he had slept, like this, in the armchair in his baby girl's room. He just couldn't get enough of her joy.

Her smile, laugh, and the smell of baby powder made him want to be around her all the time. Like his older daughter, Brianna, she intrigued him with her almond brown, chinky eyes and excited laughter. Sunami wanted to cherish this alone time while Hypnotic was getting back to work. She would be flying back from New York tomorrow. Sunami would be going on his first solo tour in two more weeks. It would be short, but still. Being away from his daughters for three months, so soon, was almost unthinkable. Especially with the unidentified threat still lurking from last year!

Though he often tried not to think about it, Sunami knew that the people who had kidnapped his daughter knew people that killed people for that bag. Sunami's mind struggled to focus as fatigue overcame him. His daughter had worn him out! He tilted his head and drifted into the land of rest. He almost didn't feel the buzzing of the large handheld remote control in his lap as it vibrated, long and hard. Sunami shook out of his snooze and wondered what the hell had awakened him. Then he realized that the silent alarm, the remote, was telling him that a door had been opened in the house!

The house he had bought in Malibu, California, had come with so much cutting-edge technology, Sunami had had to bite.

And for what he was paying, it was sure worth it. He assumed, unconsciously, that Hypnotic had gotten home early. *But...wouldn't she have called me to pick her up?* he wondered.

Still not really alarmed, Sunami pressed a button that brought the television in Rain's room on. He pressed another button that brought the view of the front door camera to the screen. There was nothing! Sunami switched cameras a couple times until he came to the back door. There!! Three dark-clothed individuals with masks, guns, and goggles.

"In the house?" Sunami whispered to himself.

The thought of the danger to his daughter sent a burst of animal-like adrenaline and a super dose of fury into his bloodstream. With cat-like stealth movements, Sunami turned the TV off and left the room, not making a sound. He cleared the upstairs hall from his daughter's room to his room in less than a second and a half.

In a secret compartment made inside his closet, Sunami studied the rack of illegal guns, knives, and other artillery. He picked up a 10-millimeter block fitted with a red laser beam. "Too loud," he said to himself, sticking the gun into his waistband. Sunami chose a razor-sharp K-Bar army knife and nodded his head. He turned the light off in his walk-in closet and vanished from his bedroom. It was showtime!

Keese

Chapter 1

The hired hit team made its way into the lock-picked back door of the extravagantly expensive, fully furnished beach house, after disconnecting the phone lines to the house. Just a precaution in case an alarm connected to local police. Anything else, they could handle. They just needed time to kill everything breathing inside the house. Those were their orders. "Handle every living, breathing thing inside that house." Their employer had been very specific.

The leader of the team, the one who navigated the boat to shore from the yacht, took in the sight of the exorbitantly spaced kitchen and living area through the goggles, which made the view a bright red. Even in darkness, they could see the layout of couches and chairs, large-screen plaza televisions, paintings, and hardwood floors. They advanced through the area, ever alert, but not noticing the dime-sized camera cleverly blended with the rare, expensive painting Hypnotic had bought in Paris, France, for eighty-something thousand dollars!

The three of them came to a halt, silently, in front of the stairs leading upstairs and the hall beside it leading to three of the house's five bedrooms. According to the blueprints they had studied, the house was a five-bedroom, three full-bath, two half-bathroom, two-car garage house, equipped with a gym, whirlpool tubs and showers, and a recording studio in the attic. Net worth, three point six million dollars.

All that money, the leader thought, and they had just cut the phone lines and lock picked the door to gain entrance. What a waste! But, they had no way of knowing of all the electrical gadgets and high-tech security systems that had come with the price tag! They would soon find out.

The leader signaled one of the three to continue down the hall and the other to follow as they made their way to the second level. The assassin who had the ground level silently advanced on the first room, which was on the right. The door was open and offered easy enough access. Stealthily, he entered the room only to find a room full of designer clothes and shoes for women! There was a large vanity table with a huge mirror and lights, but the lights were not on. He quickly checked the room before leaving to go to the next room. Bypassing what was obviously a half bathroom, the assassin advanced to the next room with a closed door.

In the pitch blackness of the bathroom, Sunami's intense stare followed the man as he waited to be spotted. He had planned on throwing the knife into the man's forehead before gunning down the next two, if need be. But, surprisingly, the assassin went to the next room without so much as a glance in Sunami's direction. He was oblivious to the immediate threat. Just the way Sunami liked it! Sunami emerged from the darkness, behind the masked assassin.

Dressed in cotton, gray sweatpants with the strings tied tight around the pistol he carried, soft cotton socks, and a tank top, Sunami eased up behind the assassin as quietly as the wind caressing his skin.

As the assassin tried the knob on the door, Sunami quickly wrapped his big hand over the man's mouth and violently stabbed him in the throat, below the Adam's apple, crushing his windpipe with the eight-inch knife, disabling the assassin from making a sound! The next stab went into the heart, and Sunami twisted the handle of the knife as the warm blood poured on Sunami's hand from the two wounds. The body went limp in his hold, and Sunami drug the body to the bathroom floor from which he had emerged. One down, two to go!

**

Upstairs, the two assassins separated to check the rooms on the upper level. The leader was first to find Rain's room and sensed that someone else was inside. There was a hint of masculine scent mixed with the smell of a baby. The leader quietly stepped back to the hallway and looked in both directions, seeing only the back of the other assassin as he entered the room. Temporarily satisfied, the leader turned back to attend to the task at hand. It was going to be a shitty job, morally, but somebody had to do it. She didn't notice the dark shadow pass behind her, in the hall.

Sunami had taken the stairs quietly but with the speed of light after checking all the rooms downstairs.

He saw the thin frame of the assassin in his daughter's room and was, again, filled with the hatred of the devil himself. But he had also seen the back of the bulkier assassin as it entered a room two doors down. It was the room that held his punching bags and other fitness equipment. He advanced upon the bigger target first, knowing that it wouldn't take him long to dispose of him.

Sensing movement from behind, the assassin whipped his head around, spotting Sunami. But it was already too late. Sunami capitalized on his surprise before the assassin could even raise his weapon. With a swift movement, Sunami sliced the man's throat and shoved the knife into his temple, causing the assassin's bladder to release. Before the man touched the floor, Sunami was back in the hall.

Rain was awakened by somebody lifting her out of her crib. As her eyes opened to focus on the creature holding her, amusement outweighed fear and sleepiness at the sight of the masked face with weird-looking goggles. The assassin reached for the gun she had holstered upon picking the baby up. She was sure that she heard the sound of her partner's gun and a body dropping to the floor.

"Daddy?" Rain wondered aloud. The assassin's heart almost skipped a beat at the thought of killing a child so young. But, then again, it had to be done. Orders were orders.

"I'm here, mama," a deep voice said from behind her.

The assassin automatically whirled around to see the voice that had spoken.

Surely, it wasn't one of her men. Sunami stood in the doorway, gun in hand, aiming for the center of the assassin's goggles!

"Lay her back in the crib and step away," Sunami commanded, barely able to contain his anger. Or was it fear?

"You won't shoot while I'm holding your daughter," the female assassin said, voice soft and heavily accented. "You wouldn't want to make a mistake and hit her, would you?"

"Three seconds," Sunami said, without concern for the assassin's argument. He would definitely drop her as she held Rain. There was absolutely no question of his marksman skills.

Sensing his thoughts, the assassin slowly lowered the baby girl back down into her crib. She was wondering if she would be quick enough to grab her gun and fire. Mentally, she kicked herself for being stupid enough to put it down in the first place. And there would be no way to unholster the gun in a fast manner because of the length of the fitted silencer. Damn!

By now, Rain was going crazy! She stood at the rail of her crib, bouncing up and down while laughing and calling her daddy.

"Pow! Daddy, see? Pow, Daddy, pow-pow!" Rain exclaimed from the bed.

"Yep. Pow, baby," Sunami said affectionately. He flicked the lights on, causing the assassin's sight in the goggles to distort into a blinding bright-red blur. He knew this would force her to close her eyes inside the goggles, giving him the opportunity he needed.

The assassin felt the gun being taken from her holster as Sunami's gun rested against her chin. Suddenly, the goggles were ripped off and she could see again. Her heart thumped tremendously. She could see certain death in the deep brown eyes of the target, whose name she never even knew. He stared back into her brown eyes with pure hatred. The gun was removed from her chin as he went to snatch off her mask.

Quickly, she back-handed Sunami in the throat while he was distracted. Then, she grabbed the arm with the gun, twisted it, and tried to break it with her knee! The gun fell to the floor, but Sunami's arm remained intact. He managed to reverse the twist, but the dark-skinned female kicked him full-fledged in the balls! He dropped to his knees as the assassin made a dash to the door. Sunami reacted swiftly, picked his gun up, and tilted it in her direction, letting off two loud barks. The sound startled Rain and she began to cry in fear. The assassin lay in the doorway, struggling to crawl through. Ignoring Rain for the moment, Sunami came upon the assassin and rolled her over. She was chocolate brown with a short haircut. Her lips were full, and Sunami thought she was actually kinda cute. She was either African American, Haitian, Jamaican, or pure African. Which, he couldn't tell. The accent had confused him.

"Who hired you?" he asked.

The assassin stared at him without saying a word. She wasn't dying, he had only shot her behind both kneecaps.

Sunami pointed the gun at her head.

"Who hired you? I'll let you live, but tell me who hired you."

The assassin looked away. How could she give up her employer? That wasn't loyalty. But, even if she was sent to prison in this country, the boss would have her killed anyway. There was no way to get out of it. She was as good as dead.

"Obidiah MaTimbu," she said.

"Who?" Sunami asked.

"His name is Obidiah MaTimbu. I will tell you nothing else," she said with finality.

"Thanks!"

Sunami blew the front of her skull wide open! Assuming the phone lines were cut, he used his cell to call the Malibu police as he tended to a scared Rain. He set the scene up before the cops arrived and went to make a call to his right-hand man. He had to inform York that there was a new enemy on the rise. And he wanted to find out about him. As big as his crime family was now, he was sure that it'd be taken care of. But first, he had to calm his baby down.

***

"Play that back for me, Malik," York said from inside the recording booth.

Malik, the recording engineer at Hit Factory in Manhattan, nodded and pressed a button on the large board in front of him. He and York had recorded three songs already and this was the last verse and voiceover for the last one. Malik didn't know what time it was, but he knew he was bone tired. York, even while drinking merrily and smoking like a house on fire, was a fucking work-a-holic! And a perfectionist, to say the least.

But Malik was in no mood to complain. He charged five hundred an hour for his time!

While York was waiting on the play back, he lit the half blunt that had gone out. *This would be, what?* York wondered. *My tenth blunt? More?* He wasn't sure. He just knew he'd been smoking heavily all night. Checking his yellow-gold Franck Mueller, York saw that it was ten minutes after three in the morning. He had been in the studio since eight the previous evening. Surprisingly, he wasn't all tired. Must be the Red Bulls he drank along with the Patron Silver. He damn sure was feeling a bit sluggish, though.

The door to the soundproof room burst open, and York was a half a second away from smacking whoever it was who had the audacity to enter his domain without knocking first. Then, he saw it was his queen, Pam, and she looked about ready to smack him! "C'mon, baby. We've been here all night. I'm 'bout ready to leave," Pam said, anger evident on her face.

"Hold on. I'm almost done. As soon as I get this last one straight, we're gone, okay?" York said.

"Why in the world are you making us stay up here while you work? The house is twenty minutes from here, baby. Nothing is going to happen. At least not with all the security and guns you got! We gone take a cab to the house, okay?"

"A cab? Hell no, Pam. You not putting my daughter in no fucking cab. You might fuck around and get in the car with the enemy. Fuck DAT. Speaking of which, where the hell is my daughter, anyway?"

"Ms. Cindy got her. She's asleep. The same thing I wanna be doing right now. Sleeping!" Pam said.

"I told you about leaving my daughter by herself with that white lady, girl. I don't even know why you want a damn nanny, anyway, and a gotdamn white lady at that. I dunno what the fuck is wrong wit' you," York scolded.

"She's a good lady, York! Look...I'm not about to get into this with you. Just hurry up, okay? We are ready to go."

"Gone and take the car, then. But take Raquel with you. I ain't 'bout to let nothing else happen to you, ya hear me. And I damn sure ain't 'bout to let nothing happen to my daughter."

Pam sighed in frustration as she left the booth. Nothing had happened in almost a year since the car incident in New York. Come to think of it, it had been more than a year. The shit was over with, she thought. And had York not been fucking with drugs, that shit wouldn't have happened to her. But did she blame him for it? Even though he had lied to her and kept the drug organization he and Sunami had a secret, she still didn't blame him for putting her life in so much danger without her having the slightest bit of knowledge as to why it was happening. But now that York had finally left it all alone, she was sure that whoever had been after them before, was no longer after them now. Sunami, maybe. But not them. They were safe.

Pam made her way to the mastering room and opened the door to find Malik sitting behind the board as the beat and lyrics of York's new song pounded out of twenty-something different speakers. He was nodding his head. York's cousin, Raquel, was sleeping on a black leather sofa behind him with her face in her hand. *York is exhausting them*, she thought. Malik looked over to the opened door and turned the music on the speaker down.

"What's up, Pam?" he asked.

"Hey, Malik. Just came to get Raquel. I'm going home," Pam said.

"Oh. Okay."

Pam shook Raquel, who startled awake. Her face held confusion and sleepiness as she focused on Pam.

"C'mon, take me and my baby home. Baby is gon' catch a cab or some other transportation," she said, handing her the keys to York's Range Rover. Raquel gladly followed. She was ready to go too.

***

York gave Malik the thumbs up for the last track. It was exactly how he wanted it, and now they were done.

"Go 'head and master that shit, fam. That's grade-A Wolfpack music, right there," York said.

"You want me to drop you off at the crib?" Malik asked.

"Sure."

York's phone rang as he was collecting his things from inside the booth. He cleaned up his mess after every session instead of letting the cleaning company do it. Besides, it was his studio. If he didn't care enough to take care of it, why should anybody else? He answered the call, seeing that it was Sunami calling him.

"What it is, cuz?" he said.

"Slow motion. Look, I gotta ask you a question," Sunami said, getting to the point.

"What's up?"

"Who the fuck is Obidiah MaTimbu?"

"I'm not sure, why?"

Sunami explained everything that had taken place in the past hour at his home in Cali. When he got to the point of asking the woman assassin, York's memory started to come up with a few sketchy news articles he had either heard or seen on the news. The name sounded familiar, but he didn't want to give Sunami any wrong info.

"Look, just tell me where I should meet you, cuz," York said.

"Let me put a few pieces together first. But get ready to make moves soon. Hypnotic is on her way back now. But I gotta go. The police here."

"Okay. You already know what time it is, yo," York promised, mimicking his older brother, Outlaw. Always trained to go.

Chapter 2

As the morning sun shed light over all that was beautiful in Malibu, Hypnotic stood on the front porch of her vocational home, holding a very active and playful Rain, who was excited at seeing her mommy. The tears that rolled down the naturally beautiful design of her face were not of sadness, but of frustration. She watched as the MPD and medical examiners moved about, investigating the home invasion and attempted murder of her husband and daughter. Hypnotic knew, also, that they were investigating the "self-defense" of her husband's actions!

Sunami stood in front of the house, on the street, by a Malibu police officer who was questioning him at length. Sunami had told them his story four times already. He was beginning to get pissed off.

"So, how did you manage to stab two of them and shoot one of them Mr. McKnight?" the deeply tanned officer asked, again.

Sunami could tell by his manner that this was the officer's first time dealing with such a violent event. He had the scent of an officer who hardly ever had to touch his gun for any reason other than putting it away before bedtime and putting it back on for work.

"Again, I was attacked in my room. I managed to stab the guy..."

"You did a lot more than that! But, continue," the officer said.

"As I was saying... I went to grab a gun and go check on my lil' girl. When I entered, I jumped. The gun was loose and we fought for it. I got it back, and shot the girl running, while the other man made it downstairs.

"The girl produced a gun after I shot her legs and fired at me. I shot her in the head. Then, I went downstairs and got into a shootout with the other guy. I ran out of ammo and I think he might've, too. I tried to make my way toward him and he surprised me. We fought and I killed him. End of story," Sunami said.

"And what a bogus story it is!" the officer pointed.

"What?"

"Look, I don't take bribes, Mr. McKnight."

"I never...Ah! How much?"

The officer checked to see if they were being watched or if anybody was within hearing distance. He lowered his head and put his hand over his mouth and coughed.

"Five thousand," he said.

"Number where you can be reached?" Sunami asked, not at all surprised.

The officer handed him a card with his name, rank, and numbers on it.

"Six o'clock, sharp. Starbucks at the Malibu Pier. Got it?"

"See you then," Sunami said.

"Well, Mr. McKnight. I hope you're okay, and we will do everything we can to find out who is responsible for this. The report will be filed," the officer said in a loud voice.

Another officer appeared from the side of Sunami's house. He came toward them and pulled the officer that was questioning Sunami to the side.

"Ralph, this looks like a hit, to me," the officer said, calling Detective Ralph Baker by his first name.

"Don't you mean an attempt? The guy, McKnight, slayed these guys! And from what I hear, the feds are on the way. McKnight's gotta violent rap sheet as long as an elephant's truck!"

"I was told that. But anyway, some of the guys found a motorboat down a ways on the beach. Local residents claim they have never seen it before and it doesn't belong to them. Think we should call the Coast Guard to check out there? Maybe they came from another boat, or something."

"Naw. It'll be the feds problem, soon."

A black Lamborghini Gallardo roared up the street and pulled in behind Detective Baker's patrol car. A tall, muscular, dark-skinned man jumped out of the driver's seat while another smaller brown-skinned man hopped out of the passenger side. The look in their eyes was evident. The two men made Baker shiver unconsciously!

"Excuse me, guys! This is a crime scene, you can't—" Baker started.

"Shut the fuck up. Where my nigga Sunami at? Sunami! Hey, Sunami!!" the smaller one called.

Sunami had momentarily joined Hypnotic and Rain to make sure they were doing okay. He saw Animal drive up with Zahir. He didn't know that Zahir would come acting a fool from jump street! Already, cops had their eyes on the two of them.

"I'll be back, Hypnotic," Sunami said, heading toward his two wolves.

The detective, along with two other uniformed officers, had formed a blocking wall between the house and Animal and Zahir. Sunami could just hear Detective Baker talking when Zahir got irritated.

"Bitch, you better get the fuck out my gotdamn way, yo! You don't know who the fuck you fucking wit', do you? Huh?" Zahir yelled, angrily.

"Chill, Zahir." Animal was trying to calm the situation before it turned into something totally out of control.

"Naw! Fuck chilling, yo! My nigga called and told us to come. I ain't 'bout to be held by these fake ass rent-a-cops. I'm the Graveyard General, muthafucka! I'm already dead."

Sunami stepped between the two forces and told the detective to back off. He could see that they were ready to take action against Zahir, and he could also see two bulges on Zahir's waist and one on Animal's! This was definitely not going to happen out here.

"Zahir, fall back, bruh. Y'all go and talk to Hypnotic while I holla at the detectives, real quick," Sunami told them.

Zahir, wearing a diamond-encrusted chain with a charm shaped like two crossing AK-47s, mean mugged the police a little longer. He wore a white fitted T-shirt and some Dior jeans and Air Force Ones. His hair was freshly cut.

Animal started toward Hypnotic to check on his niece, Rain. He hadn't seen her in a month. Animal wore a Louis Vuitton T-shirt, faded thousand-dollar jeans, and ice cream sneakers. His chain was modest, but the watch and bracelet he wore looked like carved blocks of ice! The Lambo sat on twenty-two-inch, black Lexani LT-706 rims. Sunami turned to the detective.

"Look, these are my brothers, man. Do yourself a favor and leave that tough guy shit at the station, ya dig? These ain't ya ordinary Malibu regulars. Muthafuckas will hurt you out here," Sunami said.

"Is that a threat?" Baker asked.

"Nope. Just useful information, that's all."

***

After making sure he wouldn't be needed for anything by the police, and before anybody else could show up, Sunami told Animal and Zahir that they were going to talk down at the modeling agency that Sunami and York co-owned. The agency was called Baby Girl Models, Incorporated. Animal and Zahir took off while Sunami showered, changed, and spoke with Hypnotic.

"What's going on, baby?" she asked.

"I'm planning on finding out, soon. Are you going to be okay for a little bit?" Sunami asked.

"Sure. Rain is going to C-R-Y when you L-E-A-V-E," she said, spelling out the words so Rain couldn't understand.

"She'll be fine. I gotta eliminate the problem before it blooms. I hate bringing this shit around her and Brianna. She actually watched me shoot that bitch today."

"Bitch! Bitch, Daddy," Rain said, mocking Sunami.

"Don't say that, Rain. Mommy will give you a spanking, okay. No bad words," Hypnotic scolded.

"She's too smart for her own good. Anyway, the reporters are already showing up, baby. I gotta get out of here. Sorry I couldn't welcome you home the right way!" he said, winking.

"There will be plenty of time for that, hunny. Go do what you have to do, okay? Just take care of it. Did you lock the gun case in the closet?"

"Yep. I think we have a new problem on our hands, bae. The three of them were African, I think. Their accents sounded crazy, and they were black as hell!"

"Is that a news helicopter?" Hypnotic asked, looking into the bright sky. Sure enough, a news helicopter circled the house as it lowered to get a better view. Reporters were starting to call out more loudly with their questions.

"Okay, I'm gone. Keep your cell on, okay. I'll call you." To Rain, he said, "Be good, Rain. Daddy's gotta bounce for a minute."

"Noooooooo! Daddy, Noooo! No bye-bye!!" she cried.

Sunami made it to the garage and slid into the sleek, black Ferrari Spyder two-seater. The engine growled and lowered the hum. Sunami pressed the high-pitch horn, motioning for bystanders to get the hell out his way. He pressed a button that folded the roof back as he pulled out and onto the street. He punched the gas pedal and the sports car disappeared like a shadow!

***

Sunami parked his Ferrari beside Animal's Lambo in the private parking spaces reserved for staff. He made his way into the building and found it as busy as ever. Few models strolled the halls, but there were mostly agents, event managers, and other miscellaneous workers. Makeup artists, wardrobe selectors, hair stylists, and the like.

Sunami was met by his personal assistant, Cherry.

Cherry was a beautiful redhead, with the curves of a black girl, who had no interest in being a model. She got her name because she loved deep-red lipstick and cherry-flavored Blow Pops! She was a student, at some college, studying marketing or something. He couldn't really remember. Her eyes were blue, her feet and hands perfect, and she carried herself like she was already a millionaire

Sunami knew she would become something pleasant. The girl, at age nineteen, also loved rap music and was a fan of Wolfpack music!

Cherry approached Sunami with a clipboard in hand and a piece of paper on it full of notes. She took her Blow Pop out of her mouth.

"Good morning, Mr. McKnight," she said with her California accent.

"What's good, Cherry. What ya got?" Sunami asked.

"Okay, first, you just received a call from Special Agent Charles Lavender, who wants you to call him as soon as you get in..."

"I'm not here and not expected to be here at all, today."

"Oh-kay! Then, Donna Karen called for some ladies to do the show for her new line. She specifically asked for Brittney, April, and Rebecca. Rose didn't show for her six o'clock shoot and Sam wants to know what he should do. Jessica Rabbit wants you to call her, anytime of day, and you've got Mr. Dodd and Mr. Bryant waiting for you in your office. "

"That's all?"

"For now. Oh, and your wife's customized Ferrari is ready and waiting for your instructions on when to send it. It'll make a great birthday gift, I think. I wish somebody would buy me a Ferrari!" She nudged him.

"One day. Okay, hold all calls until I say. I need to talk to my brothers for a minute."

"Some of us heard about what happened, Marcus, How's your baby?"

"She good. Everything's fine," Sunami assured.

"Cool. Where's my morning kiss?"

He leaned and gave Cherry a peck on the lips as he approached his door. Cherry rubbed his back before turning toward her desk where her phone was ringing off the hook.

"Coffee? Anything before I go?" Cherry asked.

"Nah. Not right now. I'll call you if needed," Sunami said.

"Okay, love."

With that, she made her way back over to her desk. Sunami entered his room where Animal had a model named Bunny Tsunami on his lap and Zahir had a model called "Amazin' Amie" on his.

"Alright, ladies," Sunami said. "Out, please. It's business time and we all know, business comes before pleasure!"

***

"Who!?" Zahir asked.

"She said his name was Obidiah MaTimbu. That's all I got," Sunami said, looking from one to the other. He had just explained everything that had happened the night before. Now, he was trying to gather information.

"I...I think I know who that is, yo," Animal said, thinking hard.

"Word? What do you know?" Sunami asked.

"Well, you know I have Ethiopians in my family. If I ain't mistaken, dude is a gang leader in Africa."

"A gang leader? What the fuck type shit is that? African gangs tryna take over shit in the states or something?" Zahir asked.

"Nah, don't get it twisted. African gangs ain't like American gangs. They're like the mafia, except different. This muthafucka, MaTimbu, is a rich ass muthafucka. His family owns some oil plants and diamond mines. He also does the black market thang, too. His gang is full of mercenaries. Do y'all know what that is? A mercenary?"

"Hell yeah," Sunami said. "They're like hired militia or military trained assassins, right?"

"Something like that," Animal said.

"So, how do you know all this shit, Animal?" Zahir asked.

"Nigga, I read! Duh. Ain't you ever picked up a newspaper? Or, maybe watch the news. See, a lot of people ain't aware of some of the activities going on in Africa. Because they are always in some kind of war or political battle, muthafuckas don't see some of the corruption. Kidnappers, murder for hire, bombings, and shit like that. That shit happens all the time over there. And with the kind of money Obidiah MaTimbu makes from oil production, nobody would think he is involved in the gangs and shit, but he is. He owns oil companies in Angola, Africa, and has a percentage of a company in Texas, I think. And he's probably worth hundreds of millions."

"My question is, what does all this shit have to do with me? Why would he hire people to kill me and my family?" Sunami asked.

"That's what we gotta find out," Zahir said.

"I don't give a fuck who he is. You fuck with one, you fuck with all of us! Your friends are my friends. Your enemies are my enemies. That's how we're living," Animal vowed.

"Look, make some calls and let's see if we can get more info on this nigga. I might need to take a trip to Africa," Sunami said.

"Nah. You'd never make it back, homie. To them, we are as white as George Bush!" Animal said.

There was a knock at the door.

As Zahir and Animal got up to go to their separate offices, Sunami called for the person knocking. He was met by Cherry, who looked pissed off.

"What is it?" he asked.

"You have a visitor who promises to lock me up for obstruction of justice if I lie to him again," Cherry said.

"Who?"

The door opened and the man in the dark blue suit smiled at Sunami. Instantly, hatred returned to Sunami's eyes. If looks could kill, he'd be arrested for a double homicide! Because he wanted to beat the living shit out of Charles Lavender.

"Mr. McKnight! Have you been ducking me?" Lavender asked.

"Do you have a warrant or are you here to jack off to my models?" Sunami spat.

"Just wanna ask a few questions about last night. That's all."

Chapter 3

Nobody ever wanted to listen until the flame was held right under their ass, York thought to himself. After a couple hours of sleep, York was back on schedule. He had showered, dressed, and met one of his security guards outside at the waiting Maybach. The driver opened the door for him and he got inside. He was booked to do an interview at Hot 97 radio station. His next album, *Understood,* was scheduled to drop in a month.

As the SUV pulled out of the private gates of his estate, York thought of Sunami's phone call earlier. For a whole year, York had insisted that they find the root of their problem and dead it. Sunami had been convinced that Cuba was dead.

"Bruh, we got money to make! We chase those muthafuckas till the sun burn out, but where will that leave us if we don't stabilize ourselves financially first? We getting paid now. Let the hired help do some dirty work. We just beat the fed charges, York! That shit don't happen but once every blue moon, ya dig? Next time, they gone try to hit us hard! Let's get money. Fuck whoever trying to end my life. It's Wolfpack, nigga," Sunami had declared.

He did have a good point at the time. But, York wasn't so sure about who was responsible. His gut told him that the bombing was a final attempt to get rid of them. But, wasn't Cuba dead? Sunami had been sure he was. But York could see the uncertainty in his eyes after he had asked. After a while, though, nothing happened. But York continued to have a sour feeling in his stomach. And he refused to let his guard down for the slightest second.

Now, with the call from Sunami, York wondered if he had been proven right. Even though Sunami had informed him of the assassin's African heritage, York wondered if there was more to it than what was seen on the surface. Could the hired assassins be on contract for some other organization? And what about this nigga, Obidiah MaTimbu? If he was who York thought he was, the man was a force to be reckoned with. And it was rumored that he dealt in any and everything from diamonds to heroin, from oil to prostitutes. Murder for hire was in that category, somewhere.

With the second attempt on Sunami's life and putting his new-born daughter in danger, there was sure to be bloodshed. If it had been his daughter, JaJa, he'd be ready to kill the world. York just hoped that they wouldn't be pressing their luck. Sure, they were street niggas, trained by their hoods in the warfare of urban living. But, they were going up against trained militias and organized crime syndicates. People with ties to ruthless murderers, hitmen, and mobsters. But those thoughts never occurred to any of them when they were slap in the middle of war!

The SUV pulled up to the radio station, and York was met by a crowd of fans. Not too bad, there were maybe twenty or thirty people, plus cameramen from news stations. York, dressed in his best mafioso suit and tie and diamond cufflinks, got out of the truck and was swarmed with questions, screams, and eager fans.

"Mr. York, what are your thoughts on the attack on Sunami?" one reporter yelled.

"I love you, York!"

"It's Don, yo! Look, that nigga fly. See his pinky ring?"

"Mr. York, do you feel like you and your family are in danger?"

York shook a few hands but ignored the questioning about his ace, Sunami. Those were not questions for him to answer. And what he thought about his family's safety was none of their business. As York made his way toward the front doors of Hot 97 FM radio station, a man grabbed him by his suit jacket.

"Y'all niggas ain't gangsters. All y'all do is rap that shit. But when a real—"

The man was interrupted by the butt of York's Beretta!

York slapped the man over, and over, and over, and over, until his entire right hand was soaked in blood. Some of the onlookers ran for help, others watched in amusement. Some people even cheered him on! The screams were overwhelming.

"Fuck is wrong wit' you? Putting yo' goddamn hands on me, like you crazy or something! Fuck ass nigga," York spat, wiping his hand on the man's shirt.

Inside the building, he went to the restroom and washed up. When he came out, he was met by the radio personality, Jane Doe. She was a very short Filipino who was very pretty. She was staring at him with an astonished look on her face.

"What?" York asked with a smile.

"You're way too cute to be crazy!" She laughed.

"Well... Thank you."

***

Jonathan Singleton sat, flipping through the lasting DuPont Registry in the small security building that sat next to the driveway behind the front gate of, rap/business tycoon, York's estate. The New York home, itself, boasted of being five acres large, surrounded by a twelve-foot concrete and stone fence. The house was a rebuilt redbrick building containing a six-car garage (that was separated from the main building), skylights, an inside pool, an outside basketball court, seven rooms, including a gym, library, movie theater and shooting range, four bathrooms, dining area, stainless steel kitchen, den and living room. It was, by far, his largest owned property.

Jonathan was the gate guard.

His job consisted of watching the camera monitors for the entire outside of the estate and radioing other guards if anything, away from his assigned perimeter, wasn't right. That, and cross checking the comings going of visitors with the appointment logs. The rule that York stressed the most was! "Nobody gets in without the permission of the residents, personally. I don't give a damn if it's the fucking president of the United States," York had said.

The job was pretty easy too. And the pay made up for the lack of benefits. After the Marine Corps had lost its appeal, Jonathan had worried about what he would do outside of military life. He had earned a degree in biology, but didn't have the patience it would take to further his education to become a doctor. And he had liked the shoot'em up, bang-bang style of the Marines, so he knew he needed to find a job that had an edge to it. Personal Security wasn't so bad. Sometimes, though, Jon did kinda wish something exciting would happen, other than watching squirrels fight over acorns and cars pass by in the rural area.

That was the reason he was a little surprised when the champagne Alston Martin Vanquish pulled up to the gate. Surprised, but not alarmed. For one, Jon knew that York was away on business, and for two, his wife hadn't contacted the front gate to notify him of any visitors that were coming, which was the normal operating procedure, according to York.

Jon turned the pages in his appointment notebook to double check and make sure he hadn't missed anything, though he doubted it.

Finding nothing, Jonathan secured his side arm in the holster and stepped out of the building to see what was going on. Lots of times, people got lost out in this area and searched for assisting at the first sign of life they could find. Needless to say, there were very few houses out this way that weren't farms or other industrial business. Good luck finding anyone to talk to, there, Jonathan thought. He was met at the black, iron gate by two of the most beautiful black women he had ever seen before in his life!

One sported a short, bob-cut hairstyle while the others touched her shoulders. The bob-cut woman held the map. Bingo! Jon thought.

"How can I help you ladies, this morning?" Jon asked, putting on the charm.

At age thirty-one, he still thought he had the build of a solid, well-trained Marine. His hair cut was short-short, almost a ceased. On the job, he wore cargo pants, his black combat boots and a tucked in "Semper-Fi" T-shirt which was the Marine Corps motto. Jon saw no reason for the all business, macho security guard routine with these two diversified divas!

"Um, yes. We're supposed to meet some friends on the Bernard campus but I think we're lost! Can you help? We go to Columbia University," the woman with the bob-cut said.

The accent intrigued Jon and he wondered if he had stumbled upon some foreign exchange students.

"Are you two from New York, or..." he asked.

"No, we're exchange students from Nigeria. This is our first independent road trip," the straight-haired diva said.

"Oh, okay, okay. Cool. What's your name?"

"I'm Dani," the bob-cut woman stated. "This is Vanessa."

"Cool, cool, just call me Jon," Jonathan said.

"Can you help us, Jon?" Vanessa asked with a smile.

Jon could see that she was clearly flirting with him. He had every intention of flirting back! "Sure, it's no problem. Let me step around here so I can see the map a little bit better. Hold on, give me a sec," he said.

"Thank you, so much," Vanessa said.

"Yeah, thanks," Dani agreed.

Jonathan headed for the reinforced step door beside the main gate. He grabbed his keys and flipped through them, one-by-one, with a bright smile on his face. That was the great thing about this job, he thought as he unlocked the first of four dead bolts. Often he got to meet very interesting people, some of them rich! But the bitches he met, dealing with York on a regular basis...Gawd!! He was surely grateful for that particular blessing. The pussy was damn sure plentiful! As the last of the locks unlatched, Jonathan turned the knob that gave access to the front of the stone fence and front gate.

The sight of PD Dani holding a black pistol fitted with a suppressor froze Jon in a kid stride! Vanessa was back at the car with her hair now in a ponytail, gloves on and a ski mask in her hand.

From his position, Jonathan noticed a submachine gun sitting on the driver's seat. It, too, had a long silencer attached to it. It didn't take long to put the pieces of the puzzle together. He'd been bamboozled! "Shit," he said, disappointed in himself.

"That's right, lover boy!" Dani said before firing two shots into Jon's face at point blank range. He was dead before the second shot hit him.

***

Willie polished the front right rim on York's black Mercedes CLK 600. He too, was a guard but he held the extra job titles of mechanic and detailer, also known as car washer. He had just finished cleaning Pam's 6 series Benz and one of York's customized choppers, some of the other cars such as the Phantom coupe, Lamborghini Murcielago, and the two "his and hers" Ferraris that didn't come out as often. Therefore, they stayed clean longer.

"Hey!" a voice whispered from behind.

Willie was interrupted from his polishing as he turned around to see a slim, masked individual. "What the hell?" he said.

The masked figure produced a silenced pistol from behind their back and splattered Willie's brains all over the side of the 600! All the washing and polishing had been in vain. The two assassins, known as Dani and Vanessa, quietly made their way across the grounds. They tried to stay out of sight but because the estate was so largely spaced out, it was proving difficult to do so.

Time was of the essence, because Dani had decided to leave the car in front of the gate after dragging Jon's body back into the security building. So, they needed to penetrate, destroy and vacate as quickly as humanly possible, all whole being thorough. As they were crossing the grounds to the main building, another guard on patrol stopped by to speak to Willie.

"Tom Kat" was probably the youngest guard on the payroll. At nineteen years old, he was in the army reserves and attending a technical college. He took this job to spend money. His name, Tom Kat, had been given to him early because of his provocative ways with women. He was quite the ladies' man, but he was capable of handling the tasks of being a security guard. It was Tom Kat who found Willie lying next to the luxury car, dead. He reacted accordingly while canvassing the landscape with his ever-watchful eyes. He spotted the two assassins as he spoke into his, now raised, walkie-talkie.

"All units, I've got a DOA. Two suspects headed to the main building. Both armed and dangerous. I'm engaging from the east.

Copy?" he spoke while he drew his gun and raised it from his crotch.

He received a copy from other guards but he was sprinting towards the two suspects.

"Hold it, right there!" Tom Kat yelled, advancing on the two with his gun drawn.

Vanessa turned without the slightest bit of thought and let a burst go from the machine gun she wielded. Tom Kat saw it coming and divided at an angle, and rolled.

He came up with his Browning 45 caliber and fired two rounds. One of which made contact. Vanessa was thrown to the ground by the impact of the slug she had taken above her right breast. Dani recovered and ran to find shelter as she fired numerous silent rounds at the young boy who had shot Vanessa! She could hear others coming.

***

Pam had been in the kitchen with Jeff, the cook, who came by three times a week whenever she, York and Ms. Cindy were around. Pam heard the sound that reminded her of firecrackers on the fourth of July, then registered the sound and reacted.

"Get down, Jeff. Get down! I'll be right back."

She said running out of the kitchen. As she crossed into the living room, she noticed a figure running across the yard towards the front entrance. The figure had been close to the house. Then she noticed one of the guards on the ground with his gun raised. The sound of firecrackers sounded again, but this time she saw the guard's gun go off! Pam dashed upstairs to the playroom where the nanny, Ms. Cindy, and her daughter were finger painting. Soft music played in the room and the TV screen showed a children's program called *The Wiggles*. They were oblivious to the shots.

"Cindy, you and JaJa get away from the windows and stay down until I tell you to. We got trespassers," Pam commanded, leaving the room. Cindy compiled without asking one question.

This was part of the drill that Mr. and Mrs. McNeal rehearsed with her on several occasions. except Pam wasn't using the code words that York used. As more gun fire sounded outside, Pam burst into her room and threw open York's gun cabinet. They had enough guns in the house to supply a small army. That was not to mention the guns that were available to the guards! She grabbed her High Point nine millimeter and shoved it into the waistband of her jeans. She then grabbed a pistol grip shotgun and ran for the stairs.

"Not on my watch!"

Pam mumbled to herself as she pumped a slug into the shotgun's chamber. Pam bypassed Jeff in the kitchen, who was crouched down in between two cabinets. She threw the front door open and noticed the young guard, Tom Kat, watching over the masked assailants. She could see that the gunman was having trouble breathing.

"Mrs. McNeal, they went that way." Tom Kat pointed.

Pam nodded to him and leaped off the front steps and took off in the indicated direction. Pam McNeal had long ago given up being a helpless victim. The hunted had become a hunter!

Chapter 4

Special Agent Charles Lavender sat cross legged in the chair on the opposite side of Sunami's desk. Sunami had explained, for the umpteenth time, exactly what happened the night before at his Malibu vocational home. Now, Lavender pursed his lips as he considered his next question. The story and the report that the police filed, was, technically, believable, but parts were sketchy. The point of Lavender coming out to question Sunami, again, was to show him that he was hot on his ass! And Lavender had no plans of letting him wipe his ass wrong.

"Do you have video surveillance at your home?" Lavender asked.

Sunami hesitated.

Then, a broad grin broke out onto his face. He reached into his desk for a Cuban cigar and a zippo lighter. Sunami offered one to Agent Lavender, but he declined.

"Is this a F.B.I. investigation, Mr. Lavender, or something personal?" Sunami asked as he rotated e tip of the cigar over the flame and puffed it to life.

"Answer the question, please, Mr. McKnight. Do you, or do you not, have video surveillance at your home, in Malibu?"

It was a question that the Malibu police had failed to ask. So, he gave Agent Lavender points for that. But, of course, Sunami was already a step ahead of the special agent.

"Yes, Mr. Lavender, I do. But, it does not record. It only shows what the cameras see for the moment. Does that answer your question well enough?"

"Yes. Thank you, McKnight."

Lavender stood, straightened his suit jacket and stared long at the smiling face in front of him. He hated Sunami with a passion. But, he could not allow his personal feelings to affect his actions. The acquittal of Sunami and York's first charges had hurt Lavender, professionally. But he would not be beaten so easily.

"I hope you'll have a nice day, Agent Lavender. Maybe one day you might put aside this personal vendetta against me, that you have for God knows why, and we can play golf or something," Sunami said, struggling to contain his laughter.

"You're a murderer, Mr. McKnight. A mass murderer, at that. Never will I ever play anything in your company, besides guess who's going to jail. And to answer your question: It's both personal and under the F.B.I.'s investigation. We know more about you than you think. So, continue being arrogant. I warned you, once. Now, I'm coming at you with everything I got. It won't be over until you're serving ten life sentences!" Agent Lavender promised.

Before Sunami could respond, his office phone rang and he saw that it was a line that only few people had the number to.

"Uh-huh, well, that's fine and dandy, Agent Lavender. But, if you don't mind, I have more pressing business to attend to. You wouldn't know about million dollars phone calls, would ya? I thought not. Again, have a nice day and, uh...fuck yourself!" Sunami said, picking up the phone.

Agent Lavender left as a familiar voice spoke to Sunami on the phone. He hadn't heard from the caller in a while.

***

Dani produced Jon's ten-millimeter Smith & Wesson pistol as she neared the steel door from which she gained access to the private estate. The guards were advancing, but she was holding them off long enough to make a getaway.

The mission had been a complete failure and now Dani just wanted to keep her life. She knew Vanessa was probably dead, by now. She slowed and turned, lifting both pistols. Pow! Pow! Pow! Pow! Pow! Pow! Pow! Guards scattered to find cover as she fired until her original weapon went empty. With no time to reload, she dropped it and continued to squeeze off rounds from the S&W at zigzagging targets.

The loud boom of a shotgun hastened her efforts of opening the steel door! Pam continued to advance. She had a routine going with the shotgun, now. Pump and pull, pump and pull, pump and pull. The barking of the loud cannon empowered her as she ran down the figure that had caused a threat to her livelihood. The figure made it through a door and into a car in front of the gate. Pam never altered a step, even as the large ten-millimeter bullets whizzed so dangerously close by her.

Another guard fell to the ground, beside her, in agony. Chest shot, Pam noted to herself as she sped up. The car's tires spun in reverse, causing a cloud of burnt rubber smoke, as Pam ran out of shells. She dropped the shotgun, grabbed her Highpoint pistol and didn't miss a beat as she riddled the exterior of the reversing Alston Martin with bullets. Two other guards were beside her, firing, also. Her twelve bullets went too quickly for her liking but there was nothing more she could do. The mask-wearing assailant had gotten away!

***

The Maybach transporting York had made the final turn onto the rural road leading to his home. He was tired but there were still things he needed to do. There was a video shoot for him in Miami, tomorrow. He still needed to choose the models he was going to use. Maybe he'd detour and go pick up some girls from Baby Girl Models, himself. The hoe surely loves that, York thought. And he wanted to see Phame, anyway.

Phame was one of the bad ass models he was fucking. He hadn't seen her in a couple months. Their schedules were always conflicting, being that she was such a top-notch model and he was such a successful artist and businessman. Halfway down the long rural road, a bullet riddled Alston Martin sped by the Maybach like a bat out of hell! York was turned in his seat, watching the smoking Alston Martin disappear in the opposite direction.

"What the fuck?..." York wondered aloud.

"Um, York...look," the driver called to him.

When York turned back in his seat, they were pulling up to the front gate. York could see the tire marks in front of the gate and backs of the guards, and what looked like Pam, headed back towards the house. The driver, Max, blew the horn and everyone turned around, quickly, ready to shoot. One of the guards ran down to the small security building and pressed the button that opened the automatic front gate. After the Maybach drove in, York hopped out of the SUV. The gate closed behind him.

"Yo, what the fuck is going on?" York asked.

Pam handed her empty shotgun to one of the guards and headed back in York's direction. By the time she made it to him he had found out that both Jon and Willie were dead. Lance, another guard, had been shot in the chest. The paramedics and the police were on the way. "York, one of the ones that broke in is up here."

She said pointing towards the house.

"Tom Kat found Willie and saw the two of them coming towards the house. They both wore masks and had silent guns. C'mon, let's go see who these people are."

"Pam, what the hell are you doing out here?" York asked as they made their way up to the main building.

"I heard the gunshots from the kitchen. When I saw what was going on, I went and grabbed my gun and came to protect what's mine! What? You thought I had you and Hypnotic show me how to shoot for no reason? C'mon, baby."

"Well, where the fuck is my gotdamn daughter, then, Pam? If you our here paying Indiana Jones, where the fuck is my daughter?" York asked, angrily.

He thought that Pam's priority was supposed to be protecting and shielding their sixteen-month-old daughter. Not out bussing guns like she is a cast member for *Boyz N The Hood*, or something!

"Baby, chill, okay? That was the first thing I did. I got Cindy and Jaja down and away from the windows, first. Once I saw that she had him and that he was safe, I came to help. Why are you getting mad?" Pam asked, getting worried.

York had a habit of blowing things out of proportion.

And she was insulted to find out that he thought of her as being capable of being that dumb. Of course she would insure the safety of her child, first. Every mother she could think of would. But, not many had the balls, for lack of a better word, to actually go out with the intentions of neutralizing or eliminating the threat. She had come a long way and she expected a little graciousness, if not pride, from her husband.

They reached the other asked assailant, who was being guarded by Tom Kat.

"He's hurt, but he'll make it till the police get here. Son of a bitch tried to take my head off!" Tom Kat chuckled.

"Well, let me return the favor."

York said, drawing his pistol. Boom!

He shot her dead in the forehead, causing Pam to release a small yelp in surprise. The other guards looked at York in amazement! Never had they seen this side of him. His face showed pure rage. And with good reason, too. His family had been put in danger. Tom Kat was the only one, besides York, who didn't think of his actions as ruthless. Besides, the mask-wearing perpetrator would've done the same thing to any of them, given the opportunity. Willie and Jon were proof.

"What?"

York asked, rudely, staring at the amazed looks of the other guards. None of them had the nerve to say a word. York bent and snatched the mask off of the face. He wasn't surprised to see that the gunman was actually a gun-woman. After Sunami's call, that morning, he had half expected it.

"Tom Kat, y'all handle the medics and police when they get here. I wasn't here when it happened, so, there's no need for them to speak to me. Tell'em what you know, and have 'em clean this shit up off my yard. We'll make arrangements to account for the two people we lost. Somebody keep an eye on Lance until the medics get here. Pam, call Jon and Willie's family and let them know what happened. Write a check for one hundred fifty thousand dollars for the both of them and have it sent to the family. I'm flying out tonight. Got shit to take care of in Cali and a video shoot in Miami. When you get done with the families, call Shodd and have him check on Angie and Sean. Then tell him to pack up and meet me here in three hours. Everybody understand?" York asked.

Everybody agreed. York dropped the bloody mask onto the dead girl's body and walked toward the house. Pam was right beside him. He headed upstairs as Pam gave Jeff the okay to resume cooking. Upstairs, she found York hugging their daughter JaJa. She could see the affection in his gaze as he kissed his first child. He turned to her, his face softened.

"I'm sorry, baby. I didn't even ask you if you were okay," York said.

"I'm fine, sweetie. Just shaken up a little. Don't worry, though. We'll be fine. The guys you hired are good and I can take care of me and mine," she said,

"I'm gonna take care of all this, soon. Hire three more guys, while I'm gone. Have everybody on point, okay?"

"Okay, baby. Aren't you gonna call Sunami and let him know what happened?"

"Yeah. But, I'll be there late, tonight anyway."

"Go ahead and get ready. Dinner will be ready soon."

Pam said, taking the baby.

"Pam...I love you, girl. I really mean that," York professed.

"I know. And I love you, too."

***

"Word got 'round that you looking for some information about somebody overseas. That's true?"

Red Rum asked Sunami over the phone. Sunami was surprised at the fact that his name was involved directly in the inquiring. Red Rum, who was way in Durham, had been the first to call offering assistance. But Sunami wondered how the info had reached this mutual friend so fast.

"Is that what the world is? How'd you find out so fast?" Sunami asked.

"Well, I saw you on the news on your way out, this morning, on the net. That Ferrari is dripping, by the way. What's the retail?"

"Two hundred and sixty grand. But I know somebody if you're interested."

"Definitely. Anyway, I got a call from my nigga who says he can help you. But it's a two-way streetcar. Ya know, like, one hand washes the other. Feel me?" Red Rum asked.

"What does he want? And why didn't he call me, himself?"

"He asked me to set it up, since I fucks with you. I told him you were good people, knowing Ace, and all. But I ain't sure what it is he wants, though. He says he can give you the info you looking for and maybe more. But he wants you to do something for him. And not for free, either. One businessman understands another, feel me?"

"Who is it?"

"Ever heard of the Byrd Cartel?" Red Rum asked.

"Oh, Birdman? I thought he retired," Sunami said.

"Not quite. After Meech got locked up, he started making more moves but quieter than before. And, when you and people started coming up, you started putting dents in his pockets. Luckily, you know me and he asked about you. Things almost got messy."

"Yeah, well, it is what it is. If he's thinking about asking me to stop my wolves from eating, he can cancel that, war or no war."

Sunami promised, determined to be firm.

"Calm down, tough guy. You can have North Carolina. That shit is small potatoes to him. He won't ask you to stop nothing, I'll be sure of that. So, what you gonna do? Let me know now nigga, I got business to take care of."

"When and where?"

"Atlanta. Tomorrow. Cars will be waiting."

Red Rum informed. "One thing."

"What?"

"I'm bringing my partner."

"Fine. One guy, my nigga. Nobody else. You ain't got shit to worry about. It's just that Bird don't trust niggas, feel me?"

"Yeah, well...That's one thing we got in common, already," Sunami said.

***

Later that night, York arrived in California. Sunami met him at LAX Airport and drove him out to Malibu to stay with him. On the ride, York gave Sunami the full rundown of what had happened at his house.

"So the shit is getting that serious, huh?" Sunami asked, not expecting an answer.

"Yeah, it is! We gotta make shit happen and soon," York said.

Sunami told Jim about the phone call he received from Red Rum. He told York that they were flying out, first thing in the morning to meet Birdman. York shrugged it off.

"It's whatever. I gotta cancel my video shoot, then," he said.

"Cool. Phame should be on her way to meet us at my crib. You know ya niece, Rain, misses you," Sunami said.

"Yeah. If she keep fucking around wit' you, she gone be a lil' killer like her daddy!"

"I ain't a killer, but don't push me!" Sunami laughed.

As Sunami pulled the Spyder up to his home, they saw Phame's Mercedes Benz AMG G 63 in front of the house. Sunami smacked his teeth when he saw that Hypnotic hadn't moved her Benz SUV. She had left it right in front of the garage door where his Ferrari was supposed to go. "Damn girl is crazy, man," Sunami said as he and York got out.

"Tell me about it! Ma went Conan on me today, trying to shoot one of the muthafuckas that got on the property!" York informed him.

"Oh, Lord. Next, she'll be jacking you up by the collar!"

Chapter 5

Inside, Hypnotic and Phame sat in the living room, both with a glass of Moscato. Sunami scolded Hypnotic about her car being in his way and they both left the room to go put both cars away. Phame's smile told York everything he wanted to know. She was happy to see him.

"Marcus, what did I tell you about having these secret meetings behind York's wife's back? Phame is a nice girl, but I don't like being involved with this shit," Hypnotic said, irritated.

Sunami was closing the garage door as she approached him.

"Baby, we've been through this before. That man is grown. And since he's my cousin, I refuse to make him stay at some expensive ass hotel just so he can get his lil' side piece of pussy when he got all this space in the house. Me and him got business to take care of, anyway. So, what he does shouldn't even concern you. Your name is Mrs. McKnight, not Mrs. McNeal. So mind ya damn business!" Sunami responded sarcastically.

"It just makes me wonder, sometimes, what you do when you're away with him...and for the record, my name is Hypnotic McNeal, thank you!"

"Yeah whatever!"

"Shut up." She laughed as they entered the house.

Phame was what Sunami, and a lot of other niggas, considered to be the perfect black woman. Technically, she was mixed with Brazilian, but who cared? She was five-foot-six inches tall, dark brown with a golden tint, gray eyes with perfect Everything. You name it, she got it! According to her modeling portfolio, Phame was twenty-five years young. It also said that her waist was a size twenty-six, her breasts were 34C cups and her ass had a thirty-eight-inch radius. To put it plainly, the bitch BAD!

As Sunami and Hypnotic were reentering, Sunami noticed his favorite feature about her. Phame sat with her legs crossed at the ankles, all ten toes beautifully decorated, matching her nail color of the moment.

Volcano Orange! She wore a colorful skirt and a Dior blouse! Sunami noticed that she wore a thin, simple necklace with a small diamond-encrusted heart, a few rings and brackets, and an expensive watch that Sunami couldn't tell who manufactured from his distance. The ponytail she wore complimented her angelic face and properly showcased her diamond stud earrings. Phame wore no makeup, outside the job, and she still out-shined most of the top models in America, fully made up! She could be the wife easily to any black or white billionaire. But, she belonged to the infamous gentleman/gangster, York!

Sunami had grabbed a bottle of Cîroc vodka and two short glasses for himself and York. He poured, keeping his eye on Phame who was now leaning against York, nestling between his neck and collar bone. York sat with his left arm around her, acting as nonchalant as he always did.

"I ain't gone keep y'all too much longer. Me and York gotta catch a flight in the morning and I know some of us want to get some...sleep," Sunami said, smiling at Hypnotic. "So, what's been up, Phame? I saw you on the cover of Go Viral Magazine. What was that, like, your fifth issue?"

"Yeah. It was actually one of my best photoshoots. I left a message for you at the office about a month ago, Sunami. I wanted to let you know that my sister is interested in modeling. We've been tryna get her to do it for a while, but she's been focusing on law school. She said she'd be willing to do some summer modeling if you still want her to," Phame informed him.

"Hell, muthafuckin', yeah!! That girl is gorgeous. But I didn't get that message, though. Or, maybe I did. You know, I got so much going on with the agency, Real Estate, Hypnotic's promotion company and the other artist that I'm overseeing. That, and tryna juggle between speeding time with my daughters, so..."

"We all know they're a handful! Especially when they are together," Hypnotic said.

"You guys have the cutest lil' girl I've ever seen in my life! Are you two planning on letting her model early?" Phame asked.

"I dunno. It's up to Hypnotic," Sunami copped out.

"Shit, she might as well model! Lil cuz got money written all over her," York said.

"Yeah, that she does. She's also high maintenance, at fourteen months," Hypnotic confided.

"She ain't that bad, Hypnotic," Sunami said.

"York, how's your daughter doing?" Phame asked.

"Oh, you already know she good! She got swag like her daddy, so she always gon be good, know what I'm saying."

They each had a few more drinks before Sunami stood and took the glasses and bottles back in the kitchen. When he came back, Hypnotic said her good nights to the two of them, eyed Sunami, and made her way to the stairs. Sunami didn't bother to sit down, again.

"Bruh, you already know where everything at. Me casa es tú casa! Phame, feel free to utilize anything you need. The kitchen is full and at y'all's disposal. I'm 'bout to take my ass to bed," Sunami said.

"Yeah, right! You going to bed, but not to sleep!" York laughed. "Well...I'll holla at you in the A.M., ya dig?" And Sunami was gone.

***

York and Phame found their way to one of the guest rooms on the first floor. There was no way of telling that someone had been brutally killed in the hallway, because Hypnotic had hired a fierce cleaning crew who had the house looking like it was just built recently. The walls were clean, the wooden hallway floor shined and the entire house smelled of the homely scent of vanilla and brown sugar.

Inside the room, Phame left York in anticipation as she went into the connecting bathroom.

"Don't you move, mister!" She had commanded.

Shortly after, York heard the shower running. While waiting, he dimmed the lights and turned on the surround system and selected a throwback Faith Evans that Hypnotic had programmed into the memory. York took the time and rolled up a nice blunt of some

Cali bud that Sunami had given him. He had just loosened his tie when he heard the water stop. York cracked a window and lit the blunt, allowing the sweet aroma of chronic to drift into the air.

Phame emerged from the steamy bathroom wearing only a white terry cloth robe. The front was partially open and York was able to see the space between her ample breast as well as her diamond pierced belly button. He had to restrain himself from looking further down. The last thing he wanted to do was get excited too quickly and end the party before it even started! Phame was the only woman that could do that to him, though he'd never tell her in her lifetime.

"Are you ready for me?" Phame asked, stepping toward him on her tiptoes as if she were still wearing heels.

York took a deep drag off the flavored wrap filled with loud and gave Phame an arrogant look.

"You asking the wrong question, ain't cha?"

Phame took the blunt away from him and put it to her lips, exhaling so deep that York thought she might choke. Then, she blew out a thick, gray stream of smoke and said,

"I'm sorry, Daddy. I meant to say, am I ready for you, now?"

"There ya go," York said, smiling.

Phame helped York undress and then let the robe fall to the ground. York was mesmerized by her natural beauty, even though he had been fucking with her for four months now, on and off. Because Phame posed nude, sometimes, her pubic area had been waxed clean. She was as bald as a baby eagle, down there. And that enhanced his arousal. Phame lowered to her knees and faced York's penis, head on. She kissed the tip and talked to it as if it were one of her best friends.

"Did you miss me? Huh? Don't worry, I never forgot about you for one second, I promise. I even dream about you! Have others been treating you kindly?" Phame asked the aroused penis.

York stifled a laugh. Then, shock waves went through him as Phame took the head in her mouth and sucked, softly. She never sucked the entire shaft. The head, she had told him, held the most nerves and that was where all the sensation came from. So, she would waste her time and tire her jaw trying to accommodate the whole dick, which wasn't small by far. And York couldn't complain with her reasoning. In fact, he could barely even speak, half the time. Phame continued to tongue kiss his dick while adding suction and rubbing her clitoris all at the same time.

She moaned continuously as her body started to react to her teasing. Already she was beginning to drip from being so wet! When she felt York tensing up, she removed her mouth from his penis and licked her lips.

"Your wish is my command, Daddy. How would you like to fuck me?" she asked.

York didn't even speak. While his build up was subsiding, he grabbed Phame by the hips and lay back on the bed, bringing her on top of him to straddle his waist. Phame reached between them and took hold of the crowbar-like shaft that was York. She aimed and lowered herself, sliding thick meat into her center. The sensation made her close her eyes to enjoy.

"Mmmmmmm, Daddy! This is what I live for, right here," she confessed.

Slowly, Phame rotated her hips while rising and falling all the way back down to the hilt. York navigated her insides with ease. The moisture was overwhelming. Phame powered herself to lean over top of him, giving him full access to her breasts. York hobbled each nipple while Phame massaged his scalp and gripped his dreads. She began putting more rhythm and bounce in their love making as the feelings got better. York grabbed her hops and took control.

SMACK, SMACK, SMACK, SMACK, SMACK, SMACK, SMACK

Their skin slapped together rapidly and Phame's climax rose to its peak. She started having hot flashes and her eyes rolled as she neared the boiling point.

"Oh my gawd, baby...ugh! Ooooh, yeah! Shit, shit, shit, shit, shit. Don't stop, Daddy, pleeez. Please, don't stop," Phame begged.

Finally, the pot boiled over and the wave gushed from Phame's insides. Her convulsions were met with York's sleeting. Both of them were panting like they had just ran a marathon without stopping. York continued to thrust inside her center, softly, as Phame lay on top of him, catching her breath. His hands explored every inch of her backside and made their way back up to her long, curly hair.

"I swear to gawd, if your wife slips one time, you're mine, nigga! Do you hear me? MINE! She is so lucky," Phame declared from beside his left ear.

"Yeah, I hear you, a'ight." York chuckled.

This was how a Hood Consigliere was supposed to live. Free of worry, free of stress, and free of drama. Just plain old free!

"So, Daddy..." Phame said, meeting York's eyes. "What's next?"

York considered this, briefly. He smiled and sat up in the bed, looking back at Phame's beauty.

"All fours, girl. Ass up, face down," he commanded.

***

The next morning, York and Phame met Sunami and Hypnotic in the dining area for breakfast. York was immaculately dressed, his suit freshly pressed. Hypnotic wore only a robe, similar to the one Phame had found in the bathroom the night before.

Her hair was pinned up on top of her head and York could see that she was still tired. His guess was that Sunami kept her busy all night, also! And with a wife that fine, who wouldn't!

York's pin striped suit almost mirrored Sunami's. Both wore dark colors with a light-colored dress shirt and a dark tie. And both suits had vests that went over the dress shirts but under the suit jackets. Their jewelry was very light, but what they did wear showed signs of wealth just as easily as wearing a couple of bank statements around their necks. They both had narrowed the ice down to just earrings, cufflinks and watches. Neither of them wore wedding bands because both wives initials had been tattooed on their ring fingers. And, as always, both wore guns! Sunami was in a slanted, right-handed holster in the small of his back. Similar to what some undercover FBI agents wore. York wore a shoulder holster as well as a holster identical to Sunami's.

Phame at breakfast in a tight gray spandex and a U-Neck T-shirt that was tied in a knot in the back. Her hair was back in a ponytail and she wore a pair of running Dior running shoes, no socks. The jewelry was gone. Hypnotic had made them eggs, turkey bacon and pancakes. Orange juice and French vanilla coffee was also available.

As they were eating, the door chime sounded. York's head whipped toward the door, his freshly twisted dreads tied neatly. Phame had greased and twisted them that morning, for him.

"It's just Animal," Sunami said. "He called and said he was coming through for a second."

"I'll get it," Hypnotic said, heading for the front door.

Hypnotic was coming back into the kitchen with Animal behind her. She was asking him if he wanted a plate to eat.

"Nah, I just got something from....Got Damn!" Animal exclaimed as he looked across the room.

Everyone had their eyes on him. Animal was dressed in casual urban clothes, as usual. But his eyes were on Phame.

"What the hell wrong wit' you, Animal?" Sunami asked, amused.

"Nothing. I just didn't know Phame was up in here. Girl, you bad as a muthafucka! You know that? Damn, you thick."

"Animal, sit yo ass down somewhere!" Hypnotic said, bringing him a glass of juice.

"Thank you, Anthony. You say that every time you see me!" Phame said, nonchalant.

"I know, but I can't help it. And what I tell you 'bout calling my government? My name is A-n-i-m-a-l! You got that?" Animal asked after spelling his name, sarcastically.

"Um-Hm, whatever."

C'mon, Animal. I gotta let you know what's going on for today," Sunami said rising from the table.

The others watched Sunami and Animal leave the dining room and walk back towards Sunami's office. Phame elbowed York, softly, with a concerned, questioning face.

"Baby, why he always do that?" Phame asked.

"Do what?" York asked back.

"You know he acts all excited when he sees me, like that. I mean, it's not like this the first time he's ever seen me."

"Nah, he just fucking wit' you, gurl. You know Animal bout damn crazy! He was like that when we was in prison up north together and he ain't bout to change for nobody. That's one thing I can say, Animal is the same person, every day, week, month, and year! He just crazy as hell!!" York laughed.

In Sunami's office, he gave Animal a rundown of what was going on so he could notify Zahir. Animal wasn't cool with the idea of them going to meet an unknown drug kingpin without the whole team.

"Sunami, it's all for one, remember dat! What if these fuck niggas try something on y'all? You and York gone be stuck!" Animal said.

"I get what you saying, Animal, but it ain't even like that. And look at who you talking about...Its Sunami, nigga! And York wit' me. Nigga we go dumb hard!! But if shit do pop off, y'all know what to do. Kill everything moving, if we don't return, ya dig? But dude is a friend of a friend. Everything is gravy, trust me," Sunami said.

"I don't trust nobody. I'm a grimy ass nigga, and I know I ain't the only one, either. But, like you said, if y'all don't come back...it's gone, be BANGA TIME!"

"And you know this! Let Zahir know and call Raquel to bring him up to date. He was supposed to come out with York but he had to take care of something with his B.M., so I dunno what he gone do. But y'all niggas keep shit moving. And I might need you to make a money pick up from Sean, next week. These birds keep flying south and the bread keeps flowing in with ease.

"We gotta clean six million dollars, man. I wish I wouldn't have waited to pick up the first three, but fuck it. It's done. We 'bout to get outta here, so tighten up. And make sure Rain and Hypnotic is straight when we leave."

"Bruh, you know we got them. I don't even know why you said that stupid shit!"

"Shut up, nigga."

Sunami left the office and got up with York. He said bye to Phame before leaving. Hypnotic had gone up stairs to change and get Rain ready to go on a morning run with Phame.

"York, call me when you get back. I'm free for a couple days if you gon' be in Cali," Phame said.

"Yeah, well. I'll let ya know. Don't get ya hopes up!" York said, leaving.

Keese

Chapter 6

The private jet landed in Atlanta, Georgia, around four in the afternoon. As promised, they were met by a stretch, white Mercedes Benz and a stocky, short bald head man. The man looked as if he had seen a few first fights in his days, and probably won them. He introduced himself as Kindu.

"I'm Bird's consigliere. C'mon, let's ride," Kindu said, leading them to the open car door.

Sunami noticed the two miniature flag posts on the car's hood. Both flags were small and colored black with a white bird in the center, its wings fully expanded in mid-flight. Inside the limo, the seats were a soft, blood red colored leather with velvet trim. York sat beside him and the man, Kindu, sat across from them. He opened a small refrigerator and pulled out a bottle of some ancient scotch.

"Y'all, niggas wanna drink?" Kindu asked.

The two of them declined by shaking their heads. The limo was now navigating the busy streets of Atlanta. Sunami covertly kept his eye on Kindu while York pretended to look out the tinted window.

"Look, yo, y'all can relax. From what I hear, Sunami, you knew David Santiago," Kindu said.

"Yeah, I was at Lanesboro Correctional with him awhile back." he responded.

"Then, you know Bird, he was there with him."

"I never knew him, personally. But, I heard of him. Did you know Ace, too?"

"Yep, that's my people. I helped him handle a lil' situation down in Florida."

"Oh, you talking 'bout the shit wit' Orellana Cartel?"

Sunami asked paying more attention, now.

"Yeah."

"You was in on that shit?"

"Yeah. Ace put me and my nigga Mac on after that, shit."

"What was that shit about?" Sunami wanted to know.

"Basically, the nigga, Javier Orellana, had sent some people at Face because Face had killed his brother while setting a vendetta with some Mexican gang. The dudes that came to kill Face got his car confused with Ace's brother, Fat Boy's, car. Fat Boy had been taking Ace's baby mother and son home when they hit. Everybody died except Fat Boy. He was in a coma for, like, three years," Kindu explained.

"Damn."

After a forty-minute drive, they reached the Birdman's estate. To say he was living luxuriously, would be an understate to the tenth degree! There was a huge fountain with a decoration of stone birds spitting water in the front yard.

The wrap-around driveway was wide and Sunami spotted several foreign cars in the driveway in front of a long building with, Sunami counted, eight garage doors! The grass was the perfect shade of green and neatly kept. The house, itself, made York's house in Jersey look like a child's play pen next to a castle. In fact, that is exactly what Bird's house was... a modern-day castle!

As the limo pulled to the front of this castle, two thick ass, dreadlock wearing, gun toting Jamaican women emerged from the front double doors. The women were extremely sexy, in their own exotic way, and they wore transparent, white linen garments. The driver opened the door for them and Kindu led the way. Before they could enter the house, though, the women stopped them.

"Weapons?" one said in a thick island accent.

Sunami gave Kindu a look that said he should've known better than to think they would meet a notorious kingpin, known for ruthless drug wars, without their own protection. And Kindu could see that Sunami had no intention of humoring him, either. But, there was nothing to even worry about.

"They are straight, Emanny. They are with me. Don't trip," Kindu said.

"But no one sees the Bird—" she started to argue.

"I said, they're straight. Okay!? I got them."

"Fine. Come."

They entered the front room and Sunami thought he was in some kind of museum, or something. Large, expansive marble floors, diamond light fixtures, oakwood stairs and railings, expensive paintings and exotic furniture.

They were stopped in front of the stairs and the Birdman, himself, appeared and began his descent. He wore flannel pants and a matching V-neck shirt. His dreadlocks were rude, but in a prearranged sort of way. His face was clean shaven, besides the thin line of his mustache. He wore a bulky diamond watch and a chunk of ice on his pinky fingers.

Sunami and York could not see his ears, but they too probably held huge rocks! On his feet, Sunami recognized, were Gucci loafers with the gold G's. Birdman smiled at the two of them. "Sunami, I do remember you! You use to rap in the cipher with Clap, from Greenville right? Won't you fucking wit' that bitch, Ms. Chapel?" Bird asked, extending his clean, manicured hands.

"Hell yeah. But I don't really remember you, though," Sunami admitted. "Don't sweat it."

"Anyway, this is my consigliere, York. Where I go, he goes. What I know, he knows, ya dig?"

"That's whass up, that's whass up. What's popping, York?"

"Counting money, fucking hoes, and busting my gun, as far I know. Anything else is just plain irrelevant," York responded, still peeping out his surroundings.

"Y'all, c'mon over here, and let's talk, man. Kindu, you ain't got my niggas no drinks, man?" Bird asked.

"They didn't want nothing in the car, shit, I figured they straight," Kindu said.

"Aw, c'mon blood. Go get us a bottle of Rozay. Don't nobody drink that ol' hard ball ass liquor you drink!"

They laughed as Kindu went into the direction, Sunami assumed, the kitchen was in. York and Sunami followed Bird into a large room that held a huge wooden deck with a phone, computer and a large room wall of books behind it. There was a real comfortable looking chair behind it, also. In front of the desk were a couple comfortable, leather resting chairs. As they settled in, the two women guards, including Emanny, stood at the door.

"I know y'all smoke loud, right?" Bird asked.

York looked to Sunami. Sunami nodded, giving his approval to trust Bird. Bird, caught the gesture and frowned.

"Look, man, I didn't call y'all here for no bullshit. I'll roll the blunt right here if you don't trust me, or you can roll the shit yourself. This meeting is all business and all love, fam. You got my word. Matter of fact..." Bird looked up at the women. "Manny, y'all can go, for now. These dudes is my peoples. They won't hurt me," he said.

"But..." Emanny started. But the icy glare that Bird gave her had stopped her mid-protest. She bowed sightly, and her and the other woman stepped out into the hall and disappeared as Kindu showed up.

"Whass wrong wit' Manny, bruh?" Kindu asked, setting down clean glasses and a chilled bottle of Rozay.

"I dunno, but she starting to get out of pocket. She gon make me slap the shit outta her island ass so hard, she gon forget how to speak English properly!" Bird declared.

"Ha-ha! You crazy. I got that thing to take care of, so I'm gone. I'll catch y'all niggas later, a'ight?"

With that, Kindu left the room. Bird turned his attention back to the two men in front of him. He finished rolling a blunt and sat it down on the desk to dry.

"A'ight, so, I done showed my sign of good faith. Now, will y'all sit y'all guns on the table? C'mon, meet me halfway, now," Bird said.

"Whoa, bruh! No offense, but I don't even know you, like that. Ain't no telling what you got planned for us. We came here for information and to find out what you wanted. Now, this trust thang is a two-way street. Sunami say you good, I'll accept that. But you wanna operate wit' York? Then, take that gun from under your desk and put it on the table, first!" York said.

Bird smiled as he slowly brought a chunky, silver .40 caliber pistol from under the table. He sat it down in front of him and placed his hands in his lap. Sunami nodded to York and stood, removing his gun from behind him and placing it on the table. York took his ten millimeter out of his shoulder holster and did the same. Before he could sit back down, Bird was shaking his head.

"The other one, too," he said.

"What?" York asked. "The gun in the small of your back... lose it, too."

"How the fuck?..."

"C'mon, I was born at night, not last night!"

York placed his compact block 357 on the table beside the other gun. He was very impressed, but shocked at the same time. Though he preferred to have his guns, York wasn't tripping. He was sure that either himself or Sunami could get over the desk to kill Birdman and get their guns by the time a threat presented itself. They were just that good.

"Now that we've made it past the introductions and the other bullshit, I hear you wanna find out about this guy, Obidiah MaTimbu. Right?" Bird asked.

"Yeah. What can you tell us?" Sunami asked.

"What do you already know?"

"He's a gang leader of mercenaries from Africa. Dibs and dabs in oil, diamonds and everything criminal. Very powerful guy, plenty of connections and he wants me and my people dead. We are trying to figure out why and where we can find his ass. The only defense I know of is a good ass offense. Feel me?"

"Well, you're right about all that MaTimbu is stupid, stupid rich. Even more so than me and I'm close to seeing a hundred mil, a year!"

"Damn, nigga!" York said.

"Yeah, well...I'm 'bout to retire. Too stressful. But his gang is more like a cartel or mob family. He's the back bone. Like they say, kill the head, the body dies. As far as him wanting you dead, all I can tell you is that he's connected with some real ruthless people. The CIA, Mexican Mafia, Cuba Mafia, Medellin Cartel and the Portellini Crime Family. Other than that, I'm sure he hates rap music, too!" Bird smiled.

"So, about the Cuban Mafia...Do you know...?" Sunami asked.

"Yeah. That's why I wanted to talk, actually. I found out about your war last year when a guy named Mario Sanchez and his family turned up dead."

"Yeah, we shut them niggas down. Conflict of Interest," York said.

"Well, I got some bad news, for ya, then."

"What?" Sunami asked.

"Cuba Sanchez is not dead," Bird said.

Sunami's heart pounded a mile second considering what this now piece of information meant. If Cuba was alive, their families were not safe, and wouldn't be until he wasn't breathing. But what he still couldn't understand was how this MaTimbu dude was coming at them from out of left field. And, for what?

"So, Cuba is still alive?" Sunami asked.

"Alive, and well! In fact, when you killed his decoy, it took a lot of pressure off of him from a lot of people. Therefore, he tried to settle for just getting York, here, and his family as an even scoreboard since he couldn't defeat you. That was supposed to be his last form of action before he went underground for a while to let people believe he was dead. Well, he emerged with a partnership on a deal between the Mexican Mafia and MaTimbu incorporated.

"My guess is, he found out that York's attempt had been a failure. Now, he's trying to tie up loose ends. His superiors no longer support his vendetta against you. Y'all cost them lost time and money, not to mention manpower! I gotta give it to y'all...you remind me of my nigga, Face," Bird said.

York chewed on this thought for a while. Bird lifted the rolled blunt he had set down and lit it up. As the smells drifted, he inhaled and passed it to Sunami. It was York who asked the next question.

"So, where can we find MaTimbu? Surely, if we get him, Cuba's funding stops. Then, we can fish him out and do what shoulda been done the first time," he said.

"MaTimbu is like the wind. He moves without being seen, although you can definitely feel him when he passes. In order to pin him to a particular place, I'd have to do some deep digging, which is what I plan on doing for y'all. Because y'all my niggas," Bird said.

"And what is it that you want in return?" Sunami asked, passing the blunt to York.

"It's simple. You two heard about what happened to Mac Santiago?" Bird asked.

"Nah."

"Uh-Uh." Bird explained what took place in New York with Ace, Pretty Tone and Fatboy. He told how Patrick Portellini had kidnapped Pretty Tone's son, trying to extort him. He explained to them how Ace had felt obligated to help and how helping had caused the personal feud between the two forces.

"Yeah, I was in New York when Tone was on the news! Didn't he kill that nigga?" Sunami asked.

"Yeah, he did. But he also had the FBI hot on his ass. God only knew how many of them he had killed," Bird said.

He continued with the story on the final situation with Ace. Bird told of Fatboy getting shot and how Ace and some of Bird's own lil' homes had accidentally killed Portellini's son. He told of the father, Luigi, being furious and determined to even the score. Finally, it boiled down to Luigi being in cahoots with the CIA and getting information from them to learn of Ace's whereabouts. The government was tired of the expenses of trying to put an end to Santiago's reign. Legally, they could never get him. So, they paid for the wet work to be done. He had been assassinated!

"And that's where y'all come in. I want true retribution," Bird said.

"So, you want us to kill...who? The CIA agent, the mafia boss? Who is this directed at?" York asked.

"All of them! I've spent eighty-seven million dollars getting the info I have on these bitch ass niggas. I want Portellini dead, the CIA agent that paid him, Knicks, dead. And the special agent in charge, Samuel Brown...he's a director, now. I want him dead first. I'll take care of the tracking of this MaTimbu guy, for you, and I'll give you twenty million dollars.

"York choked on the weed smoke, hearing the figure that was on the table. No matter how rich you were, twenty million was a lot of fucking money! And he damn sure wanted a slice of that shit!

"What do you know about the Portellini's, I mean, dude could be dead by now," Sunami said.

"He's not. But, his daughter is running the show, surprisingly. It'll all be set up for you to be introduced as a potential business partner. Sunami I'd rather for you to handle that, alone, because you're not in the spotlight as much. You can get close to them and then kill all of them. You'll be introduced under a false name. It's simple with our type of business. We use fake names all the time. That way, the head honchos in Italy won't be able to send nobody at you when it's done. I got all the info on the others that you need. Brown and Knicks will be a piece of cake. They're sleepers. They think their personal info can't be bought, so...you'll have a leg up, on them. What do you say to the offer? I'll get you what you need on MaTimbu and in the meantime, you handle this for me and make some pocket change, huh?" Bird asked.

Sunami wanted to accept right then, but, there were no individuals in his circle that had more power than the other. He would put it on the table with Zahir Animal and Raquel present. Then, he'd make a decision. "Let me toss it around to my Chairman of the board. I'll give you an answer, let's say, tomorrow by midnight," Sunami said. "That's kosher. I know about you and your team. Y'all got a great operation going. I hope we can make this happen," Bird said, rising.

Chapter 7

Later that night, the entire team met in a private dining room at an exclusive Italian restaurant in California. Before leaving Atlanta, Sunami and York had a couple more drinks and smoked some fire ass bud with Bird while he gave them a tour of the entire estate. Come to find out, there had been a manmade mind behind the castle that they had to reach by golf cart. Bird's estate sat on twenty something acres, surrounded by trees, a pond and green landscape.

"All that tennis and basketball shit is overrated. I didn't even play ball when I grew up in the project. So, what the fuck I need goal for, now? And I damn sure ain't learn how to play tennis!" Bird had explained.

Now, the discussion of their trip had been laid on the table for all to consider. Sunami sipped his wine and waited for their opinion. The five of them were waiting on the main course meals to arrive. On the flight back, York had told him that he was game. The way he had explained it gave a good point of view.

"I'm saying...The shit shouldn't take us nowhere near as long to get it done. And, unless I've missed something since I've been gone, we don't even make twenty mil a year selling dope, yet! So, even with a percentage of the money, it'll be an easy profit for shit we're capable of doing. Four million, a piece, is a good share. I'm in. I'll cancel the tour and anything else, for that much paper," he had said.

The main courses arrived and Sunami pushed his house salad plate to the side. The two waitresses assigned to them sat plates of pasta down in their respective places. Sunami's plate consisted of penne pasta, cheese shreds, veal and shrimp slices in red, thick, spicy tomato source. A fresh basket of bread was placed between him and Zahir, and another between Animal and Raquel. All the wine glasses were topped off from the two bottles that sat in ice buckets, on stands, next to the table. Then, the waitresses left the VIP dining room. Animal spoke before he dug in.

"If it's gon get us the info we need on the muthafucka that tried to take out a hit on both of y'all's families, I'm down. The money don't matter, but, I'll gladly take my share! Call it a bonus. I'm doing it for y'all, homes. Because niggas crossed the muthafucka fucking line. Period," he said.

Well Sunami, I feel what Animal saying. But it's hard to say no to four million dollars! That is the share, right?" Zahir asked. "Of course, my nigga. Every dollar made in this will be split down the middle. The only bread we don't do that with is what we make independently," Sunami said.

"Well, I'm down."

"So, that leaves me," Raquel said. "I'm not too cool wit' hitting a CIA agent and an FBI director, especially with that bitch nigga Lavender on you, Sunami. But, since they came at my fam, and it's part of the deal to end this shot with whoever, a bitch in. The four mill will do me some good, too."

"Then, its decided. I'll let homie know, tonight or tomorrow. I'll ask for ten up front and we'll hit. This is how I see it. I need to go ahead and get put on to the mafia family so I can penetrate. Zahir, you and Animal can go back to New York and lay on the FBI man, Brown. After I tell Bird we're in, he's gonna give us homie addresses and all that. York, you and Raquel will take care of the CIA man, Knicks, when we find out his address. He wants Brown hit first, so that ain't gonna be a problem. That way the work is spread out between us.

"We all earn our keep. I don't think either of you should need extra help on those two missions because I plan to do it hood style. But after you scope it out, if you feel like you need something, just say so. If anything I think I might need you, all, for the Portellini family. It all depends, though. I'll let you know. But, I'm in for the long haul. I'm hoping to pull my part off in a couple of months," Sunami said.

"So, Bird's gonna take care of the money spent and drugs bought from the mafia, right?" York asked.

"I believe so. I'll get into all that with him, tonight."

"Then, you need to go see the connect and make sure everything is straight on that end."

"I'll send Hypnotic with the message. She'll holla at her uncle and handle the leg work while we're M.I.A, ya feel me? It'll work. This is what we do," Sunami boasted.

"That's whass up, then," Zahir said, taking a big drink of red wine.

They finished eating and paid the tab. They all left a hundred dollars, a piece, for a tip.

York was stopping by Phame's to stay the night, then catching the red eye flight back to New York. Raquel would go with him. Sunami was going to visit Cherry for the night and going home early. He didn't know what Animal or Zahir had planned but he was sure both of them had bitches they could visit or homes to go to. Animal sled into a Benz jeep outside and honked the horn on his way out the lot. York and Raquel left in a rented Bentley Azure. As Sunami was climbing in Hypnotic's SUV, which he had driven to the airport, Zahir pulled up in a black Maserati coupe. They would all get some rest before taking on this job. Nobody knew what the outcome would be, but they all held their hopes high. Four million dollars was on the table.

***

"So, you are telling me that you failed, correct? And Vanessa is dead, right?"

The tall dark-skinned figure asked calmly. Dani had barely escaped from the property of her assigned target with her life. She felt she and her partner had been poorly informed and wasn't equipped for such a difficult task. Now that she had made it back to, what was considered as, "safety," her actions and account of what happened were being questioned. How ridiculous could this fool be, she thought, watching Obidiah MaTimbu pace in front of her. He hadn't even paid her in advance! Now, he was upset that she had saved her own life to be able to fight another day?

It was his fault that Vanessa was dead, for underestimating the target and misinforming the two of them.

Because of this imbecile, they had practically gone into a blazing inferno with squirt guns! "Yes," Dani spoke with dignity.

"The mission was a failure. And Vanessa was killed in action. We were poorly prepared for..."

"SILENCE!!" Obidiah yelled, interrupting Dani's excuse.

The man, MaTimbu, was a true chameleon, Dani thought as he glared into her steady stare. On the outside, in front of cameras and questioning eyes, he presented himself as the intelligent, ambitious businessman who would stop at nothing to control and manipulate what he set his eyes on. As long as it was legal. But, she knew, truthfully, he would stop at nothing, period. And to his members of highly respected, elite and feared gang of trained, born and bred mercenaries, he showed a merciless contempt for anyone who couldn't complete their assignments. Dani knew that she had been taking a huge risk, coming back to him instead of making a run for it. But there was no place to run, or hide, when the "MaTimbu Tribe" had its sights on you. She had figured that she might be able to gain a bit of leverage since she had been intimate with MaTimbu on several occasions.

Nevertheless, she was far from afraid of him! Dani held and incredible resume that boasted over a hundred successful assassinations. If MaTimbu wanted to kill her, she thought unconsciously, he would have to earn it.

Because she had every intention of fighting fire with fire. She was no pushover.

"I've listened to your tale of ambush and being under equipped," MaTimbu spoke with a thick east African accent.

"What I don't understand is, why, if you discovered such a high amount of security, did you not covertly eliminate each one of the guards before advancing on the main building? If you found one, you knew you would find two. If you killed two, why not just kill them all? My reports show that there were six guards, in all. SIX, Dani!! You, a highly trained military soldier, who has experienced tough decision making under worse circumstances, acted in a way that I could have NEVER imagined you would, before now. And, for you to bring this failure back to my door, at my feet, expecting sympathy, only shows me how truly foolish you are."

"Obidiah, I—"

"Listen!"

"No, *you* listen!" Dani screamed in frustration.

Obidiah struck her with a blow that, had she not been a trained soldier, no woman would've been able to take and still stand! Before she could control her reflex, Dani short jabbed MaTimbu directly in the chin and followed it with a right cross. They were engulfed into an all-out brawl that lasted all of ten seconds. MaTimbu's security man subdued a furious Dani, who continued to struggle against his hold. Tears ran down her face in frustration and disappointment. She entertained the thought of actually loving MaTimbu, at one time. How could she have been so stupid?

MaTimbu was right, she was foolish. Obidiah wiped the trickle of blood from his lip with a small cloth he produced from his pocket. His eyes locked with those of Dani's.

"Just the type of behavior I expected from an incompetent cunt!" He chuckled.

"The only thing you were ever good for was a good fuck and blow job."

Obidiah produced a large knife and advanced on the subdued woman, quickly. He rammed the blade into her stomach, below the navel, and ripped her up to her breast plate. Dani choked on her own blood, for a moment of surprise, before dropping to the floor of the warehouse, which MaTimbu owned in Newport News, Virginia. She died, there, in a pool of her own blood and feces.

"Dump the body, Rojo."

MaTimbu ordered while opening the face of his cellphone. Killing Sunami and his consigliere was proving to be much more of a challenge then he had first anticipated. First, MaTimbu had sent out three capable, reliable assassins with Rojo, out in his yacht. When Rojo returned the next morning, alone, MaTimbu turned on the news. Marcus Knight, aka Sunami, had been the topic of every top ten station. Even CNN was talking about the attempt on his life. Obidiah MaTimbu had been shocked, first, then impressed with the young black man. After making a few calls, he had found out that two of his assassins had been brutally gutted and the other shot. Who the hell were these people? The phone rang. Obidiah wanted to ask one of his partners, the one who had given him this task, what he wanted done about this change of events. The answer came after four rings.

"MaTimbu," the voice said.

"Yes. Team two has failed, also," Obidiah informed.

"Have you taken care of the failures?"

"Yes. What would you like me to do? Continue with the efforts?"

"Not quite yet. I have a feeling that our little problem will fall right into our hands, soon."

The call was disconnected. Obidiah MaTimbu didn't know what his partner meant by that statement, but he sure didn't like having loose ends. MaTimbu was obsessive- compulsive about the neatness of his business ventures. Sunami and York would have to be taken care of, eventually, if business was to be conducted in an orderly manner. It didn't matter what they had achieved, they weren't that good! Were they?

***

Sunami ended his phone conversation with Birdman as he pulled into a parking space a couple yards away from Cherry's apartment building. He had agreed to the terms of the negotiations and gave Bird the account number to one of his overseas bank accounts. Bird agreed to advance him half the payment, plus another two million to handle expenses for the dealings with the Portellini family.

"I want you to meet me out in New York in a week and we'll introduce you to them and get this thing started, ASAP! I figured you might want some time to get ya mind right," Bird said.

"Whatever works for you. Go 'head and fax the info on the two other targets to my Tenth Street Entertainment office in New York, now. I'll have my niggas get on that. Ain't no telling when the fire-works will start, because I like for my homes, to know what's going on before they move. But, they'll go on and get the ball rolling, though," Sunami had promised. Bird had told him that it was a done deal. And he reminded him to check his account the next day and verify the secret money transaction.

Sunami assured him that he would and they signed off. Then, the imaged of seeing Cherry's sexy ass, again started playing through his mind. Cherry was a great assistant, but she was an un-believable lover! When she had come to work for Sunami, recently, he could not help but charm his way into her panties! But, unlike most woman, Cherry hadn't been star struck by Sunami, even though she highly enjoyed his music. They just connected on a level that Sunami couldn't explain. It wasn't about money, either.

Cherry had actually protested when Sunami had offered to place her in a better apartment than the one she had been living in previously. He had wanted her out of LA because it was so danger-ous and she was so beautiful. Sunami believed that her swag alone deserved better. Now, Cherry lived in a lavish apartment and went to school part-time. Sunami wouldn't let her pay rent, much to her resentment, but he just didn't go off buying her any and everything, either.

Like the joke about his wife's customized Ferrari that had been ordered for their upcoming anniversary... Cherry had said she wished someone would buy her one. But Sunami knew that she had been kidding. And even if she hadn't been, there was no way in hell! But he liked her appreciation of his gifts and she respected his mar-riage. Cherry knew that what they shared together was temporary, if it was anything. But she enjoyed it as much, if not more than Sunami. Sunami pressed the button that secured the locks on his wife's car.

He made his way to the assigned building and took out his keys. He thought he could hear some talking! Sunami unlocked the door and let himself in. There, in the front room, sat Cherry and two other beautiful white girls. They all locked eyes and Sunami saw registra-tion come on their facial expressions. They knew who he was.

Cherry sat on the camel skin love seat near the patio door while the other two women were on the long couch. Cherry was wearing something and a T-shirt that read, "I love Wolfpack music."

He knew, from past conversations, that it was her sleeping shirt. Her feet were bare and her toes were painted a sea blue color. She smiled her beautiful, white smile when she saw him. She was pleased by the surprise visit.

"Oh, my god, Cherry! That's...that's...isn't that..?" the brown headed girl asked.

"Sarah, calm down! Baby, close the door and come in," Cherry instructed.

Sunami compiled and hung his suit jacket on a coat rack he had bought for the apartment when he had the interior decorator furnish and decorate the place. He made his way over to the love seat and sat down beside Cherry. She leaned over and pecked him on the lips before setting her pretty feet in his lap. She turned back towards the two young women.

"Sarah, Kimmy, this is my personal friend, Sunami. I would call him by his birth name, but he might spank me!" Cherry giggled.

"Baby, these are my two best friends. Sarah and Kimmy."

"Whass up, ladies?" Sunami said, smoothly.

"Oh my fucking god, I mean, were sitting in the room with Sunami, the rapper!! Can I get your autograph, or is that something you only do when you're like, out doing shows, or whatever?" Sarah asked.

Sunami smiled as he eyed Sarah. She looked to be about five foot ten inches tall, but she was sitting down. She had deep brown hair, green eyes with flecks of gold and pretty, pink lips. She was wearing a pair of white shorts with gold letters spelling the name of her college on the backside, a small tank top and some of those colorful socks with toes on them. Her thighs are what caught Sunami's, ever wondering, eye. She was tanned and thick as a slice of pound cake!

"I'll be right back!" Sarah said, jumping up and running to the backroom.

Cherry shook her head and laughed. The three of them, Sunami, Cherry and Kimmy were left in the room as Sarah went to go find a souvenir for Sunami to sign.

Kimmy reached over to shake Sunami's hand.

"Are you Cherry's boyfriend?" Kimmy asked.

"Well, I..."

"You don't have to tell me, or nothing. It's just that, I never see her with any guys and lots of guys like her at our school. She's always talking about how she doesn't have time for boyfriends, and stuff. Honestly, I was starting to think she was a lesbian!"

"Bitch!!" Cherry said in amazement.

"I'm only kidding, Cherry, gosh!" They laughed.

Kimmy was a short, sexy woman with dirty blonde hair. Her face was fuller than Sarah's and her bottom was fully bloomed! She had teal-colored eyes that were the perfect mixture of blue and green. She wore her hair in a ponytail and Sunami noticed the small mole on the left side of her neck. She wore gray sweatpants that had lovely curves and a long, blue "Surfer Chicks" T-shirt that barely contained the two melon sized breasts underneath! Sunami's imagination was running wild with thoughts.

"I said, we're personal friends, Kimmy. Let's leave it at that." To Sunami, she said, "We were having a girls night. Since we don't have class tomorrow, we decided to have a couple drinks and watch some movies. But, I didn't know you were coming. Why didn't you call?"

"Well, I just got back from a meeting in Georgia. Then, I had a meeting a couple hours ago when I got here, so. I didn't feel like making the trip to the Bu. Thought I'd come surprise you. But if you need me to go," Sunami said.

"No, no, no. Don't go. But my girls are staying over..."

"That's fine. I'll stay outta y'all's way."

"No. You're good, Sunami. Believe me, she needs this!" Kimmy said.

Sarah came back with a camera and a notepad in hand. She looked like she half expected Sunami to disappear while she had been gone! Sunami signed a personal letter to Sarah and took several pictures with her and Kimmy. He promised to see them again, when the pictures were developed, so he could sign them, also. Sarah had offered to go get and find an open store that would do it then. But Sunami promised to see them and told her that it wouldn't be necessary to go out close to midnight to develop a couple pictures. He even invited them out to the modeling agency an offered them summer jobs as assistants for his other board members.

The four of them watched a few sappy love story movies while Cherry snuggled up against Sunami. To his surprise, Kimmy and Sarah came to sit at their feet, constantly touching one or the other when something sad happened. Soon, it was time for bed. Sunami and Cherry said their good nights and disappeared.

Chapter 8

Sunami closed the master bedroom's door behind him just as Cherry was putting her hair into a ponytail. Sunami went unbuttoning his shirt and taking off his jewelry as he watched her. Memories of their last sexual encounter had his penis extending inside his slacks.

"How was Georgia?" Cherry asked.

"Some bullshit. Business, basically," Sunami said.

"Is this gonna be a pit stop, or will I actually see you when I wake up in the morning?"

"I'll be here. I'm tired as a dawg, baby."

"Not too tired, I hope." She smiled, taking off her shorts and exposing the red thong she wore.

"Never too tired for that!"

Sunami dressed down to his boxes and black socks. Cherry stripped down to just her flesh. Even the bra was tossed onto the floor. Her perky pink nipples accused Sunami as she walked over to him and kissed him softly on the lips. The next kiss was full of tongue and passion. Sunami continued to grow stiff and Cherry let her small hands creep inside his boxes to take hold of the object that had been provoked by this thick, brown slab of meat!

"My friends like you," Cherry said between kisses.

Moaning has Sunami's fingertips lightly caressed her butt cheeks.

"Well, I like them, too. They're nice chicks, I guess," he said, lowering himself to one of her large, light pink nipples.

He ran his hot tongue over it slowly and felt her shiver. The smell of her wild cherry body lotion drove him crazy!

"No. I mean, they like you, like you," Cherry said, caressing the waves on top of Sunami's head. She was rubbing her thighs together, causing her pussy to moisten more and more.

"I mean, okay. They're attractive. Why are you telling me this?" Sunami asked.

"Do you like them? I mean, would you have sex with them?"

"Are you suggesting a threesome? Sure. I'm game, ya dig?"

"NEVER!" She laughed.

"Share you, enough already. But, it would probably change their lives to get a piece of you. Sarah has never been with a black guy before. She'd fall endlessly in love with you, if only for sex!"

"Fuck them. It's about us, right now. Shhh."

Sunami picked her up and carried her six or seven feet to the bed. He laid her down and pulled her G-string with his teeth. The smell of her sex was overwhelming. He kiss the clitoris and parted her lips with a stiff, slow stroke of his tongue. Cherry's thighs clamped on to the sides of his face. The sensation was unimaginable!

"Relax, baby. Relax," Sunami soothed.

He took his time, kissing her inner thighs, down to each of her toes. Her moaning grew with each kiss that sent waves of pleasure throughout her entire body. Sunami turned her over onto her stomach and kissed the back of her thighs, ass and went all the way up to her neck. He came back down and ate her pussy from behind, causing her to moan loudly into her pillow. He probed her anus with his thumb as he licked the juices that seeped from her dripping wet vagina. When he couldn't take it anymore, he enter her from behind, gripping her waist and pulling her to all fours. He plunged deep and found a steady rhythm that was comfortable for them.

"Aaah, I swear to God, I love you. Marcus, I love you so much, baby," Cherry vowed as the dick made her dizzy with ecstasy.

"C'mon, let's give ya girls a show, baby," Sunami said, speeding up the pace.

Sunami's balls slapped up against the hood of Cherry's pussy as he picked up the pace. He slapped her on the ass as he pounded harder, and harder. It was an all-out war on the queen size bed. Cherry started to throw the pussy back at him as she panted and stared down at her pillows. She could fill the length of Sunami reaching up into her chest, it felt like. All of him filled her up to the max. The juices from Cherry's pussy drenched Sunami's trimmed pubic area. The little hair that Cherry had was matted down from sweat and body fluids.

"Put it in my ass, baby! I'm 'bout to cum. Put it in my ass!" Cherry ordered.

Sunami switched holes and plunged into Cherry's anus. Now squatting over her, Sunami stuck his dick into her tight, wet asshole. Cherry went completely nuts!!

"Aaah!! Fuck, yeah. Hit it, baby. Fuck me, like that! Oh, shit, that feels fucking wonderful! Aah, ah, ah, ah, ah!! I'm cumming! I'm cumming! Marcus, ah, I'm cuuummmmmmmmming, yeeeah!" she screamed as white cream foamed out of her ass and a clear skeet shot out of her pussy.

Sunami, on the verge of nutting himself, pulled out, and Cherry turned around to meet him.

She jacked his shaft and sucked on the head until cum shot rapidly into her mouth. She swallowed every bit and continued to lick the head clean until there was nothing left. Cherry sucked Sunami off until he climaxed again, which took another hour or so. Then, she sucked him soft and fondled his balls with her tongue. The last thing Sunami could remember, before drifting off to sleep, was the sight of Cherry licking on his nipples and grinding her pussy on his crotch. He was gone!

***

The next morning, Sunami awoke to Cherry coming back into the room wearing his dress shirt only. Instead of unbuttoning it, she pulled it over her head, after closing the room door, and climbed back on the large bed. She was all smiles.

"Guess what?" she said, removing the covers from his naked body and massaging his limp penis.

"What's that?" Sunami asked, eyeing the tattoo below her navel that read "W.C." It was the initials of his crime family, Wolfpack Cartel. Cherry was his crime family mistress. Meaning that she recruited females who showed loyalty, discipline, and ambition to get paid by all means. So, for all the women that were recruited, they wore the tattoo on a part of their body, seen or unseen. So far, there were about twenty women who served as traffickers and shell company owners who were trusted with goods and money and lots of information. Sunami could smell bacon in the air. As his penis grew, his hunger did, also.

"They heard every last bit of it, last night! They were very impressed. Kimmy said that we sounded so exotic, she had to masturbate!" Cherry laughed.

"That's what's up. Glad to be of service to the needy." He laughed.

"Maybe, just maybe, I'll let them gang bang you! See if you can take all three of us. But, not today. You belong to me."

"I'm always up for a good challenge."

Cherry took him into her mouth again and hummed. Sunami lay back and enjoyed the early morning massage. As Cherry started to get into it, the door swung open. Sunami's eyes opened at the sound.

"Oh, I'm sorry, guys. I was just gonna let you know that the food is ready. I didn't know y'all were going at it, again!" Sarah said, eyeing Sunami's extended cock.

"It's fine. We'll be out in a sec," Cherry said.

"Yeah. Thanks, Sarah," Sunami said.

"No, thank you! Thank you very much." She laughed, leaving the bedroom and closing the door.

Cherry turned to Sunami and smiled her perfect smile. She shook her head.

"She's never gonna stop talking about you now. You're gonna have to fuck the poor girl's brains out!"

"Well...don't mind if I do!"

***

Sunami had spent the rest of that day with them taking the three women to the beach and out to eat. They had traveled in Kimmy's Jeep Grand Cherokee because it had tinted windows all the way around. She also had some little twenty-inch rims on it! Pretty fly, for a white girl. Then, Sunami spent the next two days with Hypnotic and his two daughters, Brianna and Rain. Calls were made in between taking his daughters to the park, strolling them along, and walking them both in the water at the beach.

It was set up for Hypnotic to handle the transactions between Sean while Sunami and the others went to work on the other tasks. Brianna and Rain would go to his mother's house in North Carolina while they were away. The documents needed to gain knowledge of the government agency's workers were sent, and marked confidential, to Sunami's New York office for the record label. York and the others would pick that up when they reached the Big Apple.

After putting Rain in the car seat of the Range Rover beside Brianna and Ms. Cindy, Sunami and York followed the others back onto the plane. All tours and video shoots had been put off until further notice. Hypnotic, Raquel, Zahir, and Animal were already settled inside. It was agreed that Sunami would stay in a hotel room, alone, under his wife's name. Hypnotic would be staying at her uncle's home until she went back to Malibu, which wouldn't be that long. Zahir had a fake ID, as well as Raquel, so that the two groups of them could be inconspicuous. They would go to the office to pick up the fax and start on their missions.

Sunami would be met by a friend of Bird's in three days and taken to a private invite event, where they hoped to introduce him to the acting underboss of the Portellini family, Carmen Portellini. As far as he was told, the name that they would address him by, and introduce him as, had been mentioned to the female crime boss, already, on several occasions. Supposedly, he had been recommended as a potential business partner. In New York, several cars waited for the plane to touch down. After deplaning, Sunami kissed Hypnotic as she wished him and the others luck on their missions. She was escorted to a waiting Mercedes Benz Sprinters by one of her uncles Yakuza henchmen. A simple Cadillac sedan awaited Sunami. York and the others would rent cars under false names and fine hotels to stay in, after the fax was picked up and properly distributed between them.

***

There was a knock at the door. Sunami rose from the bed in the hotel room where he had been checking his email. He was dressed in casual khaki pants, a black Polo sweater and Timberland boots with tan soles. There was a gun tucked in the front of his pants, unseen. He wore a simple diamond bezel chain with a white gold and diamond-encrusted watch made by Marc Jacob. Sunami opened the door, ready to take action. The Italian man at the door was Sunami's height.

He wore a casual three-button, collared shirt and dark-colored slacks. His jet-black hair was stylish and he wore an earring in his left ear. He also wore a light leather jacket, black in color. Sunami noticed the Frank Muller watch on his left arm, as well as the bulge in his jacket pocket. The man extended his hand as he came into the room.

"Sly, right? I'm Giovanni, the financial adviser for some of the wise guys in this city. Bird's your peoples?"

Giovanni asked in a thick New York accent. It had been told to him that he would be introduced under the alias, "Sly." Bird had told him that Portellini women might recognize him for who he was, given his celebrity, and not deny if she called him out. But he believed that she would respect the alias, given the type of business they we're planning to conduct.

"Yeah, what's good, Giovanni? Birdman, that's my fam right there," Sunami said, shaking his hand.

"Yeah, yeah. We go way back, me and Bird. He's good money. You ever need financial advice, you call, ya hear? I'll give you the same discount I give Bird, straight up."

"Cool."

"So, you ready to ride out, or what? You gotta jacket? It's pretty chilly out there for a southerner, like ya self. And, call me Gio. Everybody else does. C'mon."

Sunami grabbed his coat and followed Giovanni out the door. On the elevator, Sunami put on a wave cap and tossed a black and gold New Orleans Saints fitted cap on. Giovanni was telling him about the little get together that they were going to.

"It's Carmen's sister's birthday party. I think she's turning thirty-eight, or something like that. There's gonna be a lot of power at this party. Plenty of mafioso to rub shoulders with. Your organization, Wolfpack Cartel, is well known, so once I introduce you as a goodfella, you'll be good to go. There has been plenty of talk about you, already. So just be yourself."

Giovanni said as they exited the elevator.

They crossed the lobby and exited. Giovanni handed a ticket to one of the valet boys and they rushed off. Sunami was mentally preparing himself for the event. Giovanni produced a Black & Mild and lit it. Soon, a silver BMW 760i was brought to the curb in front of them. Giovanni tapped Sunami on the arm as he started to move.

"C'mon, this is us," he said.

They got into the car and drove off. As Gio navigated the car through the crowded city, Sunami was trying to put together a game plan. He didn't want to make himself look too eager in the presence of the Portellini woman, so he planned to play the noncommittal role. He would just be the smooth, cautious person that he was, keeping an eye on everyone and listening, as people spoke to him, for every little detail. When business was brought up, he planned to act nonchalant as if he didn't need anything from anybody, which he didn't! The most important thing he kept reminding himself was not to answer too many questions. The less they knew about him, the better.

And his tight lip policy would show them that he wasn't a mouth piece, as some called it. Meaning that he didn't run his mouth all the time and that he knew how to keep to himself. The two of them ended up in New Jersey. The area was a suburban area with huge, high-priced mansions and plenty of top end cars. Nothing too out of the ordinary, Sunami thought. Just a few Mercedes, your average BMW's and some nice Porsche's.

Sunami saw a Maserati here and there and one Maybach Benz, so far. They pulled up to a gated estate with two guards out front. Both wore black and had weapons in plain sight. Sunami could see plenty of cars beyond the gate, in the driveway.

"Okay, we're here. Stick your gun in the glove compartment. They're not allowed in the house."

Giovanni said, placing his block inside the middle console. Sunami took his Heck & Koch and put it inside the glove compartment. Gio whistled at the sight of the high end, massive weapon. "That's some piece you got, there," he said. "Yeah, well Gio, this is a helluva business we're in, ya dig?"

***

While Sunami was entering the mafioso party, Animal and Zahir were following the FBI director. Zahir had wanted to get a feel of the man's routine, so they followed him from work to see if he had any habits that they could capitalize on. Already, they had identified the house belonging to Samuel Brown and had witnessed his wife and kids come home from their busy day. That was yesterday. Today, Brown left the Federal Plaza early for lunch. Zahir stayed in a crowd, several yards behind him, as the man walked down the crowded streets of New York. Animal followed on the opposite side of the road, keeping his eyes on the man as he entered a small deli advertising kosher foods. Animal stayed while Zahir went in and joined the long line of people. Brown, a black man, was several people in front of him.

So far, Zahir hadn't been noticed or directly looked at. He moved up in line as it moved along. The FBI director ordered himself a sandwich and a kosher pickle before heading to the back of the deli and finding a table. Zahir picked the first thing on the menu, when it was his turn, not paying attention. He grabbed himself a Coca-Cola and found a seat. He chose not to look at the FBI man as he sat in the back with his back to the wall. Surely the man would be trained to spot someone tailing him or paying him close attention.

But, upon glance, Zahir saw that he was scanning a newspaper that had been on the table. Zahir ate the food he had ordered, noting that it hadn't been bad, either. He ignored Brown, even as two other men in suits came into the deli and sat with the director. Brown engaged them in a conversation and, for a brief second, locked eyes with Zahir. Instinct came and Zahir nodded to him and turned his attention to the TV in the corner that was turned to CNN. Shortly after the eye contact, Animal came into the deli and sat at the table, opposite Zahir's. He lit up a cigarette and breezed through a paper that had been on his table, also.

Zahir was nursing his Coca-Cola and staring intently at the TV screen. Catching movement from the corner of his eye, Zahir watched the director and the other two men leaning from his peripheral view. Zahir continued to watch the TV as Animal kept his eyes on the men. When they left, Animal joined Zahir.

"I thought it was 'bout to go down!" Animal said.

Keese

Chapter 9

Being patted down at the door wasn't all that bad, Sunami thought. It did, however, remind him of his days spent in prison. That thought kept him conscious of the risks he was taking in doing the things that he was doing. Then, the thoughts of everything he had to lose came to mind.

The last thing Sunami wanted to do was be behind bars while his daughters grew up in a world of vultures! I gotta tighten up, he thought. This shit could put me in a box or in a cell at any time. He shook those thoughts away as he was led into a makeshift ballroom inside the impressive house.

The room wasn't crowded, but there are plenty of people in attendance. All sizes, shapes and types of people mingled, bringing different walks of life together in the same room. No matter what you did, in this room, chances were it was illegal somewhere down the line. Giovanni backed Sunami's theory when he started pointing and naming people, along with their sins.

"Hey, Sly, you see that older guy, right there?" Giovanni asked.

"Yeah, I see him," Sunami said.

"You know who that is?"

"Nah, Gio. Who is it?"

"That's William Elwood, the third. Also known as, federal judge Elwood! He's been on the Portellini payroll for years. And that guy, right there with the bald spot...He's an adviser for the mayor. Basically, he puts the bugs in the ear and helps make decisions. Then you got the bitch, over there. That's Tracy Cline. She's from North Carolina. You might know her. She's and assistant district attorney in New York, now. Anything pop up, she gets a call, snatches the cars and loses, on command," Giovanni informed him.

Sunami wasn't all too surprised. It was well known that people inside the justice system took bribes. He knew of Tracy Cline.

He also knew a couple Crip niggas in Durham who'd love to know where she was hiding out. Maybe he'd give them a call! Then again, maybe not. Giovanni took Sunami around and introduced him to some people. Everybody seemed to know and love Giovanni.

People greeted him with hugs and kisses on the cheek, then, turned to Sunami and did the same once he was introduced as "Sly," the good guy. They made rounds and Sunami picked up a drink. Some kind of champagne.

When offered food, he respectfully declined. Then, Giovanni brought him over to a very beautiful woman with long, black curly hair. Her face was young and naive, but her eyes told a different story. A story of betrayal and anguish. A story of loss and gains. But mostly, they told the story of leadership. Sunami knew who she was before Giovanni spoke.

"Sly, I'm pleased to introduce you to Ms. Carmen Portellini. Carmen, this is Sly, the good guy." Giovanni laughed.

The beautiful woman extended her hand to shake. Sunami took it and turned it over, leaning forward to kiss the backside. Carmen Portellini was ravishing! Her brown eyes were lovely and she had amazing curves. Her hands were clean, manicured and soft. She wore a very stylish Marilyn Monroe print sweater dress made by Betsey Johnson with a belt made by Cos that hugged her midsection. She wore it with black tights by American Apparel and black, thigh high Christian Louboutin boots. Carmen wore a golden cuff, bangle and two rings, made by Kara Ross.

Her pinkish lip gloss enticed Sunami and made him curious about what she tasted like and if anybody was tasting her lips on a regular basis. He could find no suitable assumption by the look of guys in the room. And there was nobody sticking close to her, as he would if she belonged to him.

"It's nice to finally meet you, Sly. A lot of good people are saying a lot of good things about you. Maybe we could sit down and talk shop, sometime. You know, exchange tips and secrets to longevity. Haven't I seen you somewhere before? You look strangely familiar?" Carmen asked.

"Probably. I actually get seen quite a lot, unfortunately. But we can surely sit down and chat. Let's exchange numbers, later," Sunami said.

"Sure."

"So, where's the birthday woman?" Giovanni asked.

"Oh, I meant to tell you, Gio. She got sick and went to lie down inside. She's had way too much to drink, already. When she started rumbling on about our brother's death, I made her go inside. But, that won't stop the party. Everyone's having way too much fun, already. Go in and check on her. Leave Mr. Sly with me. He's in good hands," Carmen assured.

"Okay. I'll be back in a minute. Sly, you good?" Giovanni asked.

"Couldn't be better, Gio. A'ight. See ya in a few," he said, headed for a side door.

Carmen led Sunami over to a table in the corner where another couple were sitting and having drinks. With a wave of a hand, the two of them got up and left. Sunami held Carmen's seat as she sat and then went to a chair opposite of hers. "Sly...the infamous, Sly. You're a gentleman, Sly. I don't see many of those anymore. So, I finally get to meet the head of Wolfpack Cartel, huh?" she asked.

"In the flesh." Sunami smiled.

"Why the name Sly?"

"Because that's how I try to think of myself when it comes to law enforcement trying to stop me, catch me or kill me."

"Hmmm. That's interesting. And it does you good to have a name for this business, the music business and personal life, I guess."

"Correct, again."

Drinks were brought over by a man who looked like a guard. He then disappeared in the crowd without looking back. The smell of cigarette smoke brought his attention back to Carmen. She was smoking and eyeing him as he checked out the occupants of the party.

"So, what is it that you wish to accomplish, Mr. Sly?" Carmen asked, suddenly switching the conversation to the topic of business.

"Great wealth and immortality," Sunami said sarcastically.

Her laugh was beautiful and soothing. She covered her pretty white teeth with the back of her hand.

"I think I'm gonna like you, Sly. You remind me of my big brother," she said, sadness clear in her eyes.

"Oh? What happened to him?" Sunami asked.

"What makes you think something happened to him?"

"Your eyes. They tell a story. If you don't wanna..."

"He was killed. It was stupid, but I loved him. The man I was madly in love with, and he, had a conflict of interest. My lover killed him. The same man that fathered my child."

"Sorry to hear that. And what about this lover? Where is he?" Sunami asked already knowing the answer.

"In federal prison. He's never getting out. I forgave him, but my father never did. The man that helped him kill my brother is dead. I don't think I ever met him, but...That's something totally different. I meant to ask you, what are you trying to accomplish doing business with me?" Carmen asked, serious again.

"Well, I hoped the prices were going to be good enough to raise my profits. That, and immortality!" He smiled.

"What are you paying now? For the white stuff?"

"Somewhere around five a piece. Buying a hundred, at least, at a time."

"Five!? There is no way I can top that. Are you pulling my leg?"

"Yeah, I'm bull shitting you. I'm paying ten. Same deal."

"Well," she said, thinking.

"We can work something out. Who is your supplier?"

"That's confidential," Sunami said.

"Well, we'll get together in a few days. Let's have lunch, okay? Get to know each other better before we jump head first into this jungle we call business. I'll call you and we'll meet someplace."

"Perfect. Take my number."

They exchanged phone numbers and then Carmen excused herself. Coincidentally, Giovanni showed up right after she had gone. He sat down and had a drink before looking to Sunami.

"How'd it go? I see you're still alive, so, I guess good," he said.

"Yeah. It was good," Sunami assured.

"Cool. Ready to go?"

***

Special Agent Charles Lavender sat alongside four other agents inside of an FBI operation truck made to look like a U-Haul vehicle. The truck sat four houses down from Carmen Portellini's home. Inside the truck, there were several TV monitors watching the front gate of the estate. The agents had been documenting the comings and goings of the party.

"I got here as soon as I could. Has he left yet?" Lavender asked.

"Nope. He's riding with a guy in a BMW. Nice car. They arrived about two hours ago. License plate number, bravo-bravo-village, three-four-nine-one," one of the agents said.

Lavender had gotten a call saying that Marcus McKnight had been spotted enter acting with known mafia affiliates. Lavender wanted all the evidence he could get on McKnight. Never had there been so much hatred for a criminal that he wanted to collar as he had for this rapper/drug kingpin/murderer. Lavender was determined to find out what was going on with him. Why the hell are you hanging out with the Portellini's, McKnight?, Lavender wondered. It couldn't be for a drug connection, could it? As far as Agent Lavender could tell, Sunami was doing very well in the drug game.

Occasionally, his name bounced off small fishes and a few decent catches. But none of them would provide the bureau with enough to get a warrant for anything. There was a deep fear or respect for Sunami and who he dealt with on the streets. It even went as far as

Lavender hearing that he had constructed a crime organization, he had been told.

"Man, that nigga got people everywhere. All it takes is one person to hear that I told you guys this much and I'll disappear."

A man who had been caught on federal gun charges had claimed, he was trying to work a deal but wouldn't tell all he knew about Sunami and company.

"We can protect you! Why are you protecting this asshole? He's a nobody in power compared to the Government of the United States of America! He'll never even find you, and he won't be out to even be able to look for you. Help us. This'll go away and I'll get you some money thrown in, too," Agent Lavender tried to bargain.

"Hahahahahaha! You have lost your mind. You just don't know what you're dealing with. I'd be dead in twenty-four hours, at the latest. No cap," he had responded.

Now, Lavender had found another possible opening. The more, the better, he knew. You're slipping, Mr. McKnight, and I'm hot on your ass every step of the way, he thought.

"There! That's it, Lavender. That's the car he's in," the other agent said, pointing to a screen.

"Zoom on it fast!" Lavender ordered.

As the BMW pulled out, they were able to get a good view through the side mirror. Then, when it turned towards them, they could see both men. There, Sunami sat next to the pretty Italian boy. They looked like they were talking.

"Take a couple snaps, for me, real quick. I might need those later. I'm building my case," Lavender said.

Sunami and Giovanni were photographed several times by the FBI.

Neither one of them were aware of it.

***

"It's BANGA TIME, it's BANGA TIME, it's BANGA TIME!"

Animal continued repeating this as he followed the Ford Sedan at a distance. It was time to take care of the FBI director, Brown. They had followed him for a whole week and decided that going for him on the street would be too risky. So, they were following him to his house in a small, modest neighborhood in Peekskill, New York. Sunami had called last night and told them to get it done, soon.

Now was the time. The rented Chrysler Concorde waited at the light, three cars behind the Ford. Zahir sat in the backseat, crouched down, holding a sawed-off shotgun. His ski mask was in his lap. He and Animal had rehearsed the scenario over and over, already. Even before Sunami had called, they had went over how the hit would be done when the time came.

As the car pulled off, Zahir started to slide the mask over his head. He knew they were close.

"We 'bout to turn on the street, Zahir. Just hold everything down till I can get in there with you, a'ight," Animal said, making a right turn.

"I know, Animal. You just drive. I know what I gotta do. But when I'm out, pull in quick and back me up," Zahir said.

Animal reached over and grabbed the MP-5 from the front seat and sat it across his lap as they made the final turn onto Brown's street. He could see Brown, already out of the car, walking up to his door.

The street was clear, Animal noted, and nobody was out and about in their yards.

"Not yet," Animal said, cruising down the street, nearing Brown's house.

Director Samuel Brown had his key in the door and he was pushing it open. As the door gave out and he disappeared inside, the door of the Chrysler opened partially.

"Go, go, go, go!!" Animal yelled.

Zahir jumped out and ran with all his might for Brown's front door. The door had just clicked closed as Zahir reached it. Not stopping his stride, he jumped and extended his foot, kicking the door with a mighty force! The door swung open, hitting Brown in the back and surprising his wife and two children who were all in the kitchen. Before Brown could reach his gun, Zahir smacked him in the head with the shotgun. He cocked a shell into the chamber and put the big barrel to the director's cheek.

"Don't do that," Zahir advised.

Outside, Animal had pulled up and backed the Chrysler in while Zahir subdued the targets. Once the Chrysler was in place, Animal took his gun and ran into the house, closing the door behind him. Zahir had already confiscated Brown's pistol. He had the four of them sitting at the kitchen table at gunpoint.

"Did you bring the ties, B?" Zahir asked.

"I got'em." Animal produced a handful of the plastic ties. Force teams used to subdue criminals in large busts. He strapped the submachine gun around his neck and approached Brown's wife.

"Don't make this worse than it is, lady. Give me ya hands."

Animal instructed Mrs. Brown to comply and was tied up. Next came her ankles. Then, Animal moved to the children while Zahir kept the shotgun trained on the director. The kids cried as they were tightly tied up and left at the table. Animal produced a thick roll of duct tape.

"Look, don't do this. Do you know what will happen to you if you hurt one individual in this room? I'm an FBI agent. You will get the electric chair! You don't want that, do you? If you just untie my family and leave, I won't pursue you. You've got my word. Let us go and I'll let you go," Brown said.

"Boy, bye! You ain't runnin' shit, in here. You'll be lucky if we let you live. Fuck the FBI, and you too Mr. Director. We know exactly who you are. Do you remember Marcus Santiago?" Zahir asked evilly.

"Marcus...Santi...Oh my gawd, please!! That...I had nothing to do—" Brown protested.

Animal slapped a slab of tape over his mouth. After he got the tape on the others, he ran out to the Chrysler and popped the trunk. When he came back, he carried two huge jugs of gasoline into the front room. Animal turned Brown's stove on high, unaffected by their cries and screams. Then, he began soaking his half of the house with the flammable liquid. Zahir took the other jug and did his half. When everything had been drenched with the liquid, Animal soaked Samuel Brown and his family, as well as left a puddle beneath their feet.

The two masked kidnappers trailed gasoline to the door.

Animal looked out and saw that it was clear. Zahir left to go start the car as Animal took out his matches and tossed his gloves and mask into the puddle.

"Well...I guess this is goodbye. It's Banga Time!"

Chapter 10

York and Raquel weren't having so much luck. Out of a week's time, that had managed to spot CIA Agent Arnold Knicks one time, so far. And even when they identified him, he had been on the move. By the time they were in position to follow him, he was gone! After watching the townhouse, in which he lived, they concluded that he didn't stay there often. Turned out, trying to track a CIA operative was harder than tying a string to a fly! Possible, but very difficult.

The news of the house fire had been encouraging, but there was little they could do. York had watched the full news report on it, going from one station to another. The authorities reported that four bodies had been discovered in the blown up, burnt down house. They were now investigating the cause of the fire because the origin was "of a suspicious nature," said the arson investigators. It couldn't be determined whether the stove blew or if the whole thing had been orchestrated. York was on the phone with Sunami, now.

"They did a good ass job, on that shit. Nobody saw shit and the whole thing is a big mystery. I expected them to shoot up everything and have the city on fire with the FBI. I'm impressed," he said.

"Yeah. That one surprised, and impressed the hell outta me! Birdman is probably nutting all over himself, on that one. So, what's the deal with duck number two? How soon?" Sunami asked.

"Man, chasing this dude is like chasing shadows on a cloudy day. I Dino what's gon jump off on this. He ain't never home, he moves like he's Osama Bin Laden, or something. Can't say how soon it'll be. We'll just have to wait him out. What about you? You in good with the powers that be, yet?"

"Close. I still gotta earn the trust of this bitch. But, Bruh, she is so fucking fine, my nigga! I think she might be feeling da kid, too. You know I'm tryna put my Casanova game down. But, anyway. Call the nigga, Bird. See what he can come up with on the dude. I'd like for y'all to be available, if I need y'all. I'm getting ready to go to lunch with ol' girl now. She'll be here, in bout, ten to fifteen minutes, so...I'ma let you go. But stay on it, my nigga, Keep me up on it, too."

"Yeah, yeah. Nigga, don't go catching feelings for this mafioso bitch, neither. Remember... When you get close enough to touch all of 'em, it's lights out," York reminded.

"No sweat, my nigga. The only woman I love is Hypnotic. Her and my two little angels, Brianna and Rain. I just figure, what better way to get close than in between the sheets, ya dig?" Sunami laughed.

"I feel you. Be safe, though."

"Yeah. I gotta go, bruh."

"One."

"One."

***

Catch feelings for Carmen?... Hell nah!, Sunami thought as he pulled his Dior sweater over his head. There was no way. She had been part of the conspiracy to kill his peoples. Won't no love anywhere around there, for her. But, he couldn't help being attracted to her, though. With eyes that brown and lips so full, who wouldn't be mesmerized? He just wanted to sample the cookie, he didn't wanna take home the recipe!

Sunami undid his wave cap and brushed his silky hair. When that was in order, he sprinkled some Apricot Kiwi fragrance oil on and clipped his phone to his jeans pocket. As he checked his pistol, his phone rang and he holstered the gun on the inside of his pants.

"Hello?" he answered.

"Sly, I'm out front. Burgundy Porsche 911, this year's model, tinted windows," Carmen voice said.

"A'ight, I'm coming down, now."

Sunami jumped into some black, gray and white Dior sneakers and decided to leave the chain, today. His watch, earrings and bracket would already be enough to find his way down a dark alley!

He didn't wanna attract too many eyes. Outside, Sunami spotted the car and headed over. He sled into the passenger seat, noticing how sexy Carmen was, again.

She showed her beautiful white teeth and put the car in gear. Carmen was wearing a forest green Burberry trench coat with a Pilar by Anya belt wrapped around it. She wore black stretch pants and Christian Dior sneakers. To put it mildly, the girl would dress her ass off. She wore an odd-shape necklace designed by Shivan Narresh and a female Rolex.

"What's up?" she asked, navigating the stylish, yet modest vehicle.

The Porsche was decked out. Touch screen LCD, top-of-the-line navigation system and great sound quality speakers all around. H.E.R. played softly as they cruised the streets of New York City.

"Nothing much, just chilling. You know, another day, another dollar," Sunami said, struggling to keep his eyes off her.

He sat snug in the premium leather interior, listening to the soothing sounds of the Bose audio system.

"Did you catch the news the other day? About the family who died in that house fire?" Carmen asked.

"I caught a glimpse. Husband and wife with two kids?" he said.

"Yeah."

"What about it?"

"He was FBI. 'Bout a year ago, he was the agent chasing down the men who killed my brother and nephew. Agent Brown was the one who shot my son's father, paralyzing him from the waist down. Tyruss told me when I went to visit him, once. He said the muthafucka had done it purposely. You know, paralyzed him."

"Damn. Do you think the death of his family had something to do with your son's father? I mean, are you suggesting..."

"I...I can't say no, because Tyruss has a lot of connections as well as people who were dedicated to him. How else could you explain a half million dollars on your canteen account."

"Damn!"

"But, then again, it's probably not related. Either way, it doesn't concern me. Tyruss has asked me to move on, so, I don't really even try to figure out what he has going on from the inside. But, never mind that," Carmen said, shaking her pretty black hair.

They pulled up at an unfamiliar restaurant. One Sunami had never had the opportunity to discover or be introduced to. Two valet boys came and opened their doors for them and they got out. Carmen came around the car and wrapped her hand around Sunami's arm. It was windy outside, Sunami noticed, and it seemed like rain wasn't too far away.

They entered the restaurant and were immediately shown to a nice table with a wonderful view out of one of the windows. The restaurant was classy, yet stylish. White table cloths covered the tables and each table had its own candles. The atmosphere of the entire restaurant was dim and secretive. Soft opera played and there was barely any noise to cover it, other than the low murmurs of the other diners. Sunami held out Carmen's chair, again, before finding his own seat. Menus were placed in front of them and Carmen ordered them a bottle of wine in her native language.

"Nice place, here. Great service and all, I wonder why I never heard of it," Sunami said. "

Not many people have, actually. And there's a month's waiting list for reservations to the place. It's very upscale," Carmen informed him.

"Are you telling me you were planning to bring me here a month ago?"

"No, sweetie." She laughed.

"But owning the place sure helps!"

"Oh. Cool, then."

Sunami allowed Carmen to order for him and fell into conversation about family and vocations. Sunami kept her knowledge limited to talks about his adventurous father and his love for music. Every time a question rose that seemed too personal for him, he'd reroute the conversation with another question of his own. But Carmen recognized the tactics for what they were. She too had once kept her private life out of others' conversations.

After all the heartache she went through with the death of her brother and nephew, then, the loss of the man she loved to the federal system while being pregnant with a child she refused to abort...it had been quite overwhelming. Especially when her father had threatened to disown her for her betrayal. The only thing that had saved her was the pleading of her mother and sister. They had convinced her father to allow her this, one, "transgression." After all, hadn't they lost enough family already? Wasn't Patrick and his son enough? Regardless of her father's disappointment, Carmen had vowed not to budge.

Never would she give up the one thing that linked her eternally to Tyruss. The baby that had been created in the throes of such passion and absolute love. No! Luigi Portellini could go fuck himself, for all she was concerned. But, that had changed... When Carmen failed to produce a confirmation or denial on whether or not Sunami was married, she took the direct approach before switching to business.

"Since you still don't trust me enough to open the closed doors of your personality, let's get down to the main topic. I've done some research on you and I'm pretty pleased at my findings, Sly. I'd like to do business with you. I saw that you were once in prison in North Carolina," she said,

"Yep. First degree felony murder," Sunami said.

"You had a life sentence, if I recall correctly. Then it was overturned. You know, a lot of people would have snitched on somebody, from the get go, to escape facing the possibility of getting that much time. I commend you."

"Well, that's not how I get down. And I can assure you that you'll never have to worry about anything with me, dealing with the police."

"Well, I can offer you a deal for six and a half thousand, a kilo. But you have to buy a hundred and twenty-five, at least."

"Perfect, then. Let's get an order for a hundred fifty, then, for starters," Sunami said.

"I really do like you, Sly, you know that?" Carmen smiled.

"I do, now!" They finished lunch and Sunami offered to pay.

Carmen shook her head and smiled as she stood, grabbing her purse.

"I own the place, remember?" she said.

"Yeah, but you'll never make any money dishing out free meals, at that cost," Sunami pointed out sarcastically.

"Sly, you just agreed to spend a million dollars with me," she said in a low voice.

"I think I can afford to toss you a free meal, every now and then."

"Good point."

Carmen drove Sunami back to his hotel. The ride was quiet, but for the soft music. In front of the building, Sunami opened his door and went to say goodbye. Carmen took his face into her hands and softly kissed him on the lips, her tongue caressing his upper lip.

"See you later. We'll make arrangements for the shipment and payment, later," she said.

"Now, go, before I change my mind!"

"Please, please, please change your mind!" Sunami begged, playfully.

"I can't. At least, not right now. It's way too early. Business before pleasure."

With that statement, Sunami nodded and stepped out of the car. He knew, to do anything else would paint a bad picture of his priorities. And he couldn't afford to fuck the mission up for a quick piece of pussy that was bound to come, eventually. He closed the car door and headed inside, wondering if Hypnotic would catch a flight to give him some coochie. Or maybe, he'd fly out Cherry...or, maybe not.

***

"I don't like leaving those two loose ends drifting in the wind, like that. Sunami and York are starting to become a headache. I admit, I underestimated them, once before. But, now that I know what type of people we're dealing with, I have the perfect person for the job. I like my friends close, my enemies dead. All the way dead!"

Obidiah MaTimbu spoke into the phone. He was speaking to another one of his crime partners. One he didn't have the privilege of seeing very often, but whose presence was clearly felt.

"Don't worry. The cocky one, Sunami... he'll be dead before the sun's down," the voice said.

"What do you mean? How?" MaTimbu asked.

"I left him a little surprised, this is sure fire. I know for a fact that his guard is let down. Now's the best time to strike, unexpectedly."

"But, I was told—"

"To hell with what you were told, MaTimbu. I don't march to anybody's drum but my own. If our friends have a problem with it, give him my number. But, I'm sure he'll be pleased after he sees the news tonight."

"What if you're interfering with his plans or operation?"

"I'll settle the difference. But, Sunami dies, tonight," the voice said.

"I don't like this. It's not right, stepping on each other's toes, like that," MaTimbu protested.

But there was no answer. All he got was the dial tone of the phone. He wondered how things would play out. If his partner succeeded, it would be great. A little frustrating, to his other partner, but still a success. But, if he failed...

***

Sunami made it up to his hotel room and took out his key card to open the door. He decided that he would take a short nap before calling and checking on his daughters. Then, he would holla at Zahir and Animal and have them get up with York and Raquel to get the CIA agent done as soon as they could. He still thought he might need them close by, soon. His sixth sense was picking at him for some reason. And, his dad had always said to go with your first feeling. As he accessed his door and pushed it open, he noticed that the room was fairly dark.

But this could be accounted for by the rain clouds outside and the lights being off inside the room. It seemed as if the house keeping people had been by. Sunami could make out his made-up bed in the dark and his laptop on top of it. The bottle of Patron Silver had been evidently put away and the room smelled of fresh sheets and...what was that? Old Spice? Who the fuck wears that? Sunami wondered to himself.

He flicked the lights switch on. BAM!!! Sunami's head was swimming. Something terribly hard had been used to smack him upside his head. Before he could balance his equilibrium, a tight piece of coil was wrapped around his neck. He could feel a body pressed behind him as the rope tightened suddenly around his neck. As his head began to clear, it registered the obvious. He was being strangled!! Sunami thrashed around, trying to break free of the hold.

He couldn't swallow, he couldn't breathe and, hell, he could barely even think! The tight coil dug into the thick flesh of his nineteen-inch neck, cutting off circulation and blood flow to the brain! He couldn't get his fingers on the inside of the coil to loosen the grip. Sunami wildly threw a punch over his shoulder, hoping for a miracle or something substantial. It connected. But, he was becoming so weak that the blow had little effect on his unseen attacker. Sunami was dying of strangulation! And there was little to nothing he could do about the shit, either.

Then, the thought hit him like a bucket of ice-cold water. THE GUN!!! Sunami grabbed for his pistol, weakly, and got it out of its holster in the front of his jeans. He slightly twisted and angled the gun behind him, on his left side, and pulled the trigger. Boom! In surprise, the strangler released the coil. He had been shot in the left thigh.

Sunami gained enough room to gasp for air! His face was strangely discolored. He turned to see a stocky, tall Mexican man wearing a leather jacket overall tucked in black T-shirt and jeans. His black leather boots looked to be like the ones that were slip resistant that you could order when getting a job in a kitchen, somewhere. Blood rushed back to Sunami's brain and he was starting to think more clearly. He pointed and shot the Mexican twice more, in the chest. The eagle talon bullets ripped through the man, splattering blood on the back of the room's door.

For a minute, Sunami stood staring at the body while he caught his breath. Then, knowing he had to get out of there, Sunami opened the door and stuck his head out, looking both ways. Still empty. The room had absorbed most of the sound. He saw a cart down the hall full of dirty sheets and comforters. He sprinted down the hall and drug the cart to his door. Sunami took several sheets and comforters out before lifting the body and dumping it inside the cart. He refilled the cart and rolled it back down the hall. Now, he had to clean the blood and get outta dodge!

Keese

Chapter 11

The Federal Plaza was alive and buzzing with the sounds of determined agents on a mission. FBI Director Samuel Brown's death had caused a large disturbance and the politicians were demanding results from up high. All of this responsibility was being placed on the new, acting Director of the Bureau, Thadius Zimmerman. Special Agent Charles Lavender was oblivious to all of the above! Lavender followed Zimmerman as he swerved in and out the crowd of busy agents. In his hands, he held the photos of Sunami inside the BMW, along with a detailed report on who he had been seen in the company of and their affiliations. Then, he had a report faxed from the Atlanta, Georgia branch reporting seeing Sunami in the company of the well-known drug lord, George "Birdman" Delgado.

Then, there were Sunami's personal criminal records and bits and pieces of investigations that had started and ended without charges being filed or any convictions of suspected crimes committed. He had been trying to talk Zimmerman into giving him the "okay" to pursue it full time and the man power needed to do so. Zimmerman led him into the office he had taken over, recently, and went behind the desk.

"Shut the door, Lavender. You've got five minutes," he said.

"Sir, I have, here, enough probable cause to justify further investigation of Mr. Marcus McKnight, also known as Sunami. It is believed that McKnight had been deeply involved in organized drug trafficking and distribution, as well as a number of murders, nationwide. He was recently photographed in the company of known mafia affiliates who are tied to the Port family.

"I also received another report of him being spotted as guests of the drug lord, Birdman Delgado. It is clear that something is going on. How can you not come to the same conclusion when the subject has visited two of the U.S.'s most ruthless organized crime families, in the same month? It is also believed that McKnight, too, has his own crime family, though I don't believe they've grown large enough to interest the bureau," Lavender explained, handing Zimmerman the reports.

"Here, also is a copy of the subject's criminal history. He did time in North Carolina's prison system for felony murder."

"This is all fine, and everything, but do you have any hard evidence?" Zimmerman asked.

"Sir, with all due respect, this is more than enough. If I had anything more, we'd be ready to make an arrest. That is the reason I'm asking for funding to launch a full investigation on Marcus McKnight. The signs are there, all we need now is a vigilant team to dig deep into this thing. It would be a big bust."

"Maybe. But, you don't have any conversations recorded, pictures of any transactions or finger prints on a murder weapon! All you have is circumstantial evidence, Lavender. Now, I'm sorry, but, I've got the brass on my ass about getting Brown's murder solved. All available manpower has gone into this investigation. We got terrorists living downtown, African mercenaries trying to immigrate and a dead director and his family. There is no way I can back this. Not right now, Lavender. Under better circumstances, yes, maybe. But, there's just too much going on to drop important matters for something so small. So, continue digging in your free time. If you get something solid, call me. Until then, I have work to do."

Zimmerman excused Lavender from his office as he picked up his desk phone and started dialing a number. Lavender collected the reports and stormed out of the office, furious at the ignorance of the decision makers of the Federal Bureau. He headed to his assigned cubicle and plopped down in his chair. How was he going to get hard evidence on McKnight? The man was as careful as a fucking snail!

Lavender knew something was going on, just like last year. He just didn't know what. What he needed was a break. Somehow, someway, Marcus McKnight would let something slip. And when he did Lavender planned to be right there to catch it and nail his ass to the wall! A thought came to Lavender, suddenly. Nothing big, just a thought. He wanted to know where McKnight was staying. Something was telling him to tighten the rope around McKnight's neck, pun intended. He lifted his phone off the receiver and began dialing.

Where would McKnight stay? He could be anywhere! But, surely, he wouldn't be in the cheaper hotels. And, since he wasn't in town performing, he might not be in the cream of the crop hotels, either. That narrowed it down to a couple hundred, or so. Not great odds, but not bad, either. Something was telling him that he'd catch a break soon. He just had to find out where McKnight was staying. Where did this thought materialize from? He had no clue. But Lavender damn sure wasn't about to sit on his ass, doing nothing. Might as well search for the needle in the haystack.

***

Sunami jumped on a plane and flew to Carolina. He slept the three and a half hours it took to get there and rented a Dodge Charger when he touched down.

He called Pam and let her know that he was on his way and asked that she notify the guards. She agreed. It was around seven o'clock in the evening. The sky was getting dark.

Sunami pushed the Charger to its limits on the back roads. He just wanted to get away and have a safe place to think for a day or two. He had always found it easier to think when he was his daughters. Sunami would sit, holding Rain, or sit in a chair while the she crawled around, while talking to Brianna as if she were a full-grown adult. This seemed to relax him because Brianna seemed to listen, occasionally giving her opinion, which was mostly gibberish or just words repeated that she heard her grandmother say. But, whatever the case, that's where he wanted to be, at the moment. In the presence of his precious little angels.

Sunami arrived at the front gate of York's home and revved the powerful engine of the Dodge Charger. After close scrutiny, the gate swung open and he sped up the long, paved driveway, stopping in front of the front door. Pam met him at the door with, both, his angels. The older white nanny that York despised, Ms. Cindy, was right behind her. Sunami took Brianna into his arms and tossed her up into the air and caught her. He then did the same thing to Rain. They both beamed with joy and giggles.

Sunami hugged Pam.

"Sup, sis? What it look like, girl?" he said, entering the home.

"Nothing much. Where's York? He still working?" she asked.

"Yep. Won't be too much longer now though."

To York's son, he said, "What's up, JaJa? You getting big, girl. You been taking good care of your cousin?"

JaJa, who was York's spitting image, tugged at Sunami's leg, wanting to be held, too. Sunami picked her up and kissed her cheek. "C'mon, y'all. I need to make a call," Sunami said, walking toward the large sitting area.

Pam headed for the kitchen to finish preparing the hotdogs she was making for the kids.

"You want a drink, or something, Marcus?" she called.

"Uh...yeah, you got some Patron?" Sunami said.

"I want some," said JaJa.

"Me, too. Daddy, me too," Brianna said.

"And bring them some too!" Sunami called to Pam, joking completely.

"Yay!"

"Yes!" the kids cheered.

Sunami sat JaJa down and picked up the house phone from the lamp stand that sat beside one of the most comfortable couches he had ever sat in, in his life! Pam had discovered a designer who made them and the first time he placed his ass in one, he knew he had too have one. There was one in his home studio in Malibu, one in his Miami condo and one in his mom's home in Durham, North Carolina. Pam brought Sunami the Patron, as well as two sippy cups of apple juice for the baby's enjoyment, while the phone rang. Rain was rambling through Sunami's left pocket while JaJa drunk her juice.

"Stop, girl!" Sunami told Rain.

"Stop! Stop!" she yelled at him as he moved her hands.

"BooBoo, you gone make Daddy whoop yo' lil' ass, now! Drink ya juice and sit the hell down, somewhere. Please," Sunami warned.

Sunami wasn't listening. The phone was answered and Sunami was absorbed in his conversation with Bird.

"Nigga, have you found anything on home boy, yet? I need some solid info ASAP," Sunami said, serious as a heart attack.

"I'm still working on it, bruh. Why? Whass up, yo?" Bird asked.

"A muthafucka Mexican tried to strangle my ass when I got back from meeting with Carmen. Almost killed me!"

"What'd you do?"

"Nigga, what you think!? I sent his ass up to the virgin Mary, that what. Cleaned up and tossed him, then I got the fuck outta there."

"Okay, okay, just chill. Where are you now?" Bird asked.

"Don't matter. I'm good. The dude was a Mexican. Do you think?" Sunami asked.

"Yeah. Cuba is in connection with MaTimbu. I found that out just recently. You're not considering backing out of the mission, are you?"

"Fuck, no. I'm in the door with ol' girl. We made a deal earlier today, before I got attacked. And I don't back out of obligations, Bird. I see them all the way through. I just wanted to know if you had come up with anything I could use. I hate having to look over my shoulder. But I plan to go back in a day, or two."

"Good. In the meantime, I'll throw some feelers out for Cuba Sanchez, too. I should be able to get a line on him easily. Just lay low for a day or so. I'll call you soon as I know something, a'ight?"

"Yeah. Just hit my cell when you need me."

"Perfect. Be safe."

"Always."

Sunami hung the phone and took a long swig from his bottle of Patron. His mind kept asking where the hell Cuba came from. And how had he knew where Sunami was? If he knew, that meant, Obidiah knew, right? So, where were they, if not close by? And were they really keeping that close a watch on him? Where they so terrified that they watched him so intently and tried to surprise him with attempts on his life, unexpectedly.

Hell, Sunami would respect it more if the two main mutha-fuckas would just come and take care of him, themselves. But, it was clear that they were too pussy for that! He wished he could send MaTimbu a personal challenge. The score was, Sunami's team=5, MaTimbu=0. They had better step their game up, Sunami thought to himself. The loser wouldn't live to play again, and Sunami was close to Skunking them! He smiled.

***

York was beginning to think that they wouldn't be able to catch the CIA agent. All they had done was wait, with no more sightings of him. He and Raquel sat outside the man's townhouse, now, but still hadn't seen him. It was getting dark and starting to rain. Raquel snoozed lightly in the front seat while York watched. He was about to call it a night when a blue Honda SUV rolled to the curb in front of the townhouse. Out jumped Knicks!

He leaned into the Uber's window and spoke to the driver for a second before running into the house. The driver sat, not going anywhere. York knew that he would be coming back out soon and getting in the SUV. This might be their only chance!

"Raquel. Raquel! Get up, bitch," York called while pushing her awake.

Raquel looked over at her comrade, who was applying a snow mask to his face. He wouldn't be able to fit a ski mask over his dread, so he used the snow mask to cover his nose, mouth and chin. It was just as effective.

"Whass up, York?" Raquel asked, wiping her eyes and seeing the Uber for the first time.

"Look, dude just went inside. He'll be back out soon. It's now or never, Ra. Get ready!"

Raquel snapped out of her trance and pulled a ski mask over her face and head. She found the long-barreled Smith & Wesson 357 and placed it on her lap. She then checked a Glock 40 and pulled on her gloves. York had a black Mack-11 on his lap with a long thirty-two-round clip. He cocked the slide and stared intently at the townhouse door.

"I'ma pop dude, York. Watch the driver. If he act up, you know what to do," Raquel said.

"Already. Make sure you kill him, Raquel. I mean, kill him with no doubt in your mind that he's dead. We can't afford nobody coming out of coma's or getting blood transfusions and living. He got to go, here and now," York said.

"C'mon, man. I got it. Start the damn car." York started the car as Raquel turned the switch on the overhead light to off.

It was preset to come on when the door opened, and she didn't want that. Raquel pulled the handle on the door, opening it a crack. She held it like this and watched the door along with York. A full five minutes later, the townhouse door opened and Knicks stepped out. York pulled away from the curb as Knicks locked his door. When he turned around and headed back to the Uber, the Cadillac was five yards away. Raquel hopped out and Knicks saw the glint of the revolver, before he saw the black ski mask.

He reached for his weapon and raised it. POW! POW!! Both weapons fired at the same time! Raquel was hit in her right shoulder as Knicks took a hot slug to his neck from fifteen feet away! Raquel kept firing. Pow! Pow! Pow! Pow! Pow! Pow! Pow! Knick's body fell to the ground, his face a bloody mess.

The Uber driver was out of the car with a black Beretta now, pointing it at Raquel. Raquel froze and locked eyes. Her revolver was empty and she couldn't reach for her Glock.

"Hey! Don't you move, you muthafucka. Don't move, or I'll blow your ass to hell!" the short white man said.

FLADADADADADADADADADADADAT!! York wet up the entire SUV and the little man standing beside it! By the time the last bullet left his barrel, Raquel was back in the Cadillac, waiting for her comrade. York made his way back around the car to the driver's seat. He noticed a man sitting two buildings up, curled up on the ground. York pointed the machine pistol at the man and startled to life.

"Hey, young blood, I didn't see anything, man! I swear, I ain't seen nothing. I'm just a crack addict anyway, if you ask me. Hell, I'm high right now! Shit," the man said.

York lowered his gun, momentarily, and thought about it. He had dealt with crack heads on the regular, back in his hustling days, and most minded their business when it came to shit like this. He didn't want to kill the man because he had an aunt who was a smoker, as well. He would want a shooter to let her go, too! But, then again, we're talking about a murdered CIA agent, he thought to himself. As York heard the faint sound of sirens in the distance, he raised the Mack-10, again.

"Sorry 'bout this, bruh. Just the wrong place, at the wrong damn time," York said.

He emptied the clip into the base head as he tried to get up and make a run for his life. The man absorbed all but a few of the bullets and fell to the concrete, dead. York tossed the smoking gun inside the car onto Raquel's lap and jumped in. The Cadillac shot off like a rocket and bent the curb, heading to the freeway that would take them out of New Jersey. They would turn the car in, rent another one from a different company, then find a room in New York for the night. York thought about flying down south to his third house to see his daughter.

Chapter 12

Carmen was beyond excited. Almost to the point of nervousness, she realized as she stood in the backroom beside her father, Lugo Portellini.

His hefty frame was crammed tight into a flawless black tuxedo. His health didn't seem as bad as she had remembered it, now. And he fussed with his tie as the music in the other room started. It was the introduction to "Here comes the bride." The double doors in front of them opened, revealing a full house!

The church was packed with people who all turned to get a look at her in her beautiful, white wedding dress. As she walked down the aisle, on her father's arm, she noticed a crowd of people she knew. There was her uncle, Pete, with his wife Dana, who had tears rolling down her cheeks and a huge smile. Carmen's heart thudded as if it was trying to escape from her chest. She noticed her sister and Giovanni, Tommy Barnes, whose family had been a friend of her family for years, and Susan Veldini, who had been married to her cousin, Richard, before he was murdered.

Up ahead, a tall, brown-skinned Tyruss "Fatboy" Lawrence stood in a beautiful tailored tux with his earrings shining like the North Star. And beside him was her brother, Patrick, and his son, Anthony. Aw, how cute little Anthony was in his tux! They all smiled at her as she made her way, slowly, towards them. Her own son Tyler, stood beside his cousin, Anthony.

He held a silk pillow with two wedding rings on it, smiling. She began to cry. This was what she had always wanted her life to be. This was happiness, she thought to herself.

Tyruss's face was blurred by her tears but she could see his smile. He leaned to wipe her tear of joy away and she closed her eyes. His finger slowly caressed her cheeks and passed under her eyes. When she opened them, he stood there only...it wasn't Tyruss, anymore! The man she knew as Sly, Marcus McKnight, stood in Tyruss's place.

His smile was as genuine as Tyruss's need and he grabbed her hand as they turned to face the pastor. Carmen was overwhelmed with questions, but voiced none of them. She kept stealing glances at Sly, who stood proudly at her side. How did this happen, she wondered while still holding her smile. Is this the man I love, endlessly? Can I be with him forever? Can I trust him?

All of these questions were answered when Sly turned to her. He leaned and kissed his devotion. As the kiss ended, Carmen found herself staring into the light brown eyes. Eyes that held loyalty, pride and principle.

"I love you, Carmen," Sly's lips said.

"And I...I..."

Suddenly, the double doors burst open! Everyone's attention went to the crowd of men standing in the doorway. She could make out the shapes of large guns as they came closer. Who were these men? Why the hell were they interrupting her ceremony? What did they have planned? Carmen's mind registered when she saw the bright yellow letters on the jacket. They read: FBI. She knew, then, that she had to get out of there.

"Mommy!" Tyler called to her. "Mommy, can you hear me? Mommy, get up. Get up, Mommy, please!"

***

Carmen awoke out of her dream with a racing heart and a damp forehead! She surveyed the room and realized she was home. Her silk gown stuck to her skin and she could see that the sun was high in the sky, outside. Tyler, her two-year-old son, stood next to her bed.

"Mommy! Were you sleeping?" he asked, looking as innocent as ever.

Tyler was the perfect mix between his mother and father. His facial features resembled more of his father, but he was a light, milky brown color, being mixed with black and Italian. His eyes were the same brown as his mother's and his hair was a small, curly but thick, silky afro. His little teeth grew in perfectly straight as if he had been born with braces. Tyler wore small Iron Man pajamas. His feet were bare. Carmen's heart sank every time she looked into his pretty little eyes. She lifted him on the bed and gave him a warm hug and a light kiss on the forehead.

"You knew I was asleep, you little tickle monster!"

She smiled, tickling him until he rolled around on her bed.

"Stop it, Mommy! Sto-ho-hop! Okay, okay, okay, hey-hey!" Tyler begged, laughing mercilessly.

Carmen lay back on her bed beside her son. She sighed as the mystery of her dream faded from her mind. She had other things to worry about. What the dream meant could never properly be known. Carmen just lived her life a day at a time. She'd love to give her son a father, though. She wondered if Sly could fill in for the job.

But, then again, he hadn't even answered her when she asked if he was, or had ever been married. Carmen figured she'd just have to gain his trust and get him to open up to her. She understood that her being in the family business often made guys cautious about getting too involved with her. That, or giving up too much info. They had this idea that anything personal that they told her could end up costing them something, or someone, valuable if they disagreed with her. That wasn't how she separated, though. True, she could be ruthless when needed, but mostly she just tried to handle business fairly.

Carmen got out of the bed and took Tyler in her bathroom to get him washed and dressed. She wanted him to be able to visit with his grandpa for a couple days while she handled business with Sly. She would be contacting him soon, for the information she needed to make the transaction happen. Her family was far from poor, but Carmen had never heard of having "too much money." The statement, itself, was an oxymoron. Plus, she wanted Tyler to never want for anything. She'd do anything to ensure his eternal stability and life. And she really meant anything!

***

When Sunami awoke the next morning, both Rain and Brianna were stuck to him like a birthmark! Rain had slept on his chest, which was why his tank top was damp with drool, and Brianna had been at his side. Brianna loved her daddy to death. He slid the slob-bering lump of sassiness, which was Rain, slowly onto the bed beside her sister. Then, he checked his phone's screen for messages.

There was one from York. Sunami decided he'd listen to it after a shower. Then maybe he would go upstairs to York's attic studio and mess around with the beat machine a little. You never know when a good song will come to you. After a long, hot shower in the exclusive stall built into the guest room, Sunami checked his message on speaker phone while brushing his teeth.

"Yo, Sunami, whass good? The mission is a done deal. Last night, Raquel got hit, though. She good though. I called Bird and he connected me to a doctor he knew. I kicked him ten stacks and he straightened sis out. What's next on the agenda? And where the fuck are you? I rode by the hotel and the police was out there. Call me, ASAP," York's voice said.

Sunami threw on some fresh clothes he had brought with him. He tied his wave cap on then failed York's cell phone number. He would have to inform him of what happened. Already the body of the Mexican had already probably been found! He needed to call Hypnotic, too.

***

Special Agent Charles Lavender ran his gloved finger tips over the two bullet holes, that were chest level, in the back of the hotel room's door. There was another one approximately two and a half feet lower and slightly to his right. Around him, NYPD and their forensic specialist combed the entire room for physical evidence.

When he had discovered the room in Hypnotic's name, he had called to see if anyone had checked into the room. The clerk had been reluctant to give him the information. Lavender had identified himself as an agent of the bureau before he was allowed anything. Coming upon the reservation had been a lucky draw.

That was when he found out a body had been found and the police had had no luck, so far. Turns out, the room he suggested to the NYPD was a bull's eye! It came as a surprise to the lead detective on the case, because the relationship between the NYPD and the FBI was anything but friendly. So, when they found the bullet holes and the blood spots in the carpet that had been washed thoroughly, the detective had called Lavender back to let him know what had been discovered, as a courtesy. But, by then, Lavender was already on his way!

"Anything, so far?" Agent Lavender asked, looking up at the slim detective in corduroy pants and a collar shirt.

Detective Bryan Dade dropped his head in disappointment. He didn't like the position he was in, on this investigation. Lavender made him uneasy, even though he assured Dade that he was there, unofficially. Dade, a mixed breed Dominican and black man, military brat, didn't like anything less than progress. His eternal goal was always to leave with more than you came with, in any situation. This case did not present such an option.

"Nothing. Not even a fucking fingerprint. Not one! Fibers? None. Cigarette butt? Nope. Signs of a scuffle? Forget it. Whoever killed the guy, he sure was thorough when he cleaned. The only thing that was left were the bullets and the blood. And I'm betting that those lead us absolutely nowhere. I just got a call on the ID of the victim. He's M.M, if that means anything to ya," Dade said.

"M.M." were the initials for Mexican Mafia. Now, there was no doubt in his mind about it. McKnight was on the rampage! But there was little he could do, though. Lavender decided to throw Dade a bone and let him run with it, until there was enough to take it away from him. That is, if they found enough to link McKnight to it. It would be a start for them, since they had nothing.

"Look, Dade. I'm gonna help you out, a little," Lavender said.

"And what will I owe you, in return?" Dade asked, skeptically.

"Nothing. Just keep me updated. It's just a personal interest for me."

"Okay, I'll bite. What's up?"

"The name the room was rented in is the wife of the President of Tenth Street Entertainment, Marcus McKnight. He's not all legit, trust me. This is his work. It's got his name written all over it."

"But how..."

"Listen, McKnight and the Mexican Mafia are at war. McKnight's a different kind of killer, but a killer, nonetheless. There have been many attempts on his life and as a result, lots of Mexican Mafia men have turned up dead, including the brother of the M.M. 's first lieutenant, Cuba Sanchez, and his family. It's believed that Cuba Sanchez is dead. Did you hear of the massacre in North Carolina?" Lavender asked.

"In Durham, right? Yeah, I heard a little about it."

"Well, I was half a second behind McKnight and his people. He killed them all and still managed to slide through the cracks, on me. Supposedly, Cuba Sanchez was killed in that massacre, but the bureau is skeptical about it. May have been a decoy. That's what I believe. My advice to you, unofficially of course, is this: Interrogate McKnight. Get him to tell you what happened here. He'll probably lie, but you should run a polygraph test just for your own knowledge. Now, I'll warn you. He's very crafty and intelligent. But, I can see you aren't slow, at all."

"And how am I supposed to do this? The man's probably got more highly paid lawyers than I've got cases. And, trust, I've got plenty of cases."

"I'll tell you how. His wife. It's her name on the reservation. She'll fold if you talk to her, but he won't let you. She'll volunteer to come if you apply pressure on her. That, I promise."

"Okay, then. That's what I'll do. I like your way of thinking, Agent Lavender," Dade complimented.

"Hey. It's how I got where I am today. And, remember. Keep me informed of what happens. Take my number, and call if you need help. Team work makes dreams work!"

***

When the call came, MaTimbu had been expecting it. As soon as he had read the newspaper his assistant had handed him and noticed the small piece on the Hispanic gunshot victim, Obidiah had pinched the bridge of his nose in hopes that his oncoming headache would subside. And he knew, then, that he would be getting the blame for Cuba's fuck up!

"In our line of business, MaTimbu, it's important that we as a team are able to trust one another. Going behind one's back and dealing underhandedly isn't the way you let me know I can't trust you, now, is it?" the voice on the phone said.

"Look. I just knew you were going to blame me for this crap. I told Cuba what you had suggested. The man found in the hotel is one of his men. Not mine! My eyes are on the goal, at hand. I'm not a babysitter. We are trying to take control of half the United States drug distribution and there are certain measures that need to be taken. I, for one, don't like leaving the Sunami and York running amuck with their increasing profits in our drug organization, but, but I respect your decision. So, call the one responsible for this unwanted attention. I'm not in it," Obidiah said calmly.

He rode in the backseat of his Maybach Benz as his driver navigated through midtown Washington, DC He was in Washington taking care of other matters concerning their take over, and felt like he didn't have time for the immature bickering that occurred between his two partners.

It was always a power struggle when large organizations tried to cooperate with one another. That was why the world was going all to hell, now! Everyone wanted to be involved with everyone else.

"If you recall, MaTimbu, it is your fault that Sunami and York are running amuck in the first place! Remember who supposed to quietly eliminate them? Hmm? No comment, huh? Now, I have to deal with this asshole thinking he can just do what he wants, when he wants. I'll show you why it's best to listen to me, MaTimbu. I'll show you."

"What the hell does that mean?" MaTimbu asked, disturbed by the threat.

"Just keep your eyes open. You're not to blame, so don't worry. But I'll show you how to make progress, effectively. And, please, continue not to bother Sunami and York. As I said before, they're mine. But Cuba must be taught a valuable lesson," the voice insisted.

"Remember the important role he plays. We don't want to let this become a pissing contest and jeopardize the mission."

"Cuba is a puppet. A fucking incompetent, insubordinate puppet. Sunami should've killed him in Durham. But, don't even worry about it. Everything will continue as planned, no matter what. I'll call you in a couple days."

"Fine. Do what you like. I hate insubordinates, anyway."

The call and MaTimbu was left wondering what his partner had in mind for Cuba. It was a stupid mistake, on Cuba's part, to send such an incompetent assassin, after Sunami and the others had proven their capabilities.

At least MaTimbu's assassins had gone prepared. Hell, Cuba's man didn't even seem to find it appropriate to take a gun! What an idiot!! On well. It was not of his concern. MaTimbu had other business to attend to.

As the luxury vehicle pulled to the curb in front of a tall, thick, brick, private building, MaTimbu folded the newspaper and stepped out. It was starting to drizzle, so he opened the umbrella handed to him by his assistant.

***

Hypnotic stepped through the double doors to the NYPD's eastern precinct in her business gray, skirt suit. It was her "get down to business" suit that she wore for battles involving quick wit' and intelligence. The female officer at the front desk pointed her to an interrogation room and asked her to sit and wait while she notified Detective Bryan Dade of her arrival. Hypnotic smiled and went to the room. The interrogation room was solid concrete with a metal chair on either side of the table, neither of which looked the least bit comfortable.

The only thing that stopped the room from being a cliche, an interrogation room that you would see on some low budget, cheesy suspense movie, was the lack of the room with the one-way window. In its place, there were small speakers taped to the wall, behind the table, as small as a fly. It was accompanied by, what Hypnotic identified as, a small camera the same size. After waiting for ten minutes, the tall detective entered the room with a manilla folder and sat down.

He smiled at Hypnotic and extended his hand, introducing himself.

Oh gawd, she thought to herself, he's gonna play good cop, bad cop, with me, by himself!

"Mrs. McKnight, do you know why I called you down here, this afternoon?" Dade started.

"I'm hoping you will tell me," Hypnotic said, seemingly concerned.

"I will. But, may I ask a few questions first?"

"Go ahead."

"Do you live here, in the city?" No, I don't. I used to, but I don't anymore."

"When did you arrive here, in New York, on this visit? And, how?"

"Um, I've been here for about two weeks. I flew from North Carolina on a private jet my husband's company owns," Hypnotic said confidently.

"And did you come with anyone! Your husband, maybe?" Dade probed.

"No. l flew alone, unfortunately."

"Why do you say that, unfortunately?"

"I would've loved some company while I'm here, but business and pleasure don't mix."

"Okay. Back to the point. Where have you been staying while in New York?"

"I still own an apartment here. But, I've been staying at my uncle's, this time. He has a house out in White Plains," she explained.

"Are you aware that you have a reservation for a hotel room in east Manhattan? At the Millennium Hotel?" Dade stared intently.

"What? How? No, I wasn't aware of that. I don't believe I've ever even stayed at that hotel before."

"Mrs. McKnight, cut the crap! Your black card number was used to pay for the room the day after you arrived here. You stayed in that room, Mrs. McKnight. It was checked in the same day, so tell me what's going on."

"I don't know what you are talking about, Mr. Dade. I have never even stayed at the Millennium Hotel and never have I made a reservation for anything of the kind. You truly have me mixed with someone else!" Hypnotic insisted, applying her angry face.

Detective Dade let her anger stew, for a moment. He stared into her determined brown eyes, searching for some sign of weakness. But, despite Lavender's advice, he could detect none. He decided to go slowly again, then hit her with the whole kit N' kaboodle. "Do you own a firearm, Mrs. McKnight?" Detective Dade asked.

"Yes, I do. I own several, actually," Hypnotic said, still presenting her anger.

"What type of weapon do you carry, on a regular basis?"

"Either, a Glock 9mm, or a Ruger P-89, 9mm pistol. Why?"

"Where is your weapon, now, Mrs. McKnight?"

"It's in my car, wanna see it?"

"Are you aware that your husband is a convicted felon, and isn't supposed to be around guns?" Dade asked, ignoring her question.

"How could I not be aware of my husband's past criminal history. Look, Dade, what does this have to do with my husband? Would you please get to the fucking point! I've got somewhere to be in an hour."

"The fucking point, Mrs. McKnight, is that I've got a dead gang member in a hotel room that you reserved on your credit card. And a husband who has a past conviction for murder! Wouldn't that make you suspicious, Mrs. McKnight? Now, if you tell me the truth, I might be able to help you. Tell me you had nothing to do with it and I'll make sure the one that is responsible gets charged, not you," Dade pressed.

"How 'bout I tell you to fuck yourself! You wanna talk? Talk to my lawyer, because if you were any kind of real detective, you'd know that my black card was reported stolen the day I got here! I lost it in the Uber, Detective Dade. And, FYI, my husband is in Carolina with our daughters. And has been since I left. Find some other poor soul to frame, because you won't frame my husband. Are we done? Good."

Hypnotic left the room without waiting for Dade's consent or lack thereof. She felt good. Sunami had prepared her and she had made the proper arrangements to outsmart the NYPD. She had a meeting with her uncle next.

Keese

Chapter 13

Secretively, the Central Intelligence Agency was swarming like a cloud of disturbed hornets! The death of Agent Knicks, the Uber driver and the homeless man aroused tons of unanswered questions. The agency was pulling every case file that Knicks had handled, and were sorting through it to see if something could lead them to the party responsible for his death. The brutal assassination did not reach the news, however, because the suits who held the power prohibited the media from releasing anything having to do with it. If you didn't already know that Knicks was an agent for the Intelligence Agency, they weren't about to notify you!

Even the hobo's death went unannounced, because of the importance behind the investigation. The suits figured, if they didn't broadcast it, they wouldn't have to sort through all of the organizations falsely claiming responsibility. But, surely, they would find the person, or persons, responsible. And when they did, may God have mercy on their souls!

***

Two days after his arrival, Sunami was leaving to catch a plane back to the Big Apple. Animal, Zahir, Raquel and York had arrived the day before to get some rest and visit the kids. They all had the opportunity to share a meal together and just chill. But Sunami had received the call he was expecting from Carmen, and it was time to get back to business. He had to get close enough to Carmen so he could find out where her father was, then he could kill them all.

After that, he would hunt Obidiah MaTimbu and Cuba Sanchez down, until they were nothing but an in unmarked grave. Now that the two other missions had been taken care of, Sunami was more determined to handle his part. Needless to say, his daughters was not happy about their father's departure. And, surprisingly, neither was JaJa. But these things couldn't be helped, Sunami knew. One day, they too, would understand.

So, while Hypnotic was being interviewed by Detective Bryan Dade, Sunami made arrangements over the phone with Bird, as to where the drugs would be shipped to and intercepted by. Besides, it was his money that was paying for it, and Sunami doubted the quality was anywhere near as good as what he was buying from the Yakuza. Therefore, he had no use for the hundred fifty kilos of drugs! When the plane finally landed, Sunami was met by a two toned, silver and dark blue, chauffeured Rolls Royce Phantom. The chauffeur took his two bags and placed them in the trunk before he opened the rear door.

The sky was nearly dark, but Sunami could still see the long, creamy legs and black Gucci high heeled pumps, belonging to Carmen Portellini. Luckily, Sunami had worn a suit, but had neglected to wear a tie. Still, he was prepared for the occasion. He slipped inside the vehicle, sitting next to Carmen. She eyed him, licked her sexy, full lips and smiled.

"I figured we could have dinner. Hope you haven't ate already," she said in her sultry voice.

"Nope. Actually, I'm, uh...very hungry!" Sunami said flirtatiously.

The Phantom headed for the city and the two of them made small talk. Carmen was interested in where Sunami had gone and he didn't exactly lie to her.

"I had some people to see in North Carolina. Nothing too serious. Plus, I went and recorded a song that had been on my mind for a few weeks, now," he said.

"Oh, really? What's it called?" Carmen asked, genuinely intrigued.

"It's called 'Fantasy.' It's about a guy experiencing a night of pleasure so unthinkable, he believes it's gotta be a dream. Or, better yet, a fantasy. I've been toying with this song in my head for a while," he explained.

"So, is it a true story type of song? I mean, have you experienced a night of unthinkable pleasure to the point you believe it was all just a fantasy? Maybe, a wet dream?"

"Well...I've had my fair share of pleasure, I guess. But, to answer your question, no, I don't think I've experienced pleasure, like that! But, it sure would be nice. I mean, I often come up with ideas for songs and just write them in my point of view. And anything could give me inspiration. A movie, a book, an emotion, and even real-life experiences. Sometimes, just a thought is enough to construct an entire song, or album. Sometimes, I record them, other times I sell them."

"Ah. I see, now. Do you think you could write a song for me?" Carmen asked.

"Sure. Can you rap, or sing?" Sunami returned.

"Oh, no. Definitely not! I meant, could you write a song about me? You know, like inspired by me, or something? Maybe as a gift?"

"Depends. Can you inspire me?"

"How about I work on that. I truly believe actions speak way louder than words." Carmen smiled seductively.

The Phantom pulled up to the front entrance of The 40\40 club. This restaurant had been a new addition to New York, immigrating from Jay-Z. The restaurant was top of the line and served mostly VIPs and celebrities. Sunami knew that he was bound to see some familiar faces inside. Oh well. He could handle it.

The two of them made it past a small crowd of media and some stargazers to the entrance. Inside, they were led to a booth in one of the corners. Sunami sat across from Carmen, not paying attention to most of the recognition he was getting. He did nod a greeting to P. Diddy, as he passed his table. And he spoke briefly to Alicia Keys, who was having dinner with her husband. Other than that, Sunami focused on Carmen.

She wore a beautiful dress that stopped at mid-thigh. Sunami wasn't familiar with its designer. There were just too many to keep up with! They shared some wine and shrimp cocktails while they waited on the main courses to arrive. Carmen flirted endlessly and Sunami returned every gesture. Business conversation went as fast as it came.

"Where do you want it?" Carmen asked all of a sudden.

"Well, hell, if you freaky like that, we can hop on the table! Shit!" Sunami laughed.

"Shut up, silly! Be for real, for a second."

"Here's the number your people need to call when they reach Virginia. I'll take it from there."

"Okay, make the call and tell your people to expect an eighteen-wheeler branded with the Costco Franchise logo on the side. It'll be late tomorrow."

"Perfect."

After the calls were made, they resumed their game. Sunami was deeply intrigued by Carmen's personality. It was becoming hard to keep his distance from her, already. With every smile, laugh and touch of the hand, Sunami was pulled deeper into her vibe. He knew that the final straw could be sharing one another, physically.

But, he'd like to think he was stronger than that. And it seemed that Carmen could see into his very soul. It was like she knew his thoughts and feelings. Because, he felt, if she could read his thoughts, surely she would see the devious plot against her.

The threat covered in his subconsciousness that endangered all she loved and lived for. Sunami half expected her to jump up and point a gun at him, in realization. But, then, she did the total opposite. Carmen leaned forward and placed her hand on top of his, on the table. Her leg brushed his.

"Tonight, Sly, I'm going to break down that huge defensive wall you're built around your heart. I can see that you're struggling to trust me, but I'll prove to you that I come in peace. I come bearing gifts. And as long as you continue to be who you are with me, I'll never, ever do anything to hurt you, physically or emotionally. By the time the sun rises, you're going to trust me. And you can bet your bottom dollar on that one," she said, passionately.

Sunami didn't know what to say! He only stared into her eyes, seeing the sincerity and determination. How could he respond to such realness when he was an imposter? A snake in a grass, waiting to strike her with his venom? How could he do that to her? Luckily, he didn't have to. His phone beeped, loudly, interrupting them.

Carmen leaned back into her seat as he retrieved his phone and continued to eat. Sunami saw that he had a text message. It was from his wife, Hypnotic. He opened it and read what she had typed. His eyes grew to the size of two watermelons. The message read:

"Don't freak out, baby. I want u 2 look up and to UR left. (smile)."

Sunami slowly raised his eyes. First, he met Carmen's questioning stare and shook his head.

"Nothing serious. Just a return on an investment I made, it was way more than I expected," he lied.

Carmen smiled and nodded, saying her congratulations to him. Then Sunami glanced over to his left and scanned the area. There! Three tables over, in the rear, Hypnotic sat at a table with her uncle. She smiled and waved her fork at him. Her uncle nodded. Sunami only nodded back. He couldn't work under these conditions! He took a last big swallow from the wine glasses, draining it completely. Then, he looked to Carmen.

"You want me to trust you? You wanna prove to me that you mean me no harm?" he asked, meeting her gaze.

Carmen nodded.

"Well, show me."

They looked at each other for another full minute. Carmen nodded, placed her napkin on the table, while Sunami dropped two hundred-dollar bills on the table, and they left. When they climbed inside the Phantom, Carmen kicked off her heels. Her feet were as beautiful as anything else on her body, Sunami noticed.

"Home, Donald," Carmen instructed the chauffeur.

The man nodded and before the car could pull off, Carmen turned to Sunami and pulled him into a deep, passionate kiss. Her eyes never closed and he could see that she meant business. Sunami had a feeling that this was going to turn out to be a wonderful night! And, probably, a great morning, too!!

***

By the time they reached the doorway of Carmen's large master bedroom, Sunami was a sock and a pair of boxer shorts away from being completely butt naked! Carmen, who undressed Sunami on the way up, had come out of her clothes with no problem, at all. She stood, now, in a designer bra and lace boy shorts, only. Her mouth lay open in ecstasy as Sunami explored her harden nipples with his tongue.

As they reached the edge of Carmen's bed, she tugged at the band of Sunami's shorts with her thumbs. He allowed them to fall, removing the bra and panties Carmen wore as she laid down.

Sunami trailed more of his warm kisses down Carmen's stomach until he reached her trimmed mound of brown pubic hair. He bypassed it and parted her lips with a tongue sweeping kiss, savoring the juices that flowed from her womanhood. To say Carmen was excited would be an understatement!

She tried to gain control of her shallow breathing but Sunami was literally taking her breath away. Sunami was so aroused, his penis throbbed in anticipation. He sucked on Carmen's vagina until her nails dug into his scalp with pleasure! Then, Sunami moved to her thighs, leaving deep-red hickies in his trail.

"Dammit, baby! That feels fucking wonderful," Carmen gasped.

Sunami rose and met Carmen's womanhood with his enlarged, thick member. He caressed the opening with soft rubs of his head, up and down, watching Carmen ball up the soft, cotton sheets in her fists. Every so often, he would slide a small portion of his penis inside of her, driving Carmen completely insane. Not able to take it any longer, Carmen gripped Sunami by his cheeks and pulled him deep into her passion. The heat overwhelmed him.

"Aaaaaaah, yeah!" Sunami exclaimed.

He watched as he plunged deeper and deeper into Carmen's center. The pace was fast and passionate.

Their excitement was so worked up that neither one of them thought to pace themselves and make the occasion last. Sunami's pelvis slapped the back of Carmen's thighs and ass with fierce determination, his build up not even being considered.

"Sly, Oh my god! Sly! This is all yours, baby. Take me there! Oh, yeah! Baby, baby, yeeeeeah! Keep going, baby, please."

She moaned, caressing her own sweat dampened breast. Sunami took Carmen's ankles into the air and brought them together, causing more friction inside her vaginal walls as her thighs caused her pussy to grip Sunami's penis. With each stroke, Sunami became more and more infatuated. The juices from Carmen left them making love in a damp puddle on the large bed. Everything from his hips to his knees were wet.

Some of it could've been sweat, but Sunami highly doubted it. There was nothing he could do! It was way too good to keep his control. Sunami shot off a load that nearly caused him to pass out on top of Carmen. Her moans mixed with the hot, wetness of her pussy had his dick ready to tap out.

Surprisingly, he kept going. Now, Sunami was determined to make this a night to remember for Carmen. He wasn't sure if she had cum, yet, but if she had, he was preparing to give her another one! Sunami turned Carmen onto her side and made her bring her knees to her chest. She was panting, already, and was thankful for the brief moment to catch her breath. When Sunami reentered, it was like he had grown even larger and longer!

"Ah! Mmmm, baby, it's too big," Carmen said in her sultry, little girl voice.

It only fueled Sunami's passion. Before Carmen knew what was happening, cum as thick as gravy and as white as whipped cream seeped from her insides and she was momentarily paralyzed. It took the two of them ten whole minutes to speak once Sunami had taken Carmen over the edge for the ultimate orgasm. They locked together under the disheveled sheets. Carmen rubbed her feet against Sunami's hairy legs and massaged his flaccid penis.

"You know what?" she asked, shaking. curly strand of hair from her damp face.

"Whass that?" Sunami responded, eyes closed, enjoying her every touch.

"What question?"

"If you were married, or not."

Sunami's eyes opened slowly. Why should he tell her? Surely she could find out for herself if she did some investigating. He was suddenly grateful that she hadn't. It showed that she wasn't prying. Before he responded, Carmen spoke again.

"It really doesn't matter to me. I just wanted to know. Do I have your trust, yet?" she asked.

"Of course, you do. I'm married, and I have two beautiful daughters." Sunami sighed.

"Oh. I bet they're beautiful. I'm gonna take you from your wife, though."

"Really? How do you figure?"

"Oh, she can keep your name and ring, and all that. But, she officially has to share you wit' me, or, I'll have to take you, by force."

Sunami didn't respond.

There wasn't even a need to comment on the subject because he knew that what she was speaking was beyond impossible. Impossible and unimaginable. Carmen still didn't see the plot as it thickened against her. But Sunami could feel the weight of it as it grew, on his shoulders. And he didn't like it. Not one bit.

***

The phone woke Sunami out of his sleep. He could feel the weight of Carmen's body pressed up against him, her body heat, itself, enough to arouse him in anticipation. Sunami reached over to the night stand and picked up his cell phone. Unable to hide the grogginess from his voice, he answered.

"Hello," he said.

"It's Bird. Where are you?" Bird asked.

"That ain't important. What's up?"

"I'm faxing you the schedule of Cuba Sanchez in two minutes. He's got a meeting with a guy in Miami, today. Getting this was a pain in the ass, Sunami. You gotta handle it, today. Can you make Miami?"

Sunami sat up in the bed, awake now, sliding Carmen's body onto the bed. He shook himself awake to clear his head.

"Yeah, You're sending the exact location?" Sunami asked.

"Yep. The location, name of place and time. Get it and get down there, asap, my nigga."

"I'm gone. I gotta call my niggas." Sunami hung up the phone without another word from Birdman's end.

He hopped out of bed, heading for Carmen's bathroom to get washed. Noticing his clothes strewn by the door, some probably down the hallway and stairs, he cursed to himself.

"Sly? Are you leaving?" Carmen asked, barely awake in bed.

"I have to, sweetie. Business calls!" Sunami responded, closing the door.

Keese

Chapter 14

At approximately one o'clock P.M., Cuba Sanchez sat down to a private lunch with his ranking superior, Bruno Hernandez. The two Hispanic men greeted one another with a firm handshake as they settled into an outside patio table at "Cubano Bueno," a very popular Cuban restaurant in South Beach, Florida. Hernandez's personal bodyguard sat down at the table with two of Cuba's soldiers and they ordered some wine. Normally, it would be important to keep a keen eye on everything that went on around the ranking boss of the Mexican Mafia, who, at sixty-four, was depending less on his own abilities to eliminate personal threats and more on hired killers from his organization. But, Cuba was family.

A short, petite waitress in some cut off shorts, sneakers and a T-shirt came and took their drink orders. Cuba studied his boss as the old man admired the firm buns on the back of the young, pretty waitress. Hernandez wore gray wool slacks, loafers and an expensive, light blue, long-sleeved button-down shirt. His jet-black hair was thinning, but not to the point where he had bald spots. Cuba assumed that the man colored his hair, because he could not spot one streak of gray, besides the few hairs coming from Hernandez's ears! When their eyes met, Cuba noticed that Hernandez had a soul piercing gaze.

"How are you doing, Cuba?" Bruno Hernandez asked.

"Very good, sir," Cuba responded in his native language.

"I have asked you here for several reasons, today. First, I want to know if you have knowledge of the situation in New York City. A man of ours was discovered, shot to death, inside of a dirty laundry bucket. Personally, Cuba, I know nothing about this because I'm not in everyday contact with our lower members. I've spoken to some of my political connections and it seems that they don't have any suspects for this shooting, though, they do have a theory."

"A theory? What kind of theory, sir?"

"A theory that involves that black gangster you were supposed to dispose of, last year. In fact, the exact same one who almost killed you! The one who killed the men you sent to act in your place!! The theory is: there was a struggle, and this black gangster of yours shot and killed one of my men. Now, tell me why exactly you are still pursuing a dead issue, when it was stated very clearly that the organization wanted no more to do with this pessimistic group. Now, tell me...did you arrange for one of our men to attempt to assassinate this guy?"

Hernandez sat back in his seat as the waitress sat their drinks down on the table. Cuba took his time ordering his meal and, then, waited for the woman to leave again. Before he spoke, he took a sip of his wine and drained a double shot of tequila. Again, his gaze fell upon the wise, vigilant warlord and was met with a serious, cold stare.

"I did, sir. I sent the man out to eliminate Sunami," Cuba said in Spanish, lowering his head in disgrace.

He knew that if he showed humility, he could ease the situation to where the old man would forgive him, and continue to support his actions. The last thing he wanted was to be demoted, or better yet, cast out of the organization. Cuba knew that if Bruno Hernandez were to cast him out and all that was connected to him by blood or assassination. And that would also mean Cuba would be forced to kill the old man, here and now. There was no way he could let harm come to himself without a fight.

So, he would have to shoot Hernandez, twice, in the head before killing the personal guard. Cuba was counting on not having to do that. He really liked and admired the man. Hernandez was like an uncle to him.

"Cuba. Tell me, why did you disobey the orders I gave you? I need to know the reason for this so that I can make my own decision about what needs to be done about your insubordination," Hernandez said.

"Sir, forgive me. Night and day, I think about my brother and the family that I lost. These cowards run the streets of Durham, making plenty of money, without so much as a morsel of remorse. They attempted to take my life, sir. They've caused me to be disgraced in the organization's sight. I cannot live on the same earth as these men. I'm in a very big business deal with some other powerful people that will generate the organization close to a billion-dollar profit, overtime! And the same guys are in our way. I took the liberty to try to eliminate them on the behalf of my new business partners, us as well as for my own satisfaction. Again, I've underestimated their abilities. For this, sir, I've failed. But, if you wish, I will not do it again. Or, you, meaning the organization, can help me once again. They aren't as strong as they seemed. Just very lucky," Cuba explained.

Hernandez kept his eyes on Cuba's, weighing the options that came with leadership. He retrieved a brown, Mexican cigarette from a pocket and accepted a light from Cuba. The waitress reappeared with plates of tortillas, yellow rice and hot Chili's.

"Allow me to eat, Cuba. And, then, I will decide what is to be done," Bruno spoke, setting his cigarette in an astray.

They dug into their food. Cuba slipped his hidden gun onto his lap, under a table napkin, without being noticed. He hoped the virgin Mary wouldn't make him have to defend himself. But, he had plans, and they didn't involve dying anytime soon!

***

The green H2 Hummer sped down the freeway. York navigated the huge, gas guzzling vehicle as Sunami, Animal and Zahir loaded automatic weapons and their pistols. They were twenty minutes late, so far, but Sunami had had trouble getting the pilot to come to New York, then fly to North Carolina before going to Florida! Then, they had to wait for refueling at in Charlotte... so, now they 're trying to make up for time.

"Which way, Sunami?" York asked, indicating the exit signs for Miami, downtown exit, and South Beach.

"Take South Beach. Remember that hotel in South Beach that Diamond did that photo shoot at? The one with the inside and outside pool?" Sunami said.

"I think I—"

"Remember, Zahir popped ol' boy in the mouth and the nigga fell on the buffet table? The owners were tripping till Animal gave them another two thousand, remember?"

"Oh, yeah! Yeah."

"Well, it's not that far from there. Like six blocks, maybe. Okay, turn here," Sunami said, pointing.

York made a right and punched the gas. Zahir cocked the Calico he was holding and placed it on safety. Raquel had been left in Carolina to heal from her gunshot wound. Though she had protested, Sunami had insisted that they would need her, later, and it was important for her to get some rest. Animal checked the firing pin on a pistol grip Ak-47 he was holding. He placed it on the seat, between him and Zahir, and checked his two Desert Eagle .44s to make sure the safety was off.

He was ready to get this shit over wit' because he had been having a great time at York's crib! His girl, Talan, a fashion consultant from Seattle, had been calling him like crazy, talking about she had important news. "Sorry, shawty," Animal had said while ignoring her text messages and calls while on the plane, business came first! The Hummer speed through the crowded streets of South Beach while Sunami and the others put on masks. Sunami pointed out the hotel he had referred to when speaking to York, then they pulled onto a curb. York put his mask on and took the Ak-47 that Sunami handed him.

"It's show time!" Sunami said reaching for his door handle with his glove hand.

"Nah, It's BANGA TIME, muthafucka!!" Animal said from the back seat.

***

Bruno Hernandez sat his fork down and lit another cigarette with his own lighter. The guards were still at their table, having a good ol' time, telling jokes and laughing about the least funniest things! Bruno inhaled the smoke from the cigarette as his eyes met Cuba's, again. He had finally decided what he was going to do. Cuba sat in silence as he waited for the words to come from Hernandez's mouth. His left hand rested on the handle of his hidden gun, his right on the arm of the chair.

"Cuba, I must tell you that you have upset other members inside our organization, with you latest insubordination. There is no need for me to explain to you the effects of police attention in the areas we operate, because I'm sure you know," Hernandez stated, calmly.

Cuba nodded his understanding and tightened the grip he had on his gun. Despite his mentor's age, Cuba knew Hernandez could be as ruthless and deadly as an unseen Black Mamba Snake! He could strike to kill in less than a moment's notice. And both of his guards were completely distracted, he noticed.

"I understand, sir. It would make it hard, or even impossible to maneuver with the wrong attention in the right place. Meaning, money operations would have to be shut down for amounts of time that would put sizable dents in profits made," Cuba started coolly.

"Correct, Cuba. But, also, I understand your state of mind. The loss of your brother and the death of your family was a tragic blow to us all, believe it or not. It showed us that we weren't as untouchable as our imaginations had led us to believe. This is the reason I've decided to overlook your shortcoming, but, on a certain condition."

"And, that is?"

"Tell me all about this business."

"Absolutely. I've formed a partnership with two major forces in America's drug trade. People who were once our rivals but now have come together for the good, and profit, of our kind. We intend to eliminate as many small, or mediocre, drug distributors in the key points of the United States, where the most money is made, and supply those as with our product. We plan to control a shocking fifty-six percent of drug distribution in America!" Cuba explained.

"And that is where Sunami comes into the picture? He has an organization, correct?" Hernandez asked.

"Tell me who your partners are."

"One is an African gang leader and drug lord by the name of Obidiah MaTimbu. He holds a large share of the operation because his financing is nearly unlimited. And the other organization is..." Cuba was interrupted by the movement of a black shadow he noticed from the corner of his eye.

Suddenly, he noticed that the laughter of the guards had disappeared and nobody on the outside patio was speaking. Automatically, Cuba turned his head towards the inside of the restaurant, towards the door in which he came through to get the patio out back. His heart jumped into his throat and his stomach started doing flips! He couldn't believe what he was seeing. Or, better yet, who he was seeing!

Two figures in black stood at the opening of the patio door, holding the most terrifying horrible looking objects ever seen, which Cuba knew were Russian AK-47 assault rifles. Behind them, through the glass, Cuba could see two more men, masked holding large, ugly weapons controlling the small afternoon lunch crowd. There was no mistaking the identity of the men, though they wore masks. One of the two on the patio, the ones looking directly at Cuba and Bruno Hernandez, wore his hair in long dreadlocks; they were tired in some kind of half bun. The cold chill in Cuba's spine confirmed what he already had assured. He was going to die today!

Hernandez noticed the two men, also. It only took him a few odd seconds to guess what the situation was. When the tallest man with the assault rifle pulled off his mask, he knew that today was not going to end how he had planned!

"Cuba Sanchez... You's a hard muthafucka to find, you know that shit?" Sunami said, advancing towards their table, York behind him.

Sunami motioned to York for him to watch the three guards, who were frozen still, waiting for any opportunity to strike. As of now, though, the two men had the advantage! Cuba still held the gun under the napkin, watching Sunami for opportunity of his own.

"So, tell me...whass up with that magic trick you pulled on me, back in Durham? Hope the fuck did you do that?" Sunami asked.

Cuba continued to watch Sunami, not giving him an answer to his question. Sunami smiled at him.

"The bomb in the car...that was...that was, uh...pretty creative of you, I must say. Cost my homeboy, here, like a quarter mill, or more but it was clever. Too bad we didn't realize the credit belonged to you, and not the Latin Kings. Bout gave. Thought you did huh?"

"Kill me, or die, you fucking coward. Either way, you won't escape the aftermath. The arms of the family are long beyond imagine!" Cuba said in Spanish.

"Nah...I actually like seeing you sweat, you bitch ass pussy!" Sunami responded in Spanish. as well.

With minimal effort, Sunami tilted the assault rifle and fired a burst into the chest of Bruno Hernandez!

He was blown backwards, out of the chair and onto the floor. What happened next, Sunami had not expected. A hot pain shot through his body as the flash from the gun under Cuba's napkin went off rapidly! Falling, Sunami let the assault rifle scream as the large rounds shredded Cuba's upper body. Sunami fell to the ground, as did Cuba, at the same time, Animal ran into the patio.

York began blazing the table were the guards were and Animal helped. The guards had managed to get off a few rounds, but hit nobody intended. The screams and cries of the other customers were clearly heard outside as the firing ceased. Sunami had taken three bullets, this time. And making it didn't seem to be an option!

He was weak, but still managed to control his own legs after being helped up by Animal and York. They ran through the crowd of onlookers, some gasping at the recognition of Sunami. Sunami held his midsection, where he had been shot, as they ran. Outside, two police officers on bikes were the first to arrive at the restaurant where gunshots had been heard. Too bad for them, Sunami thought. Zahir soaked them with a hailstorm of ten-millimeter bullets from the Calico as Sunami was tossed onto the back seat of the Hummer, Animal beside him.

The first police car to arrive came two seconds before York could get inside the driver's seat. Automatically, he turned and dumped a seventy-five-round banana clip into the vehicle killing all inside and disabling the vehicle, itself.

He jumped in and roared away toward the Miami airport they had come from on the Lear Jet. In their wake, they left a bunch of grief stricken, confused and terrified fans of the rapper, Sunami, wondering what the hell went wrong! The incident would bring a new meaning to Wolfpack music. And a lot of trouble, along with it!

Chapter 15

Sunami was being tended to by a registered nurse, who also worked as a private flight attendant, on the plane, as it made its way north. The question was, where would they take Sunami? York didn't want to take him to his home in North Carolina. Not because it would draw heat to him and his family, that was the last thing York cared about when it came to his niggas. It was just that he didn't want Sunami to get hemmed up by the police in North Carolina, nor the feds.

North Carolina was one of the worst places to get caught up in the system. Sunami, York, Zahir, Animal, knew from experience.

"Man, we need to tell the pilot something, soon. I know he's wondering where to go, now," York said, watching over his nigga as the flight attendant/nurse kept him from slipping into eternal blackness.

Sunami was conscious and awake, just very weak.

"Hell, yeah. The word is already circulating down there and soon every fed with a career to boost is going to be out to get my nigga. But where can we hide him so that he'll be safe and get medical attention?" Zahir asked.

"We got plenty of places he could hide all over the world. But, he won't be capable of doing for himself for a while and that means he won't exactly be safe. You already know the feds are gonna be on our ass in a matter of days, if not hours! We need alibis, ourselves. Then, they gon watch our every move to make sure Sunami's not in contact with us. So, we can't be with him, at all, after we hide him. What choice does that leave us?"

***

Indeed, the word traveled faster than the plane. Before the team of four could make it over South Carolina, Birdman, Obidiah and Special Agent Charles Lavender knew that he had been a participant in, what was being called, the "Cubano Bueno Massacre." Agent Lavender hopped in the first cab available, on his way to Federal

Plaza to talk to the director. If this wasn't enough to pursue McKnight, Lavender thought to himself, he was going to shoot the director! But Lavender and the others weren't the only ones informed of the South Beach incident.

An associate of Carmen Portellini's was on the phone with her, from Florida, giving her the details about the incident.

"The reason I'm telling you is because I recognized the guy as the man at your sister's party. I figured he was either a friend or someone you may have an interest in. Either way, I wanted you to know as soon as possible," the woman told Carmen.

"Lindsey, I appreciate the call. It means a lot. Thanks," she responded.

Carmen ended the call quickly, before Lindsey could engage her in further conversation. She then called a number that she knew by heart. On the third ring it was answered.

"Yeah, what's up?" the man's voice asked.

"Giovanni! Have you heard anything about what's going on with Sly?" Carmen asked.

"Nope. What's going on with him?" Giovanni asked, sounding a bit worried.

It was him, after all, that had introduced Sly to the family. Being that he was only Carmen's brother-in-law, by marriage, he was pretty much expendable!

"I don't have time to draw out the whole picture for you. All I need you to do is get him here, NOW! Not now, but RIGHT this minute, do you understand me? NOW, Gio!" She commanded.

"Is everything alright, Carmen? What is it he's done? And do I need to go get him expecting trouble?"

"No, no, no, Giovanni. Nothing like that. Just get him here, to me, safely. I don't care what you have to do, how much it costs or who you need to call. I want Sly here with me by nightfall. And DON'T call me without him, do I make myself clear?"

"You got it, sis. One gentleman by the name of Sly, coming right up!" Giovanni jokes.

"This isn't the time for bullshit, Gio. I said, get him here, NOW! He may be in danger."

Carmen ended the call with Giovanni and paced the room, thinking of her next move. Something was telling her that Sly had already come in contact with trouble. Even Lindsey had told her that somebody had claimed he was injured.

"Dammit!" she whispered to herself as she thought, hard. Then, she figured out the next best move. Carmen grabbed her phone and dialed another number. She wasn't completely sure she could do what she was planning to do, but it would be worth trying. Besides, Carmen always fought hard for the man she loved!

***

When Sunami's phone began ringing, York jumped to his feet and was at Sunami's side in a second, flat. He had been startled because he thought it was the heart monitor that the nurse had connected to his chest. When he saw that it was his phone, York calmed.

"Hello," he stated.

"Yeah, Sly? Is that you?" Giovanni's heavily accented voice asked.

"Uh, nah. This his brother, man. He can't come to the phone right now, but I'll give him a message for you."

"Actually, it'd be best if you interrupted whatever it is that he's doing. This call can't wait, my friend."

"Well, its gonna have to, my nigga. He ain't coming to the phone. Period," York stated firmly.

Who the fuck did this muthafucka think he was, any damn way? Didn't he realize he was talking to the Don, himself? The phone's screen read "Gio," but York didn't recognize the name.

"Is he...is he dead!?"Giovanni asked, clearly concerned.

"Nah, bruh. He just can't talk right now. What the hell do you want, anyway?" York asked.

"Listen, kid. You tell Sly that Gio knows about what's happened, earlier today. Tell him Carmen Portellini wants to help and that I'm under strict orders not to end this call without confirming that he is on his way to JFK airport, understand?"

It only took York a second to process the information that Giovanni had given him. Frankly, it was an answer to their prayers! York shook Sunami awake and quickly laid out the situation. Weakly, Sunami gave him the okay without touching the cell phone. In ten minutes, York was back on with the man called Giovanni.

"Okay. Pick him up at the airport, but you'd better come like you're about to pick up Obama! Sly is hurt and needs professional attention, asap, without having to worry about the feds or anything. I'm gon tell you like this Gio, if my brother gets hemmed up, fucking wit' you... I'm gon kill you and that bitch!" York promised.

"Man, you dunno what you just said, but don't worry. We'll take perfect care of him. He's like family to us! But don't ever threaten me, again. And if you use the word kill in reference to Carmen Portellini again, not even Sly will be able to save you, kid. That's a promise," Giovanni declared.

"That's what you think. We'll be there in two hours. Be ready nigga. Or we'll see if you dance as good as you talk."

York ended the call and found his seat. He lifted a plane phone and told the pilot where to go. As the plane made its turn, York chuckled under his breath.

"What you laughing at, York?" Animal asked.

"Nothing. Just that niggas never learn until you start giving examples in class!" York said, thinking of Giovanni.

***

Obidiah MaTimbu didn't like the news about Cuba Sanchez and Bruno Hernandez, at all. This was not the way large operations were to work. Now, there was the after of picking up the slack and bad blood between organizations. Rarely did people make money off of war, unless it were governments who were controlling the action. It was always after the wars that the paper was made.

If there was one thing Obidiah had a good nose for, besides women and oil locations, it was war. His country thrived, and perished, off of it, at the same time! It was these reasons that MaTimbu was pissed off, while pacing the expansive day room of his Texas ranch. He had called the other partner to confront him about these mishaps and had been told that they weren't in. The nerve of this American punk.

Lying to MaTimbu was normally a sin, punishable by death! But, he knew that it couldn't, and wouldn't, be done without a war. And that wasn't something he was interested in wasting time and money on. When the phone rang, he sprung to it like the call held the key to eternal life on the other end!

"Hello?" he answered.

"MaTimbu, let my actions be an example to you. When I say I have things under control, that means I HAVE things UNDER MY CONTROL. So, don't go pissing where I lay, understand?" the voice said.

"Are you threatening me, you piece of shit!? I am tired of these crab-like habits you Americans have. Everyone wants to pull the other down into the bucket. Well, did it occur to you that Cuba's part of the bill was now unaccounted for? Who is going to supply his portion of the product? Tell me that? And why did you have to have him killed? I thought you were going to teach him a lesson," MaTimbu protested.

"He learned the most valuable lesson he could learn today."

"And just what was that?"

"There is a thin line between friends and enemies! One step, and you could become the one you search for. The hunter becomes the hunted. That, and no one is irreplaceable. Those are lessons in life that none of us should forget, MaTimbu. As far as Cuba's slack...I'll supply his part and pick up the bill. We'll split all profits, now, down the middle. Three's a crowd, anyway. You never heard that in Africa?"

"No. But we'll see if your fancy words have any merits to them. Because, as you say, no one is irreplaceable. Not even YOU!" MaTimbu said, ending the call.

He made his way over to a couch in the front room and sat down. Now, that he was thinking about it, either one of two things could come of this situation. Either they had just made a power move that ensured the both of them unthinkable profits in the future that would set them for life, or, they had turned loose a hungry Lion In a small room with the two of them and no way to escape. Which of the two was the case, was yet to be seen.

MaTimbu was just hoping to make it out of this cut throat situation with his life, when it was over. He truly believed that what went around, came around. Karma was real.

***

When they landed, York was expecting dark-colored vehicles to be close by. He was thinking that he'd have to go find the guy, Gio, and lead them to the private hangar where their plane was kept. Instead, an ambulance vehicle sat inside their hangar and three Italian men stood around it with two paramedics. Giovanni approached the plane's door as it was opening. He wanted to see the man who had given him such a hard time and issued such serious threats to him and the acting boss of the Portellini family.

York hopped off the plane in some jeans, red T-shirt, and Air Jordan sneakers. The only things that were amiss were the face mask hanging from his neck and the AK-47 in his right hand. The long seventy-five-round clip gave it a menacing look. Giovanni was suddenly speechless.

"So, are they gonna come get him or do we have to carry him out, ourselves?" York asked sarcastically, knowing the presence of his gun made the group hesitate.

"Uh...we'll, uh...Yeah, we'll get him," Giovanni said, motioning to the medics.

York descended the stairs and strapped the rifle onto his left shoulder. He held out his hand towards Giovanni as the medics practically tip-toed past him.

"You know who I am, right? I'm assuming you're Giovanni, then?" he said with a smile.

"Yeah. And you're that rapper dude, uh...I can't think of your name, though," Giovanni stumbled.

"That's good. The less you know, the better. Look, I won't tryna give you a hard time, Gio. But I love my brother, man. And, I wasn't lying. If something happens to him, we'll be playing international freeze tag until you're in a bag in somebody's freezer, ya dig? That's just how serious my bruh is to me."

"I understand what you're getting at. No harm, no foul. Sly is in perfect hands with us. We'll call you."

"Nah. Don't. He'll call me when he's better. I'm going to lay low for a couple months. Be easy. And keep your ear to the streets, Gio. There's an FBI agent after him, already. Name's Charles Lavender."

"Good looking out. We'll pull some strings."

Sunami was transferred into the medic van and driven off. York hopped back on the plane and told the pilot that he had to make a quick stop was in Atlanta. There was so much to do before the feds came, and he couldn't afford to waste a bit of time, because surely they were coming.

***

"I got two eye witnesses that can positively identify Marcus McKnight as one of the armed shooters at the restaurant, Zimmerman. On top of that, LAPD has a corpse connected to the Mexican Mafia found at a hotel that McKnight's wife had reservations for. Then, if that ain't enough, the two bodies in Miami are ranking members of the Mexican Mafia. One of which was believed to be dead, as of last year at a massacre in Durham, North Carolina. McKnight's home town. Don't give me no shit, sir!"

Special Agent Charles Lavender stated, firmly. Anything other than the consent to bring McKnight down would cause pure suspicion on the new director and Lavender was already prepared to take his evidence of a federal crime! He would not be told no, this time.

"You sure everything is in order? No loose ends, no sketchy eye witnesses, no bullshit?" Director Zimmerman asked.

"C'mon, Zimmerman. Cut the bullshit. With all due respect, sir, you are starting to concern me about your capability to handle this job, as director. McKnight is clearly an armed, international murderer. What more do you want? A fucking signed confession with every murder weapon ever used?" Lavender exclaimed.

"Stand down, Lavender! You're close to crossing the line, here. I just don't want you screwing this bust up. If we can prove McKnight committed all these crimes, the both of us will go down in history. Understand? HISTORY!"

"I don't give a damn about any of that. I just want McKnight. And, now, I've got'em. So, do I have the go, or not?"

"You have the green light...But Lavender... If you fuck this up, I'll see to it that you are finished. Do I make myself clear?"

"Yes, sir. As clear as a jar full of semen!"

Charles Lavender rushed out the director's office and began to assemble a small army. There were going to be a swarm of busts made, simultaneously, and he needed as much man power as he could muster. This was the bust that would put him in Zimmerman's chair. Marcus "Sunami" McKnight was going DOWN!

Chapter 16

Sunami awakened in a soft, thick comfortable king size bed. As his eyes adjusted to his surroundings, he had the strangest feeling that he was way out of his element. The large, opened window to his right, allowed the bright sun to shine in on him, warming his skin with its rays. There was an I.V. needle in his arm attached to a bag of clear fluid. Sunami remembered, clearly being shot by Cuba. The three bullets that had hit him had only done some minimal damage, being that they had traveled through his vest before hitting him. Thank God for Teflon, Sunami thought to himself.

Now, he only had to figure out exactly where he was and how he got there. In his opinion, knowledge was power. His thoughts were interrupted by a small boy who entered the room. Sunami determined that the young boy couldn't be more than two years of age. His coloring gave the impression that he was mixed with African American. Immediately, Sunami knew that this was Carmen's son with Tyruss "Fatboy" Lawrence.

"Hey, little man! What's your name?" Sunami's voice croaked.

It had been awhile since he had spoken. And when he tried to speak, his wounds ached intensely. Sunami felt extremely weak from the mixture of lost blood and drugs. While he was taking a mental inventory of his aches and pains, the little boy just stood in the doorway and watched him. Sunami gave up trying to make friends with him and got to the point.

"Where's your mommy, lil' man? Do you know where Mommy is?" he asked.

The little boy nodded and sprinted through the door. The boy's disappearance was followed by a loud call to his mother that he repeated, Sunami guessed, until he was met by his mother. A couple minutes later, Sunami heard the distinctive sound of heels on a hard floor, making their way towards him, it sounded like. Carmen entered the room, carrying the young boy, still as beautiful as Sunami remembered her. Sunami's brief conversation with York on the plane ran through his stored memory. When Carmen sat on the bed beside Sunami, she never allowed her eyes to stray from his.

"Hello, there, cutie! You're awake, I see," she said, kicking off her stilettos and reclining on a thick pillow beside Sunami.

The boy toyed with his mother's necklace, avoiding eye contact with Sunami.

"Yeah. Where are we?" Sunami asked.

"We're in Italy, sweetie. Good ol' Italy. I figured you'd be really safe here. Right now, you're a hot commodity in the states! And your brother made it clear that if anything happened to you, we'd all be dead!" Carmen giggled as if the statement was outrageously stupid.

"Yeah, well...he probably meant it. When did we get here?"

"Four days ago. I actually thought about taking you to my father's house, but I figured the further you were from the states, the better. So, instead of driving around New York with a wanted criminal, I had you driven from your plane to my plane. The medics worked to fix you up as diligently as possible and the plane crossed the waters to my beautiful home country. You are gonna love it, here Marcus. It's just the best place on earth to be."

"Is this your son?" he asked.

"Yep. This is Tyler Patrick Portellini. I named him after his dad and his uncle, my brother. Because I loved both of them so much."

To the boy, she said, "Ty, this is Mommy's friend, Marcus. He makes cool music that you can dance to. Say hi, baby."

The boy's shy mechanism kicked and he hid his face from Sunami. Cute, Sunami thought. It reminded him of his own child when others Brianna wasn't familiar with tried to hold or speak to her.

"What did you call me, Carmen?" Sunami asked, realizing that she had dropped his cover name and begun using his government.

"Marcus. Isn't that your name?" she asked sarcastically.

"That's what my birth certificate says, yeah. But..."

"I just felt like we were past cover names, now. Don't you think? And I don't want to call you Sunami. I like Mark or Marcus better, anyway."

"I dunno, it's just that I'm so use to being called by my alias. It seems weird to be called Marcus, to me. Sometimes, I don't even answer to it when someone called because it's become unfamiliar, now," Sunami explained.

"Well, how about I just call you baby or sweetie? Maybe I'll call you lover boy, Honey or sex god!?" Carmen teasingly.

"Now that I think about it...That does have a nice ring to it."

For the next couple of days, Sunami and Carmen carried on with conversations, getting to know one another better. Even Carmen's little boy, Tyler had taken a liking to Sunami, once he came out of his shyness. It came to the point where the two of them, Sunami and Tyler, would spend hours upon hours together, especially when Carmen was away. It was an entire week before Sunami was comfortable with standing and trying to walk. Even then, he didn't do it very much because he wanted to give his body ample amount of time to heal. The only exercising Sunami did was stretching, besides the one-sided sexual adventures Carmen took him on, almost nightly!

Over the span of three weeks, Carmen and Sunami had absorbed one another. She told him everything about her. And he meant everything. A few nights, she cried as she retold her adventures of meeting Tyler's father and falling in love only to lose him and her older brother. Sunami sometimes found himself uncomfortable listening to the intimate details of Carmen's devotion to Fatboy. It was unsettling at times, because his task, in which he was being paid handsomely to do, was always in his sub conscience.

Carmen and Sunami shared so much together that Sunami had almost forgotten completely about his own wife and two beautiful daughters. And that was definitely unacceptable! It wasn't until Carmen brought him his cell phone, which had been stored with a bunch of other personal things Carmen had taken the liberty to buy for him. When Sunami got his phone back, it had been turned off. For how long, he couldn't know. While Carmen and Tyler went out, one afternoon, Sunami checked his messages.

It had been a little over a month and his phone's storage space for messages was filled to maximum capacity. There were numbers of text messages from his wife, Hypnotic, as well as York and Cherry and other women he dealt with across the nation. There were also missed calls from the same people, as well as unidentified numbers. One of the last messages from Hypnotic caught his attention. He knew that he should've called her by now, if only to check up on her.

All the message said was, "I trust you. I love you. Call me."

"Shit!" Sunami said to himself, dialing Hypnotic's number. It must be hell for her, having to deal with the baby and the feds all on her own. And he hadn't even had the decency to call and check up on her. As the phone rang, Sunami prepared himself to be cursed out in languages unknown. Hypnotic was understanding but everyone had their limits, he thought.

"Hello?" Hypnotic answered.

"It's me, baby! Is everything okay?" Sunami asked.

"Oh my God, Marcus! I've been waiting to hear from you for forever, now. Where are you?"

"It's not safe to say, you know the police..."

"Yeah, I know, baby. I actually traded my phone for a new one and kept the same number. My uncle gave me a scrambler so that any taps on my phone would be distorted and sound like gibberish to whoever listened. They won't even be able to tell who called or where the call came from. Some kind of new technology from Japan, he says," Hypnotic explained.

"Damn, I need me one of those," Sunami mused out loud.

"Where are you? Are you hurt? Well, I'm assuming you're not, because then, I wouldn't be talking to you, now would I?"

"Baby, I'm still handling some business, but I'm fine. I was shot a few times, but it's nothing serious."

"Nothing serious!? What do you mean, Marcus? So, what everybody is saying about you is true, then? You did the thing in Florida?"

"Yeah, that was me, Hypnotic. The muthafucka Cuba... I..."

"You finally got him," Hypnotic finished for him.

"Yep."

"Then, it's over, right? I mean, that's done. What else are you doing, then?"

"I can't say right now," Sunami lied.

"No, you won't say. There's a difference. Baby, Bri and Rain are having a fucking fit that you're not around. The FBI have served warrants on three out of five of our homes, including the condo in Miami, the house in Malibu, and my place in the city. They tried to threaten you and me with possession of illegal weapons, but the only ones they found were registered to me in each state."

"How? Didn't they find—"

"Nope. York gave me the heads up, and my uncle and I had it taken care of. All your guns are safe. But they still want you for the shooting and some other charges. I don't see how you're going to get out of this one when they claim they have two eye witnesses that saw you with your mask off and a perfect description of the murder weapon in your hand. Plus, you're gonna have to explain you being shot and your absence when the entire nation is looking for you. I'm worried, Marcus. My uncle says he'll do whatever he can, but…"

"Don't worry. We'll take care of it, no matter what happens," Sunami assured her.

"I don't like the sound of that. I miss you so much, baby. We still haven't made love in almost two months! Whose panties are you pulling down now?"

"What do you mean?"

"Just that, when you're on these secret missions, you normally get away for a day or two to give me what I need. And I really need it right about now! I don't care if you're fucking that pretty chick I saw you with at the restaurant. She's gorgeous, baby. Was she good in bed?"

"Hypnotic, you tripping," Sunami said, beginning to sweat.

"Babe, I really mean it when I say I don't care. She can't marry you or nothing because you're mine. But I don't mind if she experiences the goods that I get whenever I want. Chances are, if you're working and she's involved, you're either gonna kill her, or get her killed. Am I right?" Hypnotic asked, knowing she was right.

"Next subject, please."

"Exactly. I just want you to not lie to me, sweetie. Don't ever lie to me. Everything else is petty! Anyway, when will I be seeing you?"

"I dunno, sweetie. Soon as I can get all this shit under control and finish what we're being paid to do. I think it'll be real soon. But, I still have to find this guy who sent the assassins to our home to try to kill me. After that, and a few other things, I'll be home free."

"And don't forget about the FBI, honey."

"Yeah, well, them too."

Sunami heard his name being called from out in the hallway. It sounded as if Carmen was on her way up to his room, so, he had to end the call with Hypnotic. Not because he feared being caught or anything. But, because Hypnotic was a reminder of the unthinkable fate that awaited Carmen. That was too much for Sunami to deal with, at the present moment.

"Baby, I gotta go. I'm gone hit you back when I can, though. Okay?" Sunami said.

"Oh, the cutie's back, is she? Don't wanna get caught on the phone with your wife? Huh?" Hypnotic teased.

"Hypnotic McKnight. Stop it. I mean that shit, girl."

"Okay, okay, baby. But at least, ask her if we can get tighter for a threesome before you have to...well, you know."

"I'll think about it. Tell my angels Daddy loves them."

"Sure will. And I love you too, Daddy."

"And the same for you, Mama. I love you, times a million. Gotta go though. Bye."

When Sunami hung the phone up, a little piece of him hung up with it. But he didn't have time to allow his emotions to pour out of his pores. Carmen came into the room bearing gifts from her day out. The look in her eyes told Sunami that she was thirsty. But what she was thirsty for wouldn't be found in a soda machine or a fountain! It was time for bedroom gladiator class!

***

"Mr. York, do you know that lying to a federal agent and interfering with the investigation can put you in prison for a long time?" Agent Charles Lavender asked, pacing behind York's chair inside the interrogation room. "In fact, with your record, it's enough to see you gone for a minimum of twenty years. All I have to do is add on a conspiracy charge, along with possession of a firearm by a convicted felon, ain't that right, Director Zimmerman?"

"Sure is, Agent," Zimmerman cosigned.

York didn't even flinch. The FBI had searched each one of his properties, high and low like they were searching for a microscopical cell that could destroy the planet! Everything had been in order, or so York had thought. After leaving Sunami with Giovanni, he had gotten straight to the task of clean up. Everything that could be charged as a crime had to go, is what York had told his wife, Pam, and four shooters from their crime family, whom he had called in to help. York had made it clear that he didn't want a speck of a bud of marijuana anywhere within a hundred thousand feet of his homes! And just as he had suspected, the FBI came in full force.

Luckily, he had remembered to call Hypnotic from the plane and give her the early heads up. So, when the authorities came, they were greeted with big smiles and soft drinks! All was clear. That is, all but the unregistered pistol left at York's Las Vegas condo! And that had been enough for Agent Lavender to swoop down upon him like a hungry hawk.

Now, the agent thought he had some kind of hold on him.

"Are you even listening, York?" Lavender snapped.

"I hear you, man. Damn."

"All we want to know is, where Marcus McKnight is. We know you two were in contact, recently. Tell me where he is, and I'll just forget about the petty stuff. Don't you want to see your daughter grow up to become a woman? I know I would."

"Listen, yo. It's like I told you, already. Dude holla'd at me early the other morning. I haven't seen him since, though. All I got was a phone call that day," York lied, calm faced.

"I don't believe you. And you're gonna wish I did, trust me."

"Well, do what you gotta do. My lawyer will be here in less than five minutes."

And at that very moment, the interrogation room door opened and York's attorney walked through the door with a look on his face that could peel paint off a wall! He eyed the two detectives with menace in his gazing, telling them to back off or die, without ever speaking a word. Allen Mason was a well-known lawyer who demolished prosecutors and police witnesses. York left less than five minutes later.

Chapter 17

As the nationwide search for Sunami continued, Carmen and Tyler Portellini were becoming more and more attached to him. It had come down to the point where Sunami went weeks, and sometimes a whole month, without contacting anybody in the U.S.

In fact, most times when he did call, it was to speak to his daughters so they wouldn't be so distressed with him. That, in itself, was hard for Sunami. Every time he got ready to hang up the phone with them, they would throw a fit and cry as if they were being tortured to death by some sadist! Sunami hated himself for putting them through so much at a young age. But, while he spent time in Italy, Sunami learned to speak Italian and got the privilege of being able to see what it was like to have a son. Sure, he often treated Shadow's son like his own, but somehow, it just wasn't the same.

Tyler Portellini took to him like a fish takes to water! They played in the park, on days that Sunami felt up to it, and Sunami was learning that Tyler was very aggressive and rough in his way of playing. On the days that Sunami's body healed intensely, the two of them would play XBOX 360 or the PlayStation 3. Tyler was a game god, for his age. He continually spanked Sunami in all sports games. From *Madden* to *NBA 2K10*, Sunami had no wins. *Fight Night*, though, was a different story, entirely.

While Sunami was in this exile, he learned plenty of valuable information. Like the fact that Carmen's father, Luigi Portellini, had purchased, and was remodeling the same Mansion in New York that had been used in the 1972 mobster film, *The Godfather*. He had heard that the mansion consisted of eight bedrooms in all, two fireplaces, a basement pub, four car garage and an in-ground pool!

Carmen mentioned that they had scooped it up for a measly 3.2 million. And that included the remodeling costs that would better suit their needs. After hearing this, Sunami had restrained himself from sending his wolves, immediately. Why? He still couldn't figure that part out. Often, he told himself that it was because of all the FBI heat that Zahir, Animal and York would be getting, right about then.

But, inside, he knew the truth was that he was having second thoughts about what had to done, involving Carmen and Tyler. His orders were clear. No Portellini was to be left alive. And a part of him resisted the fact that the sooner Luigi was dead, the sooner Sunami would be obligated to die pose of Tyler and Carmen. Besides, Sunami thought to himself, what's the damn rush?

The nigga, Birdman, hadn't even produced his end of the bargain, yet. Sure, Cuba and his boss were delicious appetizers, but Sunami wanted the African. And he wanted him bad! There was no real reason to jump the gun on his part of the payment when he hadn't been given what he wanted, yet. Right? Since that settled the decision he had to make, for the moment, Sunami continued to rest up and heal. It wouldn't take much longer now, though. He was walking regularly, talking, breathing and even doing a bit of exercising in the gym, not to mention with Carmen, too! But, still, in the back of his mind, the conviction of what must be done eventually weighed heavy on him.

Sunami sat the bar from the weight bench back on the rack. He had been struggling with 225 lbs while thoughts ran through his mind. As the sweat dripped from his brow and his breath came out uneasily, he dabbed at his forehead with the bottom of his shirt. Carmen was upstairs in the shower and Tyler was being taken out to play by a nanny. Sunami knew that at some point Carmen would make him breakfast and then they could make love. This had become an everyday ritual, and still, Sunami couldn't see the plot thicken in front of his eyes. When his phone rang, his mind was elsewhere.

"Hello?" he answered, trying to sound as normal as possible.

"What's popping, lil' homie? I just wanted to check on you and make sure you're doing okay, still. I heard you took a couple for the team..." Bird's voice said through the phone.

"Yeah, nothing new. Just comes with my lifestyle, that's all. What's good with you?"

"I got some good news and I got some bad news. Then, I got a question."

"Okay, what's the good news?" Sunami asked, straightening himself on the edge of the bench.

"The good news is, I know where Obidiah MaTimbu is, right now."

"That's whass good! Where?"

"Wait. Don't forget the bad news, Sunami," Bird said.

"Oh yeah. What's that?"

"The bad news is, he won't be there much longer and the feds are still hot on your ass. My connects are telling me that some smart ass down there is wondering if you had anything to do with the old director, Brown, getting burnt."

"Man, I ain't tripping off that. Can't I get this muthafucka out the way, real quick? The sooner I do this, the better," Sunami said, impatiently.

"I feel ya, bruh. But, how do you plan on getting here and to him that fast? You're all the way in Italy!"

"Wait. How do you know where I'm at?"

"Nigga, I know everything! You talking to George Delgado, nigga. I do this shit!"

"Whatever. What was the question you had?"

"What's the status of your mission? Do you have a line on the fat muthafucka who killed my nigga?" Bird asked.

"Kinda. I know the area he's in, but I haven't gotten every detail I need. When I know, you'll know."

"What the fuck do you mean, Sunami! You've been under that bitch's roof for months! Haven't you fucked her, yet? And if you have, why hasn't she given you keys to everything she own, by now? I may have overestimated you, Sunami"

"Check this out, muthafucka! You want me to do this? Then, shut the fuck up and let me do it. Don't you ever question how I move, nigga. I said it'll get done, and it will. You just make sure you got what you promised me! Ya dig?"

"Calm down, fam. I got a plan for MaTimbu. Go ahead and handle the bitch and her daddy. Then, you'll be able to fly in and cancel the African. That's my word. I'm 'bout to put some real power moves into play, for you. Let's get this all taken care of so we can take care of the FBI situation for you. Then you can go home to your family and get back to the money, ya feel me?" Bird said.

"Yeah, I hear you. I'll get on that, ASAP! Give me a couple days and it'll be done."

"A'ight. Holla at me, later."

"Yeah."

Once again, Sunami was face to face with reality. But, he already knew, business was business. What had to be done just had to be done. Sunami then called Animal and Zahir. He knew that they'd let York know what was up. He didn't wanna take the risk of putting York in some deeper shit, if he could help it. Soon, Sunami thought to himself, this would all be over. Then, he would be able to tell the difference between his real friends and his enemies. But, for the time being, he was still terribly confused!

***

When Animal got the word from Sunami, he put the others on point about what was to go down. This would be the first time that Animal would be in full control and he had everything planned out inside his head as to what would happen and how. It was decided that each of them would move around frequently for a week before making the move. They needed an opportunity to see if the FBI were on them as hard as they suspected they would be. So for the following seven days, after Sunami's call, Zahir, Animal, York and Raquel traveled separately, all over the United States. And just as they figured, the feds kept a close eye on them for the first four days.

While York met with A&Rs, producers, and managers across the states, undercover agents tried blending in with his surroundings, all while listening in when they could and keeping an eye on the suspected rapper. But, they stuck out like sore thumbs in the atmosphere that York had grown accustomed to. Zahir and Animal made power moves in the modeling industry, as well as the promoter scene, all while watching the ones who thought they were watching them! Although not much money was actually being made, the work that they were doing was good because it caught them up on the things they had been neglecting for other important things. But, who could be blamed for putting down a job that grossed about a million a year and a half for a job that paid twenty million for less than a year? Nobody, that's who!

Raquel was probably the one with the least attention on her. Now, fully healed, she kept up with York and was working on a mixtape, as well. Raquel never really felt like she was being watched, and truthfully, she wasn't! If she was, she could've been knocked off while checking some of the group's drug operations while in Winston Salem, Greensboro, Highpoint and Raleigh North Carolina!

While the others played "Mr. Nine-to-five," the dog food was bringing in a big bank. Raquel had spoken to Sean, aka Black, who was York's top man in the drug organization. Also, he was York's sister's husband. Sean had expressed concern to Raquel about a few other organizations that had suddenly disappeared from the dope game.

"I'm saying, ma, it's like they were here the other week, and now they just left. I mean dead gone, ya feel me?" Black was saying.

"So, what's wrong with that? More bread for us, right?" Raquel asked.

"Yeah, if it was us who were taking them off the map. But, Raquel, don't you think it's crazy that real go getters are just up and disappearing? I mean, I ain't heard shit about no sweep by the police, or nothing. I'm just tryna keep my ear to the streets, ma. But don't nobody knows what's happening. Now that is crazy!"

"I'll let Sunami and York know, when I can. We still working on something, right now," Raquel informed.

"A'ight, yo. Just make sure you do that."

But little did they know, the plot was already thick! And it would be a couple weeks before the real plan came into play. Being that they all were hard at work, it wouldn't be something of much importance to Sunami or York. Not enough for them to stop what they were doing and to investigate on their own. Hell, Sunami was fucking wanted by the feds, himself! What did he look like, looking for missing dope boys that weren't on his team!? Shhhiiit.

Black felt it, though. He knew that something wasn't right in the game and he didn't like it. In fact, he lessened his orders of dog food and told some of his key men to move cautiously. Something just did not sit right, and he'd be damned if he got caught slipping. Plus, he had his wife, York's sister, and his two sons to think about. It would be unthinkable for something to happen to them because he wasn't on his toes. Hell to the nah! If there was one thing the game had taught Black, even though he'd been successful all this time, it was, nobody lasted forever. It didn't matter how you ended. The simple fact was, it would end, at some point. And Black had intentions of leaving with possessions, not empty handed! So, he had most people fall back and observe. It was the only way to live in a jungle full of predators.

***

Obidiah MaTimbu was becoming impatient. Months were going by, and still, nothing had been done. His business partner had him killing off hundreds of small organizations that were in the way, but still the main problem remained. And his orders still stood: Leave Sunami and York to me, he had said. Well, MaTimbu was getting tired of leaving shit to "him" and nothing productive being done.

This is what he was explaining to his partner on the phone, at this very moment. The last thing MaTimbu was, was a coward. He told his partner exactly how he was feeling.

"MaTimbu, what you neglect to understand is, the only downfall of accomplishing a master plan is, it takes time! Time, MaTimbu. And in the end, it will all be worth it. But these things can't be rushed. Is that understood?" the voice asked, irritated.

"Clearly, but what about Sunami and York? The best time to take care of them is now while the government's attention is on them. We can sniff them out and eliminate them, quietly. Then, while the government is occupied by the discovery of the bodies, we can put the key power moves into play. Now, that, to me, sounds like a master plan," MaTimbu explained.

Obidiah was unaware of the aggravation he was causing his partner. Being such a pessimist would definitely bite him in the ass, later, and his partner knew exactly how it was going to happen. So, for now, he would humor MaTimbu. But, not for too much longer. Because, surely as the sun rises and falls, MaTimbu's days are numbered. The sad part was, he didn't even know it, yet.

***

One of the lead agents in the organized crimes section of the FBI made his way through the maze of cubicles towards the director's office. In his hands were pictures taken by an overseas unit that he believed would be able to help one of the special agents on the force. The agent he had in mind was Charles Lavender. Lavender, at the time, was busy getting his ass chewed by the director. Months had passed and, still, there was no sign of Marcus McKnight, also known as Sunami.

Zimmerman was furious! Time, money and manpower were being spent in vain, and that didn't make him look too good at all. Therefore, since he was feeling the wrath of the brass, Lavender would have to feel his wrath. And there was a lot of wrath to feel!

"What am I supposed to tell my boss, Lavender? Huh!? Five damn months have gone by and you haven't produced a damn thing, except hot air and unnecessary bills to be paid! Where is McKnight?" Zimmerman demanded to know.

"Sir, he's got to be hiding somewhere. But you can't expect for him to just fall in our lap! We'll get this guy, I promise. He's smart, but he ain't no fucking genius," Lavender said.

"Compared to you, Lavender, he's a modern-day Einstein! You can't out smart him for shit."

The knock on the door interrupted them. As the young agent entered the room, Lavender shot him a glare. That is, until he explained why he was there.

"Sir, I think this would greatly benefit the McKnight investigation," the agent said.

"What is it?" Zimmerman asked, extending his hand to take the photos.

"These are a couple of photos taken in Italy. We have a small team keeping track of the Portellini family and their activities. Sadly, sometimes they're a bit behind. But, it seems as if McKnight has gone into exile with the Portellini woman. They seem to be quite, uh.....friendly with one another."

Zimmerman passed the photos to Lavender as he looked at each one. It was clear where McKnight was. Now, they just had to take him down. Zimmerman fixed his glare on Lavender again and leaned in.

"Lavender. Get him in here, NOW! And I swear to god if you fuck this up, I'll kill you, myself. Put a team together, the best men. And go. GET MCKNIGHT!" Zimmerman commanded.

"Done, sir. It's done," Charles Lavender vowed, leaving the room.

Chapter 18

It was crunch time for Animal and the team. The four of them, without Sunami, flew to New York City to plot and execute the plan to kill Luigi Portellini. After days of undivided attention from the feds, it seemed like they just lost interest and disappeared. It had happened just as the four of them suspected it would!

Animal was the leading general on this one. It was decided that the mission, itself, would be a risky one and with the feds not far behind, they all needed to be on point while being effective at the same time.

Therefore, York was acting as the consigliere, watching their backs while Animal put his ruthless ways into action. Zahir and Raquel would improvise, should something unexpected occur. The Sprinter van that York had made arrangements for was in place when they landed. Guns, locked and ready, they made their way through New York, once again, to find their target.

All the way to Staten Island, NY, York kept his eyes on every single detail. What cars turned when they turned, who was standing where on what street, who switched lanes when they did one to another. To the normal mind, it could get a bit confusing, after a while. But to the born hustler that York was, it was all done by nature. His mind never functioned on the same wavelength that everyone else's did. That was what made him who he was!

A totally different breed of thug. When they entered the neighborhood of the four-acre Staten Island mansion, not much of it could be seen from the roads of the neighborhood. York circled the neighborhood three times before he found a place to park. Animal informed everyone that the plan was to enter from the backyard, and he was expecting some sort of security.

"That's why we gon keep the silencers on. Hopefully, we can make it inside without alerting nobody. If somebody does hear us, we might be in for a real shootout. That ain't something we want in this area. I bet the cops would show up in two minutes or less. Keep y'all eyes open, and not just for y'all self. Let's get it poppin'!"

Animal led the way as they advanced to the back side of the property. The streets of the neighborhood were fairly dark and not many people could be seen out and about. Animal made a note to himself, mentally, not to get too excited or carried away as to alert the neighbors. He was expecting resistance, already. There was no need to increase the threat by making their presence known to more people than were already bound to find out. That's why everyone would stick to their silencers!

At the back of the house, York was lifted onto the stone fence by Raquel and Zahir. York was the shortest, so he would have the most trouble climbing the ten-foot fence. After York got into position and scanned the yard, he gave them the "okay" and Animal WS helped over, followed by Raquel. Zahir jumped the fence last, hitting the ground a few seconds before York, who had watched for any movements while the others got situated. To their surprise, nothing happened.

Keeping an eye on the entire backyard and pool area, the four of them slowly made their way across the yard. Their guns stayed ready to hose down anything that didn't seem right to either one of them. Again, surprisingly, they made it to a back, sounding glass door.

While they grouped, Zahir scanned the exterior of the house.

"Find the phone connection, Zahir," York whispered.

"I'm looking, bruh," he replied in hushed tones.

Zahir walked east, against the main building, searching for the box that held the wires to the phone and security lines. After five minutes of fumbling around in the dark, he found them. Zahir took some wire cutters and cut all lines available. Then, he met back up with the rest. Raquel had been picking the lock while Zahir was gone.

"Did you get 'em?" Raquel asked.

"Yeah, they cut. We're good to go, ma," he replied.

With that Raquel turned the knob, holding his breath and hoping Zahir hadn't fucked up. No alarm sounded, that they could hear, and with the swiftness of a snake, they entered the house. Immediately, they spread out to cover the entire lower area before advancing to any other levels. The four of them checked each room but came up with nobody of importance. To York, it seemed almost as if the entire mansion was deserted except for the four of them! He wondered if Sunami had gotten the correct information.

After the four bedrooms of the lower level were searched, they headed upstairs. It was then that they encountered the first sign of life since being on the property! On her way to the restroom, Sophia, one of the live-in nurses that took care of Luigi Portellini, bumped right into Animal. Before she could even grasp, she was struck, gagged and pinned to the wall by the strong hand clutching her throat!

The entire team was alert now.

"If you moan, if you scream or even breathe loudly, I'll kill you and bring you back from the dead just to kill you again," Animal stated calmly.

"Do you understand?" Sophia nodded, trying to contain the pure adrenaline and fear that was the cause of her heart beating in her throat!

All of her senses were on fire and she was afraid that she would disgrace herself by urinating down her leg, and dying because of it.

"I'm going to ask you some questions, a'ight? I want you to answer quietly. Don't try to talk me to death, either, or I'll just get bored and shoot you for the hell of it."

"Animal, just ask the bitch the damn questions, man!" York whispered.

"Okay. How many people are here, right now?" Animal asked, releasing his grip, slightly.

"Five, including me," Sophia said quickly.

"Who are they?"

"One other nurse and two guards, other than Mr. Portellini."

"Where are the guards staying?"

"They both guard Mr. Portellini's room, from the inside," Sophia told.

"What kind of weapons do they have?" Animal asked.

"Guns. Pistols, I think."

"Okay. Good. And where is the other nurse?"

"In that room, over there. She's the daytime nurse. I monitor Portellini throughout the night."

Animal thought about the information he had just received. He was trying to come up with the best possible plan of action. Zahir, Raquel and York were already over by Portellini's door, listening to see if they could detect any movement inside.

Animal figured that the guards would be up and alert, guarding their boss at all times. If the door just burst open, they'd probably wet up the opening before anyone, or anything, got a chance to make a move, he thought. Therefore, he would have to be smarter than them.

"You're going to take us inside. If you blink wrong, I'll kill yo ass. But, listen to what I say and I'll let you live," he lied.

"But sir, Mr. Portellini is a very sick man. There is barely a reason for him to have security, at all, besides his wealth! If I had to guess, I would say that one, if not both, of the guards are probably asleep on the security cot. There is hardly ever a threat to Mr. Portellini, which is why I don't understand what this could be about," Sophia whispered hurriedly.

"It's not for you to understand. Just open the fucking door and you can go."

She had to lie, Animal thought as he made silent eye contact with York. The only thing keeping her alive was that he wanted to use her as a decoy. There wasn't a way that the guards of a notorious mafia boss would be sleeping while all kinds of deceitful plots and plans brewed with conspiracies of his demise! Animal was no dummy. Maybe a little slow, at times, but no dummy.

The feeling that the nurse was trying to play him for a fool angered him to the fifth power. With his gun in hand, Animal shoved the hesitant nurse towards the door. Sophia glanced back at Animal and the others as they prepared themselves, guns raised and ready for a wildfire fight. She turned the knob and pushed the door open to a darkened, larger master bedroom. The only light inside the room came from the moonlight through one of the large windows. Animal nudged Sophia into the room and awaited a greeting or some indication of where, exactly, the guards were positioned. Surely, they would be close by the door, or more likely, in the blind spot behind the door.

But, after a long ten seconds, Animal realized that Sophia was just standing there in the middle of the darkroom, nobody saying anything! Without another thought, Animal tapped York's arm and they all stormed the room, quietly, in squat, still expecting the unexpected. It was the only way, Sunami had explained to them once, to stay alive. Once the four of them were inside, a MUX between surprise and shocked emotion overcame them. Inside the room, over on a small military like cot, a guard was sound asleep, his gun on the door, sat out of reach! And another, in the corner behind the door, sat in a comfortable recliner chair, sleeping like a newborn baby.

It took them a second to register what reality had dealt them. In the center of the back wall, close to a floor-to-wall window, a huge white bed held a lump of a figure in which labored breathing was coming from. Occasionally, a cough, or two, rattled the body as the noise filled the room with sound. Animal recovered quickly and signaled to Zahir and Raquel.

"Yo, get the guards. York, let's do the old man so we can get outta here. Fuck it, if its gon be this easy, let's get this shit done!" Animal said, heading towards the large master bed.

Without question, Zahir and Raquel sprang into action. The spray of their silent weapons were more quiet than the hacking and wheezing coming from Luigi Portellini. The guards never knew what hit them. It was Zahir who turned back to Animal, when the deed was done, as he and York prepared to eliminate their priority target.

"What's good wit' ol girl?" Zahir asked.

Sophia's eyes grew to the size of basketballs when she realized that the tall, evil looking man was talking about her! She looked to the one who had snatched her by the throat as she had been going to the restroom, which she still needed to use.

"But, you said...I thought..."

Sophia stumbled over her words, fear rushing through her like a hot flash! Animal looked up and smiled the smile that had the power to terrify those who weren't accustomed to his ways. He shook his head at Sophia.

"Sorry, baby girl. I lied," he said.

Before Sophia could protest or make a dash for the exit, her body was riddled with bullets that traveled as quietly as a thief in the night. The last thing she saw was the automatic weapons being raised at the bed in which Luigi Portellini rested.

***

His heart pounded with the fierceness of a bass drum in a marching band as he paced the darkened room.

Sunami was not normally a man who was easily disturbed. But the rapidly occurring events of the past couple of months had him more stressed than a man awaiting an HIV test results! Only a few months ago, Sunami had been sitting in his youngest daughter's room, watching her sleep, when a hit team of assassins came to eliminate him and his family. Now, he paced the master bedroom of a mansion owned by Carmen Portellini. A woman who had taken the large responsibility of running her family's business.

A woman who, by doing so, had placed herself in a seat to take responsibility for the death of Marcus Santiago Jr., a street legend, loved by plenty. A woman who Sunami was charged to kill, along with everything in her immediate bloodline. A woman who Sunami, also had fallen deeply in love with!

"But how!?" Sunami whispered to himself, angrily.

Sunami was a married man! A happily married man, at that. So, how, he wondered, could he have fallen in love with the woman he was being paid four million dollars to kill? The question seemed to be rhetorical, because he sure as hell didn't have an answer for it! Glancing at the bed, quickly, Sunami noticed that part of Carmen's leg had come uncovered. Again, they had spent the night making passionate love and whispering meaningless words to one another.

Except that Carmen continually dedicated herself to Sunami. And sadly, Sunami had wanted to do the same. It was strange because it seemed as if the more Sunami and Carmen shared one another, the better, more pleasing she got to him. Earlier, Sunami could have sworn on a stack of bibles that Carmen was as wet as an ocean polluted with K-Y Jelly! And her discharge from her orgasm was thicker, more rich and more intense than he could ever imagine.

Even now he couldn't help but notice every part of her that was visible. The curve of her smooth heel, her perfectly shaped toes, the silky skin of her leg! Even her hair was arousing.

"Stop that shit, Sunami!" he told himself, shaking his head.

For a moment, Sunami just stood, staring, at the sleeping figure in the bed, wondering what he would do. Wondering if he could do what he was paid to do. He was stuck between the decision to get it done, or just walk away from it, once and for all. But the ring of his cell phone made the decision for him.

"Hello?" Sunami whispered, leaving the bedroom.

"Sunami, its Bird," Bird said.

"I know."

"Listen, I just got a call from your partner and them. Luigi is dead. Now, all you have to do is kill the bitch and her little boy, and get the hell out of there."

"So, they got out without a problem?"

"Yeah. But, listen. I got Obidiah MaTimbu right where we want him, so, if you hurry the fuck up, you can get him."

"How the hell do you got him where we want him? I thought you said..."

"Fuck what I said. Kill the bitch and get to the fucking airport. The plane should be there in less than a half hour. So, get the shit done, NOW!" Bird demanded.

"Man, what I tell you 'bout talking to me like dat, nigga?" Sunami said, pissed off.

"Listen, Sunami. You're not understanding me. I can't get in contact with any of my agency connects, right now. And the only time that happens is when something big is about to go down. Think about it, who's their number one target, right now, besides Osama Bin Laden? YOU!! So, hurry."

"You think they might be..."

"I don't know, Sunami. Do you wanna sit around and find out for yourself?" Bird asked.

"Good point. I'm on it."

"Don't forget, Sunami. Nobody lives. Nobody! The lil' boy dies, too. Then, get on the plane. MaTimbu is next."

Chapter 19

Sunami ended the call and turned his phone off. The time, in which he had dreaded so diligently, had come. He went back into the room and found some dark-colored clothes to wear. After getting dressed, Sunami went into Carmen's walk-in closet and rambled around. He found the gun and silencer that had been covertly sent to him weeks prior. As he screwed the suppressor on, he stared blindly at Carmen's sleeping figure.

How he was going to find the will to harm her, he still didn't know. Sunami decided he get rid of the help, first. He left to go find each house maid and the cook. The last person he silenced before heading back to the bedroom was the mechanic, a nice guy whom Sunami had learned a lot from and also had grown to like. Back inside Carmen's room, Sunami, sat on the end of the bed with the gun in his lap, staring at Carmen as she slumbered.

He checked his gun, took a deep breath and cocked a bullet into the chamber. The offending sound echoed off the quietness of the room's walls. Sunami raised the gun at the still figure on the bed, his hands trembling violently.

"I can't do this shit," he whispered to himself.

But he had to do it! And there wasn't much time left. In less than an hour, he should be on a flight back to the states, leaving the bodies of Carmen, her son and every employee of the house behind. So, why couldn't Sunami do the one thing that had always come so easily to him? The answer was plain, but Sunami refused to acknowledge it.

Then, the unexpected happened. Carmen's eyes opened and focused directly on Sunami. Then, they focused on the gun pointed at her.

"Baby, what?...What's going on?...Why do you have that gun pointed at me?" she asked, confusion in her eyes.

"I'm sorry, Carmen. I'm so sorry. I have to, baby...I'm so sorry, but, I have to," Sunami confessed.

"What? Have to what?"

"I'm sorry, Carmen. I'm not at all who you think I am?"

"What the fuck are you saying? I know who you are, I know your name, social security number, everything! How can you not be who I know you are?"

"Not like that. I mean, I was sent to kill you. I was never supposed to get so close, Carmen. I was paid to kill you, and your son."

"My son?...But, why?" Carmen asked, tears rolling down her cheeks.

If what Sunami was saying was true, she knew this could truly be the end. In some of the inquiry Carmen had done, it was well known that Sunami had murdered plenty and his team of wolves was notorious for assassinations. Carmen would have to lay all her cards on the table if she were to make it out, alive, with her son.

"Marcus Santiago. The man who was with Tyruss when they killed your brother. Your father acted with a government agency and conspired in Mac's death, Carmen," Sunami said.

"Well, kill them! Why can't they take responsibility? What about my father? He's the one who did that," Carmen protested, grasping for any leverage.

"Carmen, your father is dead. I'm sorry. There's really no way out of this. I just wish I hadn't led you on, so much, and gotten so involved."

"But, Sunami, I mean, Marcus, I love you! I really love you! I know you're married and it's all my fault, but I can't live without you. I mean, what about Tyler? Can you honestly kill me and my son?"

"Carmen, I'm sorry. I love you, too, it's just—"

"If you love me, help me! Don't do this, please, Marcus. Just let us go."

"I can't. I… I can't, Carmen, it'll never stop."

"Who wants me dead? Who is it? At least tell me that."

"Birdman," Sunami confessed.

"What? That conniving, self-centered, disloyal sonofabitch! You're working for him? I never thought..." Carmen said.

"I'm sorry, Carmen. I'm...I'm..."

"Stop saying that! Can't you see? Marcus, I'm fucking pregnant!! I'm two months pregnant with your child! And you're going to kill me!?"

Carmen began sobbing uncontrollably. Sunami was stunned by the new piece of information. Then, he was angry at himself for not noticing it sooner. The intense, emotional sex, the nonstop eating, Carmen's devotion and catering. It was all there, laid out for him to see, and he had overlooked it as blindly as a bat in the sun!

The gun lowered, slowly, as Sunami sat on the edge of the bed. He couldn't believe the drastic turn his life had taken. Carmen continued to cry at the top end, but now it had lessened a little. For an entire thirty minutes, they sat in silence, except for Carmen's sniffing. It was she who couldn't take it anymore.

"What are you going to do?" she asked, looking at Sunami with a mix of worry, fear, and love in her eyes.

She reasoned that she couldn't really blame him for the situation he was in. Her father had killed this man, Marcus Santiago, and, of course, someone would take revenge on him, at some point. The man had ties deeper than La Costa Nostra! And, he had won battles against the FBI numerous times. Surely somebody would care when he was taken away from this world.

Carmen knew he had a family. But, what she didn't understand was why Birdman, a man she had once done business with, was the one to put a hit on her entire family! Why not just kill her father? But, then again, why not eliminate the whole Portellini bloodline? Lord knows, not many of them were left, especially after her mother had died.

She just wasn't able to take the blow of her son and grandson dying. Life didn't seem as bright, to her, after that. But Carmen wanted to live! And, regardless of her father's death, she still wanted to live and raise her son. It was him she was most worried about.

"How long have you known you were pregnant, Carmen?" Sunami asked, rebooting the fear inside Carmen's belly.

"Almost three weeks. I was waiting for a good time to tell you. I didn't know how you would take it, ya know, with your wife and all," Carmen admitted.

"Fuck!"

"Marcus," Carmen said, taking a deep breath. "I know what my father has done. And it has to be avenged. That is the Italian way, also. So, I don't care if you have to kill me. But, will you...can you let Tyler live? I know it's crazy, but he hasn't even lived yet. Give him to the foster home or a nice family. I just don't want him to die, Marcus. Will you do that for me?"

Sunami closed his eyes in frustration. This was not how things were supposed to be going. Carmen held her breath, awaiting his answer.

"No," he said.

The answer rendered Carmen speechless. This man, who she had shared her love and her body with, had just crushed her soul with one little word. Carmen couldn't even breathe for a moment. That is, until Sunami continued.

"I can't kill you, Carmen. And I would never harm Tyler, or the seed growing inside of you. But I don't know what the fuck we're going to do," he said.

"I hope you don't trust Birdman, Marcus. We did business together before and he never seemed to have a problem with me then," Carmen said.

"It was probably because he was trying to get information about you, so he could kill you. Ever think of that?"

"What I'm saying is, he tried to sleep with me on many accounts. But I wasn't interested, though he's very smart and business suave. I had been hearing that he was dealing with some really bad people. Ya know, the M.M, Medellin Cartel, The Orellana Cartel, and some Africans."

"What!?" Sunami exclaimed, thinking rapidly.

"What?"

"Who told you this?"

"It was just information that was floating around. My contacts picked it up and gave it to me while I was dealing with him."

174

"Do you know about the attack on my family in California?"

"I told you, only what I saw on the news. Why? What does that—"

"Never mind. We have to go."

"But, why? What are we gonna do about..."

"Shhh! Listen."

"What? What is it?" Carmen asked worriedly.

"You don't hear that?" Sunami asked, straining his ears to hear the faint sound.

Carmen put all her concentration into hearing what Sunami had claimed to hear. At first, there was nothing but the sound of their breathing and the tension easing into the air. As Carmen's heart calmed, she could feel the steady thud inside her chest. Only...it wasn't her heart that continued to thud! The sound was far off but was slowly increasing. It sounded like several drums in a marching band being played all at once.

Sunami got up from the edge of the bed and walked over to a window. He yanked the curtains wide open and caught the sun peeking over the mountains. It was already dawn. But in the distance, right above mount Etna, the 10,902-feet-tall mountain in southern Italy, four tiny black dots hovered, or flew, toward them.

The realization of it hit Sunami like a bucket of cold water in the face, in hell!

"Oh, my muthafucka gawd!" Sunami said, barely audible.

"What is it, sweetie? What?" Carmen asked, rising to look out the window.

"Get Tyler, now! We have to get outta here."

"But, who could that be? Do you think..."

"Get your son, Carmen! Let's go!" Sunami screamed, scrambling to grab what he would need.

Carmen ran out of the room to get her son. Sunami stuck the pistol he had meant to kill Carmen with in his waistband. He then grabbed a leather jacket and tossed it over his shoulders. After that was done, he began searching. When Carmen came back, she had Tyler, who was barely awake, in some mix-matched clothing and she was carrying a large Chanel tote bag. She was startled when Sunami appeared from her closet.

"Do you have any large guns, or guns of any kind, here?" Sunami asked urgently.

"Yeah. There's an M-16 over here and a shotgun under the bed. I have my pistol. But how—"

"We don't have time," Sunami interrupted.

"Get the shotgun, grab your keys, and meet me in the garage. We're gonna need something that is real fast that can seat us all. Your Ferrari won't do, it's a two-seater. Tyler will need to be strapped in. I'll drive. Now, go!"

"Please, just tell me who's coming, Marcus," Carmen begged.

"The FBI, Carmen! And they're probably pissed to the twenty-third degree. Now, let's go."

***

"I refuse to take no for an answer, Bird! Either tell me where Sunami and York can be found and I'll dispose of them, or, deliver their bodies to me in the next forty-eight hours. I'm done taking your excuses. Cuba was right, this is a situation that should've been handled from the start. After the first attempt, there should have been more until the job was successfully completed," Obidiah MaTimbu spoke into the phone, deciding to put his foot down on the Sunami situation.

He had to give Bird proper credit, though because as he said, the mafia man had turned up on the news, dead. And, now, Bird was guaranteeing the daughter next. That would leave Sunami and York, only, in their way of accomplishing their goal. MaTimbu thought it would be best to handle Sunami and York while taking care of the mafia woman, but Bird had other plans.

"I told you, MaTimbu, to let me handle this. I've been delivering haven't I? Damn. I promise you that within the next day or two Sunami and York will be dead. The woman should've met her end a few hours ago. If Sunami isn't dead in two days, he'll be on his way to federal prison for ten life sentences, I promise," Bird told MaTimbu.

"Mr. Delgado, I don't condone dry snitching, or any other kind, for that matter. Just kill both men. If you do not keep your word, I'll be pulling out of this arrangement, we have. I'm sick of the American games that are being played," MaTimbu said.

"Oh it'll be handled. By the way, aren't you still taking care of business in Washington, DC?"

"Yes. I have a nice condo here, you know the one. Once things are completed on your end, I'll set things in motion, immediately, from here."

"Perfect. See you soon," Bird mumbled deviously.

"What? Why?"

"Huh?"

"You said you'd see me soon, why would you see me? You're not supposed to be coming out here," MaTimbu said.

"Oh, it's just a figure of speech," Bird lied.

And with that, the call ended. But Bird did plan to see Obidiah, soon. In fact, he'd be seeing him real soon. On the six o'clock news, with his head in his lap! As soon as Sunami called him, he would point him in the right direction. His scheme had fallen into place, piece by piece. Now, if only Sunami would call him... Birdman decided he call his own boss while he awaited Sunami's call. Everyone had to answer to someone!

***

Charles Lavender and his partner sat side by side in one of the choppers carrying the entire anti-terrorist task force that was stationed in Italy.

The team totaled to, about eighty men, give or take ten or twelve. They were flying over the rural area of South Italy, where Carmen's Portellini's getaway home had been discovered. It had been a long flight for Lavender, but with six cups of coffee in his system, plus the pure adrenaline that ran through his entire body, right now, he was ready for the world! As the choppers gained ground and the mafia woman's mansion came into view, Lavender gave everybody the signal to prep and check their weapons.

He didn't expect McKnight to be prepared for the surprise attack, but then again, he wasn't taking any chances! Guns were loaded and the thumbs up signal was passed around the passenger hold of the massive helicopter containing nearly twenty special agents.

"Remember, if you even see a gun lying around, anywhere, you have full permission to neutralize any and all threats. If McKnight draws a weapon at any time, take him down! And I mean, take him down fast! This guy is Bin Laden's third cousin, or something. He won't hesitate to kill you, so don't you give him the benefit of the doubt. I promise, if you do, you won't be riding back as you are now. It'll be in a body bag in the cargo area!" Agent Lavender warned.

Lavender prayed silently that he would make it out of this with his own life! Then, he loaded the AR-15 assault rifle and readied himself as the chopper lowered towards Portellini estate.

Chapter 20

Sunami closed the door behind him as he entered the building that held a slew of Carmen's personal vehicles. The modified garage was a completely separate building from the exclusive mansion, that sat in the rural of Adriano, a nice sized town in Sicily. Searching for Carmen and Tyler in the large garage, Sunami passed a silver Jeep Grand Cherokee Overland 4x4, a BMW 7 series, a Jaguar, a Mercedes Benz SLS AMG, and an Audi, among other exotic vehicles. It was at the Audi that Sunami found Carmen strapping Tyler into a new technology car seat in the back. She heard him approach and turned around.

"Okay, look. The R8 is the best choice I could come up with, because it's capable of safely holding Tyler's seat and it has gray airbags," Carmen said, indicating the red, sports-like vehicle.

"Great. Is it fast, enough, though? Chances are, these feds are about to chase us, we need to ride!" Sunami said, taking the silencer off his pistol and tossing it onto the ground.

"Hell yeah, it's fast. It's got a dual overhead can 48-value V-10 engine that's been modified. 6-speed manual."

"I'm not exactly a mechanic or nothing like that, Carmen. All I want to know is, if the bitch is fast?"

"Put it this way, babe, it tops out at about two hundred miles per hour. I bought it for $150,000. Now, it's probably worth, at least, $175,000. But there's one problem."

"And what could that be, besides the fucking fact that the feds are about to land at any second, Carmen?" Sunami asked angrily, heading to the driver's side door.

"You don't know this area and I'm probably not as good a shooter as you. Therefore, I'm driving."

"Ain't no way!"

"We don't have time, Marcus. I'll drive, trust me, I can move this bitch like you've never seen. It's what I bought it for. Just keep the FBI at a distance. I'll have us at the airport in Catania in an hour, give or take."

Without another word, Sunami went to the passenger door and yanked it open. The woman had a point, after all. He definitely didn't know the area of southern Italy and he'd do better with the gun than she would. Besides, Sunami didn't even know which way Catania was! The sound of the helicopters were deafening, now. It sounded like they were only a few feet above the ground, as Carmen closed the driver's side door and pressed the button that would open the garage door in front of the Audi R8. Sunami checked one of the forty-round clips and slapped it into the M-16 and loaded it, rolling down the window as the powerful V-10 engine came alive. As the door rose, dust and leaves scattered across the grounds of the estate. Eighty yards in front of them, a chopper touched the ground and the side door opened, revealing armed agents.

"Mommy! It's a helicopter!" Tyler exclaimed from the back seat.

"Not now, sweetie," she said, turning toward Sunami.

"Ready?"

"Let's go!" Sunami responded as the car jerked with a high-pitched squeal.

Just as the agents were coming out of the chopper, they noticed the 217 fire-red R8 lurch from the garage toward them. The chopper had landed on the front lawn, to the right of the exit, which was about a hundred and thirty yards off. Before any logical decision could be made, the sound of the automatic M-16 had the agents scrambling, Special Agent Lavender included!

"Get down! Get down!" Lavender yelled as bullets whizzed by, Striking the exterior of their helicopter.

The R8 hissed by and sped towards the entrance at sixty mph. The all-wheel drive vehicle was out the gate and around the corner by the time Lavender made it back to his feet!

"C'mon! Back in the chopper, Now! Now!" Lavender yelled.

"Simons and Vahn are down, sir. I think Vahn's gone already, and Simons is fading fast. We need..." an agent was reporting.

"Leave him! In the chopper. Now!" Lavender interrupted.

The team of agents rushed back to the helicopter as two of the other three began to rise back into the air. Lavender commanded one of the teams to secure the house and garage. So, while Lavender's helicopter lifted into the air with the other two, a team of special armed agents stormed the garage building and broke down the front door of the mansion! When they found the first body, the mechanic in the garage, they knew that they had come to the right spot.

***

"It's okay, sweetie. Look, Mommy is right here, see?" Carmen tried soothing as Tyler screamed and cried in the back seat.

He had been terribly frightened when the large automatic rifle had given the loud report as bullets scattered, and wounded, the FBI agents. Now, his sobbing was uncontrollable and there wasn't much Carmen could do, driving at 80 mph, as she headed towards the city called Paterno, which was past the Simeto River, on the island of Sicily. Sunami, on the other hand was busy checking the M-16. The sighting was a little bit off, but otherwise, pretty good. He just wasn't satisfied with the limited ammo capacity of the magazines Carmen owned.

Had he had his own weapons, he would've, at least had two or three, hundred-round drums! Forty and fifty-round clips just weren't cutting it, for him.

"Carmen, if we make it out of this, you need to remember that in a fire fight, you won't have enough time to keep changing clips. Especially with the feds! This forty-round shit is garbage," Sunami complained, watching the large agricultural land and farm houses pass by in a flash.

Carmen swiped a lock of her curly, brownish black hair from in front of her eye and switched into fifth gear before looking at Sunami. She gave him an irritated look while rounding a sight curve.

"Sorry, Sunami, but this isn't something I do, on a regular basis, have you ever thought of that?" she asked sarcastically.

"I'm just saying, step yo game up! I got guns for sell all day long. With your type of money, you should invest in the best. It is really the only way to stay alive in our businesses. We have to be prepared for the worst, especially you!" Sunami returned.

"Well, I never would've thought the man I fell in love with would be hired to kill me, Marcus. This ain't no James Bond movie! How am I supposed to know?"

"You're not! That's the whole point. But you should be well-prepared, worst-case scenario."

"In the brown bag, back seat, there should be six extra magazines for the rifle, including two seventy-five-round banana clips. Also, grab an extra clip for my nine, please."

Sunami opened up a bag on the back seat, while also trying to calm Tyler, who's crying had subsided, slightly. He found the magazines and gathered them in the front seat with him. The seventy-five-round clips weren't exactly hundred-round drums, but they were better than the forty rounds! Sunami was satisfied for the moment.

It was then that a large, black helicopter flew overhead and turned sideways, revealing a man wearing a helmet and carrying a large rifle. The gun was pointed at the audio as Sunami realized what was about to happen.

"STOP!!" he screamed at Carmen, who slammed on the brakes as she held the clutch in.

SCCCR REEEEEEEEE AAAHHH!!! As the audio jerked to a halt, the large rifle sounded off and took a chunk out of the pavement a few yards in front of the vehicle. The helicopter flew a distance more before heading back their way. Two others circled around and advanced towards them. Sunami had the one to their left in his sights. He switched the rifle from fully automatic to semi-automatic and began squeezing off round after round in odd patterns and bursts.

"Drive, drive, I can still shoot," he yelled.

BLAOW, BLAOW, BLAOW, BLAOW, BLAOW BLAOW,BLAOW, BLAOW!!! The M-16 barked at the circling chopper as the R8 took to the road with claw like tires.

Sunami couldn't tell if he were landing any shots or not, because the helicopter rose higher into the air to get away from the firing.

But, as the R8 approached the helicopter from which the rifleman had taken a shot at them, a machine gun opened fire from the sky! TAT, TAT,TAT, TAT, TAT, TAT, TAT,TAT, TAT!! Carmen swerved the sports car as a spray of bullets rippled through the right-side quarter panel! Smoke poured from the holes, immediately, and Sunami was worried that something vital had been hit. Carmen jerked the wheel, again, missing a Honda Odyssey van by mere inches, as she got back into the appropriate lane.

She switched gears, again, and continued to gain speed s Sunami's heartbeat inside his throat! The helicopters were, once again, behind them.

"Use the sunroof, Marcus. Keep them back there, okay? They could easily shoot the engine out, or shoot me and cause a fatal crash?" Carmen instructed.

"Ya think!?" Sunami responded sarcastically.

Luckily, the smoke dissipated and they continued to move with celerity. Sunami took Carmen's advice and rolled back the sun roof to see if he could get a better shot at the choppers and keep the helicopters at bay.

***

C'mon, c'mon, c'mon, get closer," Lavender urged the helicopter pilot as the chopper continued its cause of the Audi and its occupants.

"Sir. With all due respect, a man has just opened fire on us, and you're rushing me to get closer? Please, allow me to pilot this aircraft in the safest manner possible while following your orders. We do have other agents aboard, mind you," the pilot retorted.

"You'll do as I tell you to do, pilot. The agency cannot afford to lose its primary target. Now, get us closer so we can take another shot," Lavender ordered.

The car sped down curvy roads, passing few compact settlements but plenty of open space. Out in the southern parts of Italy, plenty of wealthy Italians owned large estates or farms with ranch houses and livestock. For some odd reason, the mountain area of

Sicily was very popular with prominent, prosperous Italians. Lavender could see the outline of the Simeto River in the distance as they gained on the fast-moving vehicle. The other two choppers kept pace with the sports car at each side while keeping their distance, awaiting an order from Lavender.

It may have been unprofessional and selfish, but Lavender had decided that he, personally, would be taking McKnight down! Not sitting in the background talking through a microphone the entire time. He didn't have to necessarily take the killing shot, but he'd be close enough to feel the thud of McKnight's body hitting the floor, he figured. Plus, McKnight was a lot too dangerous to want to actually be too close up on him. But the big fish would definitely be Lavenders! The pilot got into position for the shooter to take aim at the vehicle. He figured it would actually be best to stay behind the vehicle, instead of putting everyone in the line of fire.

Well, that was until the sunroof opened and out came the M-16 assault rifle! The helicopter was hovering, only, about seventy or eighty feet above the vehicle. At the moment the machine gunner on the helicopter opened fire, so did Sunami, whom had taken his time on the precise angle and aim of the shot. The first couple of thirty-millimeter bullets from the helicopter's machine gun ripped the trunk area of the Audi, but otherwise did minimal damage. The very first bullet from the M-16 struck the machine gunner in the center of his chest and knocked the machine gun's aim off.

The bullets that followed clanked and clanged the helicopter as the pilot pulled hard on the controls, sending the firing machine gun astray, shooting bullets holes into a nearby helicopter and sending it to the ground in a wild, smoking spin! The shock wave of the crash could even be felt inside the speeding Audi as Carmen made the turn to enter the expressway that would take them to the city, which the two private jets were awaiting. While Sunami had sent her to get Tyler and prepare the vehicle, she had made some quick calls and had managed to arrange a separate destination for her and her little boy. Carmen loved Sunami, and all, but at the moment, he was entirely too hot! All those thoughts ran through her brain while watching the smoke cloud from the fallen chopper and keeping an eye on the other two, which were altering their course to continue pursuit.

With another long blast of the M-16, which never seemed to end, the lead chopper pulled away and did not seem to be planning on returning.

"Where the hell are you going, pilot!? He's stopped shooting now. Catch up!" Lavender screamed over the loud beeps and rings coming from the pilot's panel.

Not to mention the rotors, themselves, being so loud.

"No, sir. I can't do that," the pilot responded, maneuvering the large aircraft away from Carmen and Sunami's vehicle.

"That's an order, pilot!! Turn this goddamn thing around, now!"

"Take your order and suck it! We're losing fuel fast, and I believe it's from a leak in the main tanks. We have taken far too many bullets, already, and unless you wanna die in a helicopter crash, I suggest you sit your little scrawny ass down! Fire me, sue me, I don't give a fuck. But, I love my life, you inconsiderate prick!" The pilot scolded.

He lifted his radio and gave the official cease and desist order, reporting seeing smoke come from the other chopper's main engine. Safety, to him, always came first. The last thing he had to worry about was Lavender's ranting and raving. His place, in the bureau, as a pilot was secure, anyway!

***

It was the most surprising thing to see the two helicopters turn away from them. Sunami took the opportunity to lower himself back into the sunroof and change clips on the assault rifle, in case it was a bluff and the feds were going to be waiting for them elsewhere.

Carmen kept it hot! Her foot never let up on the expressway. She figured, if the feds wanted to take a break or ease up, it would be a great opportunity for them to put more distance between them. And maybe, just maybe, they could shake them and make it safely to their planes! In the city of Catania, Sicily, Carmen found a vacant alley behind a homemade bakery shop. She pulled in and cut the engine, before Sunami could even process what was going on.

When Carmen began grabbing her things and unlocking her door, Sunami grew alarmed.

"What the hell are you doing?" he asked.

"C'mon. If the feds are letting up, we can probably lose them. The car is too obvious and they'll identify us by it at the airport. We can't take it," Carmen explained.

"How do you expect us to get to the airport, then?"

"An Uber. The airport is only about ten miles from here."

"I can't take no M-16 into no Uber, Carmen. Think!"

"No, you think!...I'm sorry, look. Just leave the rifle, Marcus. You won't need it. Besides, we still got the pistols."

Sunami followed her and they caught an Uber to the airport. When they arrive, Carmen led Tyler to the hangar where she was told her plane would be waiting. Not once did she look back or say goodbye to Sunami. Sunami figured goodbyes aren't easy for her. He found his way to the hangar where Bird's planes was waiting for him. As he was entering it, his cell phone beeped once. It was a text from Carmen. The only thing it said was,

"Be careful. Make sure you know the difference between friends and enemies. Love, C.P."

Chapter 21

Carmen prayed nothing bad happened to Sunami, as she flew to the location of another one of her "safe houses." Her house, the cars, her dead staff members, none of that mattered to her. In fact, those thoughts were the furthest from her mind at the moment. Reflecting on everything Sunami had told her, Carmen was still a bit perplexed about the reality of the threat against her. George "Birdman" Delgado was the ultimate snake in the grass, she thought.

That sonofabitch had conned and manipulated his was around her and into her circle. Luckily, she had had more common sense than most idiotic women with unthinkable amounts of power. Carmen wasn't one to go around sleeping with everyone who looked and smelled like money. Those whom she did choose to share her bed, or a relationship, she remained as discreet as was possible, given underworld celebrity. She had seen right through Bird's smile like his face was made of glass!

She only hoped that Sunami... No, she liked Marcus, better. She only hoped that Marcus was as vigilant and thorough as his reputation claimed of him. The sheer thought of Sunami brought a warning to her belly. Carmen reclined the seat next to her that Tyler was sound asleep in. She had put him through one hell of a day, for a toddler! But, for what it was wort, he was tough, like his dad. Back to her current love. Marcus.

Something was telling her that Bird had something up his sleeve. She didn't fully understand why there had been a hit out on her, given the fact that she had nothing to do with Marcus Santiago's death. But there would be no way to find out without letting on that Sunami had, in fact, left her and her son alive. And that would put him in danger, which was the last thing Carmen wanted to do. Then again, there was the factor of revenge to consider.

It would be impossible for her not to settle the score when Birdman threatened, not only her life, but the life of her child!! Now, there would be two children. She would have to eliminate that threat. Besides, Carmen was willing to bet the baby inside her that

Birdman didn't mean Marcus and his organization well. Sunami already had enough to deal with, with the FBI on him. And he would surely have to deal with them sooner or later! Hell, she may even have to deal with them.

When the solution popped into her head, Carmen knew she needed to act fast. Thirty thousand miles in the air, she dialed the first of two numbers on her plane's phone.

"Yo, whass up?" Gio's voice came on.

"An eye for an eye..." Carmen said.

"A tooth for a tooth!"

"Fifty men. Two helicopters," she ordered.

"Jesus, Carm! Who are we going to war with, and when?" Gio asked.

"Tomorrow. The Byrd Cartel. This isn't a joke, Gio. My father's dead, my house was destroyed, and Tyler and I almost lost our lives."

"What happened to Sly?"

"He saved us. Bird Delgado was behind it. I want to burn every feather on his fucking body!"

"I'll get right on it."

***

The brown-skinned flight assistant nudged Sunami out of his sound sleep. As his eyes adjusted to her vanilla-colored uniform, she extended a phone towards him.

"Mr. Birdman would like to speak to you, sir. He says it's of most importance," she said, apologetic.

Sunami took the phone and cleared his throat as the assistant walked across the way. She turned shortly after and handed Sunami a bottle of Spring water. He wanted to pour the bottle over his head. Sunami felt like shit! Running from the FBI on pure adrenaline would do that to anybody.

And the plane, coming to get him in such short notice, hadn't been able to restock on food before the overseas flight to Italy!

Sunami took a long swig of purified water before answering the phone.

"What?" he said, angrily.

"Whass up wit' you, Sunami? You sound mad," Bird's voice said.

"I'm not exactly having a great day."

"Man, get over that bitch, Sunami. We got other shit to do. Bigger fish to fry."

"Whatever. What is so important that you had to deprive me of my sleep?"

"Look, Animal, Zahir, and all of them are about to board a flight to Washington, DC. They will meet you there, and—"

"Wait, wait, wait. DC, for what?"

"Obidiah MaTimbu is held up in DC, Sunami. I told you I was gonna make some shit happen. Well, I did. So, we can end our business deal once this is completed. You've delivered, now I'm doing the same."

"Can this shit wait a couple days, Bird?" Sunami asked.

"Why?"

Sunami told him of the events that took place early that morning in the rural parts of Sicily. Bird listened in amazement at the story of Sunami's "Italian Adventure." Of course, Sunami left out the parts about Carmen's involvement and the fact that she and Tyler were the only two that left the house, other than himself! That would ruin Bird's morning coffee if he knew that the two of them were also on another plane at that very moment.

"Bruh, taking on four helicopters is a helluva breakfast, Sunami! But, unfortunately, this can't wait. I ain't sure I can keep this African muthafucka in place for too much longer. And, you the one who wanted this nigga so bad, so, take care of it. All the info y'all need will be in DC. A car, guns, vests, all that."

"Yeah, whatever. In a couple days, I'm gon meet up wit' you so we can talk," Sunami said, thinking of Carmen.

Something would have to be done between him and Bird.

"Man, worry about today! You could die or get twenty years fed time. Tomorrow ain't promised, nigga. Always talking 'bout later, later, later. Get this shit done and I'll holla."

"What the fuck you say to me, nigga!?" Sunami yelled, causing the assistant to look over at him, concerned.

But there was no answer. Bird had hung up the phone on him.

"Stupid ass nigga," Sunami grumbled.

He made a mental note to straighten that situation when the right opportunity presented itself. They were doing each other favors, but Bird acted like Sunami was one of his hired help or something. One thing was for sure, Sunami thought he wouldn't let him continue to talk to him in any kind of way. He didn't give a damn who Bird thought he was! Switching gears, Sunami tried to mentally prepare himself for what was to come in Washington. He didn't know much about the city besides what little he'd heard through the years of school. And there were plenty of times, throughout those years, that he wasn't listening, at all!

From what little he could recall, Washington DC had a pretty large population. He knew it was between Maryland and Virginia on the Potomac River and was the only American city, or town, that isn't part of a state. That, and the fact that it's the headquarters of the United States government. But, that was it! Fuck it! There wasn't much he needed to know, now, about the place, anyway.

There was an African gang leader there who had placed his life, as well as others, in danger. And that was all that he needed to know for the time being. Sunami closed his eyes again, hoping to get more rest before making it to the U.S.'s capital city. He wanted to be fully alert when he got there. As sleep weighed in on him, he thought about the FBI, Carmen and other stressful circumstances.

Then, he thought of how he wished things could be. Peaceful, calm, and prosperous. Hopefully, he'd be able to get things back that way soon. But he knew there were three obstacles that needed to be removed before he would be able to do so. Charles Lavender, Obidiah MaTimbu, and George Birdman Delgado!

***

Director Zimmerman was boiling with rage! Two of his task force agents had been shot, twenty more had died or been seriously injured in the copter crash, millions of dollars had been destroyed with the down helicopter and what did he have to show for it?...Not one damn thing! Charles Lavender stood, explaining the situation the best way he could, in front of Director Zimmerman.

Upon hearing about the expensive failure, Zimmerman altered a business trip flight to the Middle East to fly to Italy and get the report straight from Lavender's lips.

One of the first people he had encountered upon arrival had been the pilot of the helix that flew Lavender and others. He had filed a formal complaint and gave Zimmerman an ear full! Now, Lavender was trying his best to explain why the top-secret mission to catch McKnight with his pants down had failed. So far, nothing said was convincing Zimmerman.

"Wait a minute, Lavender," Zimmerman said coldly.

"So, what you're telling me is that McKnight, Carmen Portellini and her two-year-old son managed to murder two field agents, crash a multimillion-dollar aircraft killing twenty plus agents, critically injure another aircraft, and flee pursuit? Is that what you are standing here, into his room, telling me?"

"Sir, you must understand the circumstances—"

"I don't have to understand shit, Lavender. But, the bad part is, I do. I do understand that the bureau made a terrible mistake in hiring you, I understand perfectly. I do understand that you are the most insubordinate, incompetent field agent I've ever laid eyes on in over twenty years of law enforcement. I understand—"

They were interrupted by a knock on the door, which only infuriated Zimmerman even more!

Without acknowledgement from either of them, the door swung open and one of the agents in charge of running the Italy division stepped into the office and closed the door behind himself. Agent Debra Hardy was five feet nine inches, almost a hundred sixty pounds, and not very easy on the eyes. At forty-two, she was an overweight, single, Caucasian woman with a knack for problem solving. The only problem she couldn't solve was how not to be lonely at night!

Director Zimmerman's gaze clearly showed that this was not a time where he was welcoming interruptions. He had a tongue lashing awaiting Agent Lavender and probably some demotion, too. But Agent Hardy ignored his stern, unwelcoming gaze and stepped further into the room.

"Mr. Zimmerman, forgive me for the interruption but I believe there is something that I have to say that can't wait," Hardy stated firmly.

"I'm sure it can, Ms. Hardy. Right now..."

"RIGHT NOW, I have a message from a highly respected confidential informant who claims that Marcus McKnight and some associates plan to murder the business tycoon and gang leader, Obidiah MaTimbu in our nation's capital. So, would you like to continue insulting Agent Lavender, or would you like to do something productive? Sir."

"Zimmerman held eye contact with Hardy, sending a clear message that she was barking up the wrong tree. Then he turned to Lavender, who was now standing, with a scowl on his weathered face. Son, somebody somewhere must like you for some reason. You've just been handed the chance of all chances. Do not fuck this up," Zimmerman ordered.

***

Somewhat rested and ready to get the job done, Sunami got off Bird's phone as ready as he could be, given the previous circumstances. A black Kia Borrego Limited 4-wheel drive SUV pulled into the private hangar and Sunami could see York in the driver's seat. Zahir sat beside him in the passenger seat. Before either of them could get out, Sunami got into the back alongside Raquel who capped him up.

"Whass poppin, Sunami?" she said.

Sunami nodded and settled inside the roomy SUV. York had plenty to think about and the other four could sense a bit of tension coming from their homeboy. York followed the instructions of the navigation system past a shopping center called Greenaway which held on uppity restaurant called Jasper's. He had been to DC a couple times on tours. He'd been to the United States Botanic Garden, southwest of the capitol, with Pam. They had viewed more than ten thousand varieties of plants, including rare species. They had also visited the mall, which had turned out to be a narrow park that was two miles long, stretching west from the capitol to Lincoln Memorial.

York had overheard some lady telling a group of people that it served as the nation's "front yard," or something of that sort. Because York was a tad bit more familiar with the capitol than the others, he drove.

He knew that the silence of the car was probably because Sunami hadn't wanted to kill the mafia bitch. But, oh well. York had learned early that in life you were required to do plenty of shit that you really didn't want to do. That is exactly what made life what it is! The five of them ended up North of Kennedy Center, across the street from the famous "Watergate."

Watergate was a complex that included condos, offices, a hotel and other shops. It became famous in 1972 when some campaign workers for President Richard M. Nixon, Republican, were caught breaking into Democratic political headquarters there.

"The instructions Bird left was a condo and an office here at Watergate. I got the number to his place in my phone. There was a spare key left for us, too," York said.

"How the fuck he get that?" Sunami wondered aloud.

"I dunno. But the vests and guns are in the back. Since it's so cold out, nobody will pay much attention to the coats and shit. I dunno if he's in the office or the crib, but, I say we try the crib and if he ain't there, we wait. Whatcha think, Sunami?"

"I don't care. Let's just do it." Sunami opened the door. York got out and the others followed to the back of the SUV. It had to be at least thirty degrees outside. York pulled Sunami to the side by his sleeve. "Yo, you straight, bruh?" he asked.

"Yeah. I'm straight. Italy was some bullshit, that's all."

"Are you capable of doing this, cuz you know you can fall back and we'll take care of it, right?"

"Nah, I'm good. This is personal, remember. But I wanna run something by you when we leave."

Chapter 22

The five of them made their way onto the building, separately, clad in thick coats with hoods, toboggans and gloves. Little did passing pedestrians know, they were strapped to the teeth under their jackets! York had made extra sure his features could barely be seen. The Watergate building was sure to have a very sophisticated security system that included video surveillance. He was a fucking celebrity, for god sakes! Sunami, too, covered up real good.

He didn't need anybody seeing his face at all with him being wanted nationwide for a shooting death in Florida! Taking separate routes to the eighth floor, they met up and York led the way to the condo door belonging to Obidiah MaTimbu. At the door, Sunami knelt and leaned his ear against the door to see if he could make out any sounds coming from inside while the others watched the hall, alert. Dead silence. To Sunami, that could mean only one of a few things: one, that nobody was inside the condo, which he highly doubted. Two, that the door and walls were soundproof so as to keep sounds from coming in and going out. Three, MaTimbu was either sleeping or not in a room close to the door. And four, they had the wrong condo. Sunami hoped it wasn't four.

Any fucking thing but number four, please! There was only one way to find out, though.

"York, gimme the key," Sunami said.

York retrieved the key from his pocket and handed it to Sunami before producing a Mack-10 submachine gun with a silencer that was almost twelve inches long fitted to the snubbed barrel. Raquel and Zahir produced identical weapons and quietly loaded bullets into their chambers, keeping their eyes open. Sunami produced a 10mm Glock handgun fitted with a silencer and Animal produced one of two silenced Glock 40 cals. They all held their breaths as Sunami slid the key into the knob and turned it softly. The door lock clicked.

Sunami, then, unlocked the bolt lock, as softly as possible. Sunami aimed his pistol at the crack of the door and turned the knob. He gave it a soft push and heard the sucking sound of an air tight sealing door opening. The next sound that met him was of Miles Davis playing on a stereo. From what Sunami could see from his crouched position, the front area was vacant. He turned to the others and nodded.

"Let's do it. Search every inch!" he whispered.

The five wolves disappeared into the house and the door was closed, softly, behind them. The door was locked. They all spread out to hunt for their prey!

***

"What's on the menu for tonight, Rojo?"

"I've got a craving for some duck served with French lentils and celery raisin relish, but I don't really want to deal with the weather. It's up to you, tonight, we can order something or I can call the driver and make a reservation. What do you think?" MaTimbu asked as he clicked his briefcase closed and reached for his jacket. The big, highly trained mercenary turned bodyguard shrugged his big shoulders, nonchalant.

"Aw, c'mon, Rojo. Make us a choice, in or out?" MaTimbu urged.

He had a drawn-out meeting with the head board members of his oil manufacturing company that had taken way longer than he expected. MaTimbu had made more decisions today that would either cost or gain him millions of dollars annually. For once, he just wanted somebody else to make a simple ass decision. What to do about dinner. But the tall, muscle toned bodyguard didn't budge. He could care less what they ate, though he did appreciate the opportunity to choose.

The way Rojo had seen it, there were plenty of times of war where he was out in a jungle, alone, with nothing to eat but bugs, plants and whatever he could kill and cook! If MaTimbu wanted duck from some fancy schmancy restaurant, then duck it would be. If he wanted to order shrimp fried rice and sweet and sour chicken, Rojo would be satisfied, either way. His job was to ensure the safety of his boss at all costs, not to regulate the calories of his diet!

MaTimbu made his way to the office door and produced a set of keys to lock it behind them. Rojo stepped into the hallway.

"No suggestions huh, Rojo? Okay, then. Take it out! It's too cold out anyway," MaTimbu declared.

The two of them made their way towards the elevator, down the hall of the fifteenth floor. MaTimbu checked his messages as they walked and the conversation changed from food choices to unsolved problems.

"I'll bet you a thousand dollars that Bird still hasn't taken care of those rapping bastards! A thousand dollars," MaTimbu said, pushing the eighth floor button on the elevator.

"That asshole is as useless as a third armpit," Rojo said in a foreign language.

"I wouldn't dare take such a foolish bet. We both know he has done nothing."

"We'd be better off letting you take care of them."

"It would be a pleasure. I despise their luck. I could end it with a flick of my wrist," Rojo boasted.

A business-type woman who joined the elevator got off on the ninth floor. The elevator dropped one more floor and the two of them got off and headed to Obidiah's door. Rojo took MaTimbu's keys from him and unlocked the door. He pushed it open and stepped inside, MaTimbu right behind him. The music was a slight destruction but a man appeared in the hallway and Rojo's eyes locked on him the moment he appeared.

MaTimbu was still oblivious, as was the individual. Rojo's gun appeared in his hand just as the individual noticed him, and his arm shot out to shield Obidiah from harm as he raised his weapon. Raquel, who had been searching rooms down the hallway, dived for the lamp table where she had temporarily sat her gun down upon finding the condo completely empty.

The chunky Glock held by Rojo barked loudly inside the condo and blew a hunk of Raquel's head onto the wall behind her!

***

The gunshot startled Sunami. It had sounded like it came from right behind him. But in the half second it took to realize he wasn't shot, he raced from the master bedroom and into the front. He was only steps behind Animal and York who reached Rojo and Obidiah MaTimbu first. Amazingly, Rojo put them in his sights automatically, managing to get another shot off.

The loud bullet tore the plaster out of the wall to Sunami's right as York dived out of the way while spraying a hailstorm of silent bullets. Animal dropped to a knee and commenced pumping the huge guard with bullets from his pistol. Rojo took at least sixteen bullets before he dropped to his knees. Sunami's gun was finding Obidiah, who had produced a Browning nine millimeter from nowhere, when Zahir appeared from the kitchen behind him and knocked him unconscious! MaTimbu dropped like a sack of potatoes and the shooting stopped.

That's when Sunami noticed Raquel's body at his feet. His eyes met York's who looked as if he were about to lose his mind! Before anything crazy happened, Sunami turned to Zahir and Animal.

"Tie him up, put'em in the kitchen," he said.

"For what!?" Animal asked, angry beyond reason.

"Chill, Animal. Just do it. I gotta find out why he attacked me and York, and who sent him after us," Sunami said, turning to York.

"Yo, just chill for right now. You'll get ya chance in a minute."

Zahir and Animal drug Obidiah into the kitchen and restrained the unconscious man with duct tape they found under the sink. They undressed him as Sunami instructed and sat him in a chair.

Sunami found a filet knife and pulled a chair in front of MaTimbu while York walked into the back room to shed his tears for his dead cousin.

"Animal, check the hall to see if anybody heard the shots. I gotta get some answers and I need to know if people outside can hear this nigga if he scream," Sunami said.

Animal ran to check the hall while Zahir filled a pitcher full of cold water. Something told Sunami to take care of business and get the hell out of there. But Sunami had questions and needed answers.

***

Charles Lavender climbed down the ladder of the wildcat fighter jet that expedited him overseas at more than two hundred miles per hour. The jet had landed on the private airstrip that president Obama often used. He was met by a large group of agents surrounded by ten black Yukon trucks. One of the agents ran over to greet him.

"Lavender, right?" the agent asked.

"Yeah. What do we got?" Lavender asked.

"Twenty-six agents, ten vehicles fully loaded. The orders from the top say you're in charge."

"That's right. I want those men suited up in full body armor and ready to take down our suspects at any cost. The subject that our guy is after is an African gang leader, drug lord and famous business tycoon. We are not obligated to take any kind of special precautions for him. He's scum just like McKnight! Do we have a location?"

"Yes sir. Records show a condo leased to an Obidiah MaTimbu at the Watergate complex, as well was office space. Casualties are likely, if we don't evacuate the building."

"Too risky. That could alert our guys to our arrival, but I will tell you what...Get who you can get out there by the DC police departments before we get there. Tell them to avoid the eighth floor at all costs. When we arrive, all bets are off," Lavender declared.

"But sir..."

"The only butt you need to be concerned with is yours, and I can promise it'll be fried if you do not follow my orders to the very letter! Is that understood, agent?"

"Yes sir, it is."

"Good. Let's suit up and get ready to move. Time is of the essence."

***

The pitcher of water Zahir doused Obidiah in brought him back to consciousness with a few raid blinks! As his eyes focused, he noticed that he was wet, nude and bound to one of his dining room chairs. Luckily, his condo was fairly warm. He also noticed the familiar look of death in the eyes of the man sitting in the chair directly in front of him. Then he noticed the knife!

"Mr. MaTimbu, I believe you know who we are, so I'll skip the introductions," Sunami said.

"I know that you are supposed to be dead. But yes, I know exactly who you are, Marcus McKnight, aka Sunami. Hip Hop artist, producer, co-owner of Baby Girls Models Incorporated and minor drug kingpin and leader of Steady Wolfpack Cartel" MaTimbu said.

"Pretty good. I believe that sums it up. So, here's what's about to happen. I'm going to ask you a few questions and you're going to answer every single one. If not, I'm going to cut each of your testicles out and make you eat them. Then, I'll ask you again. If you still don't answer, you'll be eating your dick. After that, I'll move to your toes, fingers, lips and ears until you eventually bleed to death in this chair. Then, I'll set this bitch on fire on my way out. So...the choice is yours, Mr. Obidiah MaTimbu. "

"Sunami, just for the record, I'd like to let you know that this won't end with me. When I'm dead, there will be hundreds upon hundreds of highly trained killers who will hunt you and your friends down until none of your family is left. But, on the other note, there won't be any need for dismemberment. Ask your questions and I will answer truthfully. But in return, I would like a question answered, first."

Sunami looked over to Zahir and raised his eyebrow before turning back to MaTimbu. York entered the kitchen with fury in his eyes. He was curious as to what Sunami had planned with the man and the knife.

"Go ahead with your question, Mr. MaTimbu," Sunami said, leaning back in the chair.

"How exactly did you find me? And how did you get into my apartment without forced entry?" Obidiah asked.

"That's all you wanna know? Well, my connection tracked your movements and got you to stay here in DC Then, we were left instructions on your location as well as the key to your door."

"Him!!. Who exactly, may I ask, is this connection of yours?"

"Have you ever heard of the Byrd Cartel?"

"That is quite interesting. Yes, I have heard of him."

"Okay. Now, Mr. MaTimbu, I've answered your questions. I want to know why you sent people out to kill me and my family and who was behind the order?"

Obidiah's smile was as bright as that of a Colgate model. He tilted his head to the side and looked Sunami into his eyes.

"Would you believe that the organization teamed up with a couple organizations in America to eliminate growing drug Cartels in certain areas, so that we could overpower those areas and control almost half the drug importing and distribution in the U.S.?"

"Damn!" Sunami exclaimed.

"And you were trying to move my organization out the way, correct?"

"Yes."

"Who ordered those hits on us? Was it your idea?"

"As much as I would like to take credit, Mr. McKnight, I cannot. Would you believe that it was George Birdman Delgado?"

Sunami's face went slack and his heartbeat sped a few notches. Zahir, Animal and York gasped at the answer.

"Bullshit! Don't lie to me, MaTimbu," Sunami demanded.

"Sorry, kiddo. How else would I know that you killed the former Director of the FBI, and you just came from Italy because you killed Carmen Portellini and her father in New York? Bird played us both. I suspected it and you confirmed it. He'll probably turn you into the FBI when I'm dead. Don't believe me? Pick up my cell, press three, and send. You'll see."

Sunami snatched up the phone and did as instructed. The phone rang twice before being answered.

"What is it, MaTimbu? I told you shit is under control! The bitch is dead and Sunami and York will be soon, so, I'll call you later. Go home and wait," Bird's voice said.

The phone call was disconnected and Sunami had all the evidence he needed. Bird was going to die!

"Well, you kept your word, sir. But, unfortunately, your guard killed my nigga's cousin and our fellow homegirl. So, I'm gonna leave your fate in his hands. Good luck," Sunami said, handing York the knife and taking the keys to the SUV.

To York, he said, "Do what you gotta do, but make it quick."

"You'll be dead in a month, tops!" MaTimbu declared calmly.

Sunami turned to Animal and nodded toward the door.

"Where did Zahir go?" he asked.

"To get the cash we found. It's probably two hundred grand in there, in an open safe," Animal said.

"Oh. Well, look. I'm taking the back stairway. You and Zahir take separate ways downstairs and get rid of y'all gun and shit. I'll be waiting in the car. Tell York, too."

"A'ight. Go 'head, bruh."

Sunami headed out the door and down the hallway to the emergency stairs. As he emerged from the building and crossed the street, he noticed the fleet of black SUVs with flashing blue lights. They surrounded Watergate with the quickness! "Shit!" Sunami exclaimed.

Chapter 23

From across the street, Sunami watched the swarm of FBI agents attack all entrances and exits of the building. He sat inside the SUV, dialing Zahir's cell number. There was no answer. Next, he tried Animal's and got no answer again.

"Muthafuckin Bird!" Sunami snapped. He dialed York's number and got it ringing. After three rings, York answered.

"I'm 'bout to come, now, bruh," York said, nonchalant.

"Get outta there, bruh. The feds just hit the building. Where Zahir and Animal?" Sunami asked.

"They left a few minutes after you," he said, sounding like he was running.

Sunami heard the door closed in the background and could hear York as he made haste toward the nearest exit.

"Bruh, toss the vest and the gun. The feds are all over that muthafucka, and police are outside with a whole lot of civilians. Looks like they evacuated the building. They must have skipped the eighth floor. But stay on the phone with me, tell me what you see."

"A'ight."

Sunami was hoping that Zahir and Animal had gotten rid of the guns and stuff. Hopefully, they just snuck out and headed away from the building. Sunami couldn't sit around for too long. Eventually he would be spotted or look suspicious to one of the authority figures. As much as he didn't want to, he may have to leave the others, temporarily. York was still navigating his way out of the building. Sunami wondered where the hell Zahir and Animal were!

***

Zahir had taken a different stairway than Sunami. He had come out almost ten minutes behind him, at about the time Sunami had seen the agents swarm the building.

Zahir heard a door open at the bottom of the stairs and it was followed by the clatter and hard shoes and orders being given. Zahir looked over the edge and noticed a jacket with the "FBI" letters illuminated in white.

"Fuck!" he whispered, turning the opposite direction and opening the door leading to the fourth floor.

He tossed his gun into a corner, stripped his vest off and tossed it before sprinting to the other end of the hallway. He burst through the emergency stairway door and was met by a crowd of armed agents!

"GET DOWN! GET DOWN, SIR!! GET ON THE GROUND, NOW!" They screamed at him.

Zahir obeyed and was placed in cuffs as other agents ran past him to check the hall for more suspects. He never received Sunami's call because his cell phone had been turned off the entire time they were at Watergate!

***

Animal, the normally outrageous one in the group, decided that he would take the elevator. He had simply dumped his gun in an ashtray bucket in the hallway and left his vest on the floor. On the elevator, he pushed the button to the ground floor. While he waited, Animal checked his phone and saw that he had a missed call from Sunami. He dialed his number and got a busy signal.

Animal wondered what Sunami had wanted. He would be seeing him, soon, so for him to call must mean he needed something important. Probably forgot something, Animal, thought. When the bell chimed and the elevator doors opened, Animal was greeted by five agents with guns drawn.

"What's your name? Where are you coming from?" one of the agents demanded.

"I, uh, just left a meeting with my manager, why? What is going on?" Animal asked as if he were worried.

"Get out of the building, sir. We have a terrorist threat inside. Leave, now! Don't look back, just leave, quickly."

"Yes sir! I will, thanks."

And with that, Animal rushed out of the building like a scared little black man! He saw Sunami in the SUV and hurried over. He wondered if Zahir and York would make it out.

***

"You say Animal just came out?" York asked, making his way down the stairs.

"Yeah, he's with me now. Can you make it, Bruh?" Sunami asked, sounding worried.

"I dunno. I hear muthafuckas moving below, hold on."

York passed the sixth floor and saw Special Agent Charles Lavender, himself. Their eyes locked for a second and Lavender raised his gun. York managed to tell Sunami to get the hell out of there before he was subdued.

"GET DOWN, McNeal! GET DOWN, ON THE GROUND, NOW!!" Lavender yelled, rushing towards him.

"A'ight, muthafucka, damn! I'm down. Don't shoot."

Lavender grabbed the cell phone out of York's hand and put it to his own ear. But, it was already too late. The call had ended.

"You got three seconds to tell me where he is, or you're gonna need that expensive lawyer, McNeal. Where is McKnight?" Lavender asked.

"Three seconds, huh? Suck my dick, you bitch ass nigga," York exclaimed.

"By the time I'm done with you, you'll be sucking dick for canteen," Agent Lavender promised.

He was notified over the radio that they had another suspect in custody. Sliding between two agents who were lifting York off the ground, Lavender lifted his radio to his mouth.

"Can you confirm identity?" he asked.

"Uh...hold on," came the reply.

Lavender made his way up the stairs towards the eighth floor and pushed the door open to the hallway. He made his way to the numbered address of Obidiah MaTimbu and knocked, forcefully. After several knocks, he twisted the knob and invited himself in. Upon entrance, he noticed the bodyguard's body as well as another medium body resembling a black female on the floor, near the hall.

"Lavender," the radio chirped.

"Go ahead."

"ID of the suspect reads Alonzo Taylor. Not McKnight, sorry. Want me to let him go?"

"Negative. Cuff him and put him in a squad car, I'll speak to him soon."

"Sure thing."

"Oh, and send a medical examiner and forensic specialist team to the eighth floor, asap. It's a mess up here."

Lavender moved over to the kitchen and the smell of blood was very strong. Once in view, he saw Obidiah MaTimbu completely naked and bound to the chair. There was a large knife jabbed in his left pectoral, about where the heart was and what looked like a penis hanging from his mouth. His body was covered in blood, as was the floor and chair. Lavender gagged and tried extremely hard not to puke! There was a lot he didn't know about what went on, but, one thing was for sure: Marcus McKnight had gotten his revenge, tenfold.

***

Sunami navigated the Kia SUV through the streets of Washington, DC, at a fast pace. For the second time in less than twenty-four hours, he was running for his freedom and, the truth was, he was scared shitless!

Animal was losing his cool in the passenger seat, next to Sunami.

"Gotdamn! Sunami, this shit is getting way too crazy, homie. First we get paid crazy money for these crazy ass missions. Then, the muthafucka who paying us is setting us up to die and he keeps tryna put the man on us! What the fuck, yo!? Please tell me it's BANGA TIME. I'm gon' cut that bitch ass nigga Bird's head off. Dat's my word, nigga," Animal declared.

"Don't even trip, bruh. We gotta lay low, for now. I know the feds probably got the airport on smash, but, we gon get that muthafucka," Sunami promised.

"Bruh, we need to hurry up and get down there to ATL, because if he was planning to get us to kill Obidiah, then, get us knocked for it, he'll know by sometime tomorrow that all of us didn't get caught. Especially you, because if the FBI apprehended you, it'll be all over the news."

"But we can't rush, Animal. The airport is a hell no, and unless you want me to drive down to Georgia, starting right now, we will have to lay low for tonight. But you got a good point, though."

"No, we have to go now! Sunami, they are gonna comb this city looking for you. Get on the muthafucka highway and I will help you drive. It ain't nothing but bout eight hours of driving, or so. I got you. We'll be there by early morning, we can get some sleep on the way there and strike his ass around noon, if not earlier."

"One problem, Animal," Sunami said. "What?"

"We ain't got no guns, or nothing!"

"Nigga, you better call in a favor!! How many people owe you. I know you can get guns by morning in G.A."

"Hand me my phone."

***

Bird sat inside his office, talking on the phone with a potential business partner. He figured with Cuba Sanchez and Obidiah MaTimbu out of his way, the opportunities for financial gain were limitless. If only he could find a trustworthy, reliable partner. The man on the phone with Bird, now, had his own drug Cartel in South America and had a very strong tie to Escobar's family. Pablo Escobar, that is!

That was why Bird was trying to convince the man to partner with him, so that he could get an amazing discount on high quality products in large quantities. But, convincing him was turning out to be harder than Bird had expected. He was starting to get the impression that this Puerto Rican drug lord, Cali Ocho, didn't like him very much. And from what Bird had heard, it wouldn't be wise for him to cop an attitude with Cali Ocho, or get sassy on the phone with him. It was said that he started and ended wars, successfully, in the blink of an eye!

"Cali, just hear me out. Can I call you Cali?" Bird asked, trying for charm.

"No," Cali Ocho said, firmly.

"Mr. Ocho, this is an opportunity that I'm willing to share. I'm pretty sure you are aware that I am capable of doing this myself. It's just that there is so much food we can do as partners, with your connections and my setup."

"And you claim that you've managed to take out the muscle of the Mexican Mafia, the head and the under boss of the Italian Mafia, the African mercenaries, and, the second largest Cartel in America, Wolfpack Cartel?" Cali Ocho asked, skeptically.

"By myself. I'm sure you've been watching the news, Mr. Ocho. You can confirm the deaths of Luigi Portellini, Cuba Sanchez, Bruno Hernandez and, very shortly, the release of the news about Carmen Portellini's death as well as Obidiah MaTimbu. I guess you can say I've been pretty busy on this project. Now, the head of Wolfpack Cartel ran into a snag with the FBI. So, he's outta here, I promise Now is the time to move. We can set up shop, get some people in place around the area and start delivering..."

"Hold up, cuzzo. Maybe the news I watch is a different station from the one you watch. But what I've seen on CNN is Sunami's name wanted for the murders of Cuba Sanchez and Bruno Hernandez. And he's wanted for questioning in the death of Luigi Portellini. Now, I dunno this guy, Sunami. I've only done a little research on him and his credentials are definitely more impressive than yours. But, I'm tryna figure out how you mixed up the fact that you got rid of these people with the real story of Marcus McKnight killing these men? How is that?"

"Mr. Ocho, c'mon!" Bird laughed. "Do you actually think a man of my status actually dirties his own hands? That would be plain stupid! I orchestrated the entire thing. I paid Sunami to take care of business. I'll admit, he's done a great job, but, let's be serious, here, Cali Ocho. I, Birdman, am the brains behind the muscle. What is a strong hand without the mind to instruct it?"

"And did you happen to orchestrate Sunami and his crew into the hands of the FBI?" Cali Ocho asked.

"C'mon, Mr. Ocho! What do you take me for? I paid good money for their help. The problems they encountered while doing the job is covered in the pavement. It's no longer my problem what happens to Sunami. It's just convenient, that's all. Hell, that man got money. If he can't find a loophole, he should've never gotten into the game. It's like Denzel Washington said in the !movie, Training Day. The world is full of sheep and wolves. In order to protect the sheep, the authorities have to become wolves because the sheep can't survive on their own. My thing is this! Is Sunami a sheep or is he a wolf? If he's a wolf, he should know how to survive the most complex of situations. If he can't, he ain't no wolf. He just a sheep in wolf clothing!" Bird explained.

"Uh-huh. Well, as stimulating as that was, Mr. Delgado, I have business to attend to, here, in Puerto Rico."

"So, are you refusing my offer, Mr. Ocho? Because, I'ma tell ya, there are plenty who would like to be in, but, I chose you. I chose you because of the potential we have to succeed, together."

"Rrrrrrr, riiiight. I'll let you know in a week what I decide. Things like this have to be thought about, ya feel me cuz? I mean, I ain't no dummy. You can't jump into bed with every bitch that looks cute, right? So, I'll let you know."

"Good point, Mr. Ocho. Give me a call."

Bird hung up the phone feeling good about the conversation. Secretly, he prayed Cali Ocho didn't leave him out for dry, because truthfully, there was no one else. People were beginning to catch on to the devious ways of George Birdman Delgado! But fuck'em! That's what Bird always said. Hell, he was rich and he was on top. If niggas won't tryna win, they shouldn't play the game, at all. Bird-man, and his boss, were in it to win it. And that meant by any means necessary!

Keese

Chapter 24

Monday morning a group of armed Italian men gathered at a private helicopter pad in Panama City, Florida. At the head of the group, Giovanni stood clad in a black sweater, black cargo pants, black boots and black gloves on his hands. The other twenty or so men dressed similarly and they all wore guns in various places. Giovanni grabbed their attention.

"The boss has declared war on the Byrd Cartel. Days ago, an attempt on her life was followed by false information given to the feds that led to a manhunt of one of her close, personal friends and business associates. We will eliminate this one man who has caused our sister, Carmen, so much stress. Any living creature who stands in the way of us reaching our goal must be eliminated, also. These are orders from Carmen, herself. I don't anticipate a lot of resistance because this will be a surprise attack. But whatever resistance we encounter must be neutralized. For the sake of La Cosa Nostra. An eye for and eye, a tooth for a tooth," Giovanni preached.

Each of the twenty-plus men nodded their heads in agreement. They were all employed, or related, to the Portellini family. In fact, in that very crowd was the group of men who had carried out the hit on Marcus Santiago, previously. For the Portellini woman they would ride, and for the Portellini woman they would die. In their eyes, the Byrd Cartel was obsolete. George Delgado was a dead man walking!

***

After almost a twelve-hour drive from Washington, DC, to Atlanta, Georgia, Sunami and Animal found a hotel near the outskirts, closer to Bird's castle-like house. After a couple late night test runs, Sunami found that Bird's home was only a twenty-five-minute drive away. The two of them got rooms and slept until late morning. Sunami was putting his clothes on when there was a firm, but brief, knock at his room door. He opened the door to cool air, but nobody was there.

There was only a thick dark green duffel bag at his feet in the hall. Sunami pulled the bag inside his room and peeked out his doorway to the left and to the right where he saw the back of a medium build man, about six feet tall, leaving his hall. The night before, Sunami had gotten in contact with his wife's uncle in New York and arranged for some hardware and some ammunition to be transported to him as fast as humanly possible. Hypnotic's uncle had assured Sunami at he would be well equipped by morning and sent his best wishes. Sunami sat at the end of his bed at the Comfort INN and opened the duffel bag.

Inside, he found four handgun's, each with extra clips, two MP-40 submachine guns and two assault rifles. One Calico and one AK-47 fully automatic. There were also a couple sharp knives and two level-3 bullet proof vests, brand new. Sunami spread the items on his bed and picked up the phone to call Animal's room.

"Yeah?" Animal answered, sounding wide awake.

"The shipment just came. It's time to get even," Sunami said.

Within minutes, Animal was inside Sunami's room, dressed and ready to cause havoc! He took two Sig Sauer P-226 9mm pistols, a MP-40, the Calico, a vest and two knives. Sunami strapped up with the rest, taking two Ruger P95's and the rest of the weapons. They loaded up the SUV they were driving and went to a Waffle House restaurant to eat breakfast. Neither of them said a word the entire time they ate.

All Sunami focused on was the channel of his anger from the attacks on his life and being set up numerous times to fuel his hatred for George Delgado. Animal was just plum crazy! He didn't need fuel for his fire. He was born ready to pop a nigga ass! But it did help that he, too, had been set up to go down at Watergate and knowing that Bird was responsible for that and the attacks on Sunami and York's family. That was sure to bite Bird in the ass if Animal got a hold of him first!!

After they both finished eating, Sunami tossed two twenties on the table and they went out to the car. When they got in, Sunami took a deep breath, closed his eyes and said a small prayer for forgiveness and protection. When he was done, he started the Kia Borrego and turned to Animal.

"You ready, my nig?" he asked.

"You goddamn right, homie. IT'S BANGA TIME!!" Animal exclaimed.

***

Bird woke up Monday around 12:50 in his king-sized bed alongside Emanny, Bird's guard.

Since he and his wife split, Bird didn't find it necessary to get into anything serious, for the time being. So, he began sleeping with his guard who had lately been taking their sexual relationship too far mentally. It was like because she was fucking him, she felt as if she was entitled to an opinion, all of a sudden! The nerve of some hoes! Bird's previous wife had moved to Haiti, for good, to be with her family and her struggling people. Good fucking riddance, is what Bird said.

He made his way to his bathroom to take a leak. His right-hand man, Kindu, was scheduled to be there soon. Since they would be revising his plan on the drug distribution take over, Bird decided he'd better go ahead and eat before Kindu made it there. He had slid on some sweatpants and some Louis Vuitton slippers and was headed to the stairs when he heard Kindu's car approaching.

"That nigga don't never be late," Bird mumbled to himself.

It was beginning to feel like his life was full of the same old plans made and plans accomplished. It was like everything that happened was already expected, sometimes. What Bird didn't expect was the sound of screening tires and the metallic crash that was his front gate being run though!! Kindu, who was standing in the open front door, flinched at the sound of the crash and whipped his head around to see what was going on. By then, Bird had made it to the bottom of the stairs.

When the speeding black SUV made it up the driveway, Kindu couldn't seem to get his limbs to cooperate with his screaming instinct that was urging him to move!

"What the fuck is...." Bird started to ask, seeing that unrecognized SUV speed up his long driveway.

When the vehicle got close enough, the barrel of the Calico was stuck out the passenger side window and a loud, thunderous burst of gunfire erupted! Kindu, stuck in total shock, took two nearly fatal bullets that caused him to collapse where he stood. Bird, the opposite of Kindu, was quick to react. He wasn't sure who exactly was attacking him, but he was sure that if he didn't get out of the way, he might die! He ran back up the stairs and rang the alarm while waking the naked Emanny from his bed.

He managed to grab a gun before hearing more gun fire downstairs. It sounded louder and closer than before, as if the threat was no longer outside, but in his own house! Surprisingly, Emanny was up, dressed and armed in a matter of seconds. She rushed out of the bedroom door to help the other guards hold the fort down. Bird was only steps behind her.

He figured that nobody would protect what was better than he would. That, and, he wanted to see who was behind this early morning attack. Bird had surely made plenty of enemies in the past years, let alone the past few months! It could be anybody.

***

Charles Lavender had just walked into an interrogation room with the director to question Alonzo Taylor, aka Zahir, about his knowledge on the whereabouts of Marcus McKnight. Zimmerman was already seated in front of Dodd and ready to get some progress out of this investigation. Before Lavender could start his interrogation, though, his cell phone began to ring. He checked the screen and noticed a number that was unfamiliar. Lavender pardoned himself and answered the call, oblivious to Zimmerman's disapproval.

Lavender wanted McKnight and wanted to get him by any means. An unidentified number in his phone could mean the break of all breaks! And was he sure glad he answered this call. "Lavender," he said.

"Yeah, Agent Lavender, this is Agent Fickler, down in the Georgia branch of the Bureau. Do you remember me?" Fickler asked.

"Umm, vaguely. What's up?" Lavender asked.

"I'm the agent who called you with the report on seeing McKnight down here visiting the drug lord, Birdman Delgado."

"Oooh, oh, oh yeah! I do remember. What can I do for you Fick, I'm in the middle of something."

"Uh, it's Fick-ler, and whatever you're doing is irrelevant as of now."

"And what makes you say that?"

"Well, we've got a bit of action, down here in Georgia. It seems to me that there has been an attack, going on as we speak, on Birdman Delgado. Our surveillance indicates that the picture of a black Kia Borrego is, indeed, Marcus 'Sunami' McKnight. We're putting a team together, now, to interfere with the attack. Let me tell ya, there are surely some helluva fireworks going down right now. So, you may wanna get your ass on a plane or chopper and come on down to get your guy. We won't be waiting for you."

"Agent Fickler, I'm on my way. DO NOT move without me, do you understand? Under strict orders from the director himself, don't fucking breathe without my say so, I'm on the first thing smoking, out," Lavender ordered.

He ended the call and stepped back into the DC interrogation room. Zimmerman clearly wanted to know what was going on.

"I need a jet, chopper, spaceship, whatever! I need to get to Georgia, NOW!!!" he demanded.

"What's going on, Lavender?" Zimmerman demanded.

"McKnight is in Atlanta. He's attempting to eliminate George Birdman Delgado, as we speak!"

***

Attempt was an understatement, if there ever was one! In fact, since Sunami had come crashing through Bird's gates, he had managed to successfully kill Kindu, which turned out to be easier than anyone expected, and slaughter four guards and counting. Unfortunately, the muthafuckas just kept on coming! Animal had taken a bullet to the vest, but for the most part was perfectly fine. Sunami was having trouble reloading clips into the Ak-47 fast enough. His anger was so intense that his nerves were practically shot! The overdose of adrenaline wasn't excluded from blame, either.

Sunami was most surprised at the fact that Bird was actually fighting back along with his paid guards. The muthafucka was busting off clips like he was in an Ice Cube movie, or something. Suddenly, Sunami was overcome with the fear that he and Animal might not be enough to take on Bird and his army of island immigrants. And there was no way out of there. No surrender, no retreat!

To add even more fuel to the fire, Sunami could hear the distinctive sound of helicopters, and they signed close as hell!! Hidden behind an overturned wooden table, Sunami took out the empty clip from his Ak-47. That's when he noticed it was the last one. He tossed the rifle and cocked the MP-40 before glancing in Animal's direction. He was behind a couch that was literally being torn to shreds by bullets, seven feet to Sunami's right.

Sunami took a deep breath and popped up like a Jake in a box, spraying bullets every which way. Animal followed his lead with the last clip for the Calico and together they managed to take down six more islanders who were shooting in their direction. Bird was the best concealed behind his army. Then, one of the most craziest things happened. A swarm of gun toting figures dressed in black came from behind Bird's army. Just when Sunami thought it was more of Bird's goons, the group opened fire on the other islanders and ambushed them! The amount of gun fire in the house was deafening as the islander guards scrambled to react to the new threat on their hands.

The newcomers didn't stop Animal for one second. While the guards had their backs turned to him and Sunami, Animal stood tall and mowed them, and anybody standing in his line of fire, down.

Sunami joined him but tried to focus his aim on finding Bird and ending his career! The new coming assassins were surprised at the stray bullets hitting them from behind the overturned table and torn couch. They began to return fire. That is, until Giovanni noticed the familiar face behind the gun.

"STOP! STOP SHOOTING, STOP SHOOTING EVERY-BODY!! STOP!" Giovanni commanded his army.

When most of the shooting ceased, Sunami was able to see that Bird's guards were pretty much finished! Animal was loading another clip into his MP-40 and getting ready to begin firing, again. Hell, he didn't just stop what he was doing because somebody on the other side said so!

"Animal! Hold on, bruh," Sunami whispered across to him.

"What!? Why?" Animal asked, astonished.

"Just chill. Hold on a minute."

The two waited in silence to see what would happen next. Sunami sat down his MP and took out one of his pistols and cocked the slide.

"Sly? Sly, is that you? If it is, this is Gio," Giovanni said, his gun still aimed at the table, just in case.

"It's me, Gio. What the hell are you doing here?" Sunami yelled from behind the table.

"Clean up job. I'm after Bird."

"Oh, yeah? Me too. Did you get him?"

"He's right here. He's been shot, but he ain't dead, yet. I came here under Carmen's orders. She did this for you, Sly," Giovanni informed him.

"I'm coming out. Don't fucking shoot me, yo."

Sunami appeared from behind the couch, gun at a ready position. Giovanni's eyes met his and they both smiled. Sunami motioned for Animal to get up and they both came from behind their hiding places. Sunami heard the faint sound of sirens and panic seized him. Gio seemed to not notice.

"Whass up, man? You wanna finish this piece of shit off, or what?" Giovanni asked.

Without question, Sunami turned and looked at a suffering Bird, who was on the floor, wheezing. He had been shot in the stomach and grazed in the neck. Blood soaked his T-shirt and sweatpants. Sunami raised the Ruger and fired eight shots into Birdman's face without a single blink!

"So..." Gio started to say.

"Ain't no time to talk, Gio. Feds are on the way, we have to get the fuck out of here," Sunami informed him.

"Don't sweat it. We got choppers outside, c'mon."

"Y'all go ahead. As long as I run, they'll come after me and I can't put you in that kind of heat."

"Sunami! What the fuck..." Animal demanded.

"Take my homie wit' y'all. I'm gon turn myself in. It's better if one goes down and the majority go free. They want me, so I'll give them what they want."

"Sly, that's nonsense. We can..."

"Go, Giovanni. I'll take the heat. Just go. You, too, Animal. Call my lawyer, ASAP," Sunami commanded.

The sirens were getting closer but Giovanni only stood and stared at the man he knew as Sly.

"You are a true friend, Sly."

"We'll do better than to call your lawyer for you. Take care. See you, again, soon," Gio said.

Reluctantly, they ran through the house to where the helicopters were. Sunami sat down and waited for Charles Lavender.

Chapter 25

"Your ass is mine, now," Agent Lavender whispered into Sunami's ear.

They were back in California. The federal courtroom they were in looked exactly like every other courtroom Sunami had seen in his lifetime. Oakwood here, oakwood there, blah, blah, blah. It was always the same old shit. He sat beside his hired attorney out of Long Beach, California, Jay M. Glaser.

He was one of LA's top 100 lawyers when it came to criminal defense. He was the founding partner of his firm, Glaser, DaMone, & Schroeder and had been in law practice for twenty-two years. As an AV rated litigator and certified Criminal Law Specialist, Glaser represented clients in all types of criminal matters with expertise in complex felonies, including homicides. He also coated a pretty penny!

After Giovanni, Animal and what was left of the group of Italians got away, the castle-like house belonging to Bird was swarmed with FBI agents and police. They even had a SWAT team on standby, down the street. By the time the agents arrived, Sunami had discarded all his weapons, his gloves and his bulletproof vest. He was outside in front of the stone fountain where a big ass bird was spitting water.

When they reached Sunami, he followed every instruction they gave and was very cooperative with them as they placed him under federal arrest. All that happened after that was a big blur. That incident had been almost four whole months ago. Now, Sunami sat at the defense table with his lawyer as the federal prosecutor sat with Agent Lavender at their table. They were awaiting the judge to arrive.

The courtroom was full to capacity with family, friends, spectators and people with generally nothing to do. Sunami turned in his seat to get a look at the faces. There was his wife and daughters, on the front row. Beside them was his mom and two sisters, Giovanni, Zahir, Animal and Cherry with her two friends. In the rows behind them, he spotted Phame and a few other models from the agency,

York and his team of shooters, Mag, Life, Lamel, Lord, Salaam, Natasha, Fy Chang Lao, Pam and her daughter, some Spanish looking crazy dude in a royal blue suit and plenty of camera people from news stations.

For a moment, Sunami had sworn he saw Carmen standing at the doors in the very back, but, when he looked again, the woman was gone!

"All rise," the bailiff called.

Sunami tuned the cop out as he went through his routine introduction of the judge. All of this shit was surreal. But when the officer said the judges name, a pang of familiarity hit Sunami. He just couldn't place it. And then, the old judge came out and Sunami knew he had seen the man at some time before. But where?

The judge took his seat and the crowd did likewise, after him. He cleared his throat, straightened his glasses and took the flexible microphone at his podium and had it adjusted to his liking.

"Ladies and gentlemen of the court, as you have been told, I am the honorable federal court judge William Elwood. I would like for you all to please remain quiet while I have the floor, so if you would, please, turn off your cellphones, and iPods, or whatever," Judge Elwood said, pausing to give the people a moment.

Even Sunami had to turn his phone off! Then the old judge continued.

"I know you all came here today with expectations. Some of you expected to hear some crazy stories and accusations, while others expected an all-out showdown between the United States government versus this young man, Marcus McKnight. I regret to inform you that there will be neither."

The entire crowd gasped and people began murmuring about what was going on. Charles Lavender's face turned beet red and he began a hushed, intense conversation with the prosecutor, who stood to question the old judge. But Elwood would have none of it. Even Sunami looked to his lawyer, Glaser, in confusion. Glaser only raised his eyebrows and shrugged his shoulders.

"As I said," Judge Elwood began again.

"There will be no trial for Mr. Marcus McKnight, today. It is of my discretion whether the case has merit and I have reviewed the charges and motions filed.

"I found that the case will be dismissed due to insufficient evidence. All monies paid by the defendant for bail shall be returned to him, effective immediately! And I would like to speak to the defendant, Mr. McKnight, in my chambers. Without counsel, if you would, please. That is all. You people have a nice day and enjoy your week. Court is adjourned."

The judge smacked his gavel and motioned for Sunami to follow him out. The crowd erupted in gossip the moment the judge was out of the courtroom.

"This is Fucking outrageous!" Charles Lavender exclaimed.

But Sunami was gone, following the old man down a small hall to his "chambers." At the door, the judge turned around and instructed the bailiff to guard the door, outside. Then, Sunami and Elwood were alone inside the office. He never even spoke., at first. Elwood only handed Sunami a sealed greeting card in a pink envelope. Without hesitation, he opened it and read:

To the second man I've ever loved, I will never forget what you have done for me, Sly. And as a token, I took care of your little legal problem. Don't ever forget that you are mine. One day, I will be coming for what rightfully belongs to me! Forever in love, Carmen P. PS. Show the judge a bit of love for me! Sunami smiled at the card that had two Lions licking one another with a big heart in the background. He knew exactly what Carmen meant when she wrote "show the judge some love."

He got the address of a PO Box that belonged to Elwood and promised his gift of gratitude! With that done, Sunami destroyed the card and trashed it. No evidence. Outside, Sunami was met by his attorney, wife and daughters, as well as a crowd of people. The first question out of everyone's mouth was "what happened?"

Sunami had figured this would be the case, so, he had prepared himself.

"He just apologized for the mix up and told me to stay out of trouble. That's it!" he lied.

This didn't satisfy the crowd. But Sunami and his people could care less. A Mercedes Benz Sprinter Ultimate Limo pulled around and Sunami got inside, along with his family, York and his family, Zahir and Animal, and his wife, Dream. They were going to a restaurant in Beverly Hills to celebrate, called Spago Beverly Hills.

***

The group was so excited about their victories that they didn't even notice the small fleet of vehicles following them.

Nor did they see the familiar face of the crazy looking Spanish guy from the court house as he enjoyed his meal in the same restaurant, less than twenty feet away from them. They didn't even notice that the Spanish guy left as soon as they got up to go, themselves!

Chapter 26

The group decided to have more drinks at Animal's Grand Mediterranean style villa in Pasadena, CA. They allowed the children to play in one of the five bedrooms while they drank and conversed until York and Pam's flight to New York. The house was extravagant. It was a five-bedroom, seven-bathroom house designed by Constantine Hillman that was seated on nearly an acre of flat land with a two-bedroom, one-bathroom guest house. Animal had kicked out four million dollars for it! He had another three million dollars' worth of cars in the front yard!

"Drea, your house is beautiful," Hypnotic complimented.

"Oh my god, yes. It's wonderful, out here," Pam agreed.

"Who did your decorating?" Hypnotic asked.

"Some bitch Animal found on the net, gurl, I dunno. It is hot, though, ain't it?"

"Yeah, this shit is nice, bruh," Sunami complimented.

"So, Sunami, how the fuck did you managed to get the judge to throw out thirty-something charges, including nine murder charges? That shit was...unbelievable. I thought we was gonna have to pull a DUTCH out this bitch!" York asked.

"Yeah, baby. That was kinda off the wall. I mean, your lawyer didn't even say anything. How did you pull that off?" Hypnotic asked.

Sunami smiled at all of them as he took a sip from a bottle of Rozay. He looked at all their anticipating glares and laughed a hearty laugh.

"If I told y'all, I'd have to kill ya!" he said.

They broke out in laughter at his joke. The good-natured laugh was so deep that it continued, on and on. The only thing that stopped it was the unexpected ringing of the doorbell. That got everybody quiet.

"Animal, you expecting somebody else?" Zahir asked.

"Nigga, hell nah! I don't bring people out here to this crib. I don't know who the fuck that could be," Animal declared with seriousness on his face.

"Strap up!" Sunami commanded.

***

The front door was opened by Hypnotic, and the sound of eight guns cocking filled the air! Hypnotic held a Mossberg pump action shotgun at waist level while Sunami held two Smith & Wesson 357s. Pam, Drea, Zahir, and York held various semi-automatic handguns while Animal aimed a mini 14 at the small built figure at the door. Sunami was the first to recognize the five-foot-eight-inch Spanish looking man in a royal blue tailored suit from the federal courtroom.

"Who the fuck is you and what the fuck you want?" Animal asked.

"Please, don't do anything stupid. I got two guys behind me with AR15s aimed at y'all, right now, and I know there are children in the house. I got seven kids myself," the man said.

Sunami glanced over the man's shoulder and noticed, for the first time, a champagne Tahoe on some big chrome wheels. He couldn't see any men, but he did see two infrared beams coming from the tail end of the vehicle and behind the front of the car. The two guys were crouched down out of site but had placed dots on Sunami and Zahir's chest. The man in the tailored blue suit looked to Sunami and raised his eyebrows in a questioning gesture.

"Ay cuz, can I holla at chu for a minute? This is on some business shit. I didn't come here to do nothing to either of y'all," the man said.

"That's the last thing I'm worried 'bout. Who are you?" Sunami asked, stepping outside and giving everyone a signal to stand down.

The two men walked off and down the driveway together, and the infrared beams disappeared momentarily. "My name is Cali Ocho. But you can just call me Hoffa. I need to speak to you on a business proposition."

"A'ight, Hoffa. Speak on," Sunami said.

Hoffa laid out his entire background and gave Sunami a general idea of what it was he did. He told Sunami about being approached by Bird and doing research to find out who he was. Then he told Sunami about Bird's plans and how the open opportunity could benefit the two of them.

"When I found out the nigga was a snake, I fell back, cuz. I couldn't dare do no business wit' a nigga like that. And I respect you for your realness and hard work, and you gangsta, nigga. You did some shit out there that doesn't even need to be spoken about. Just know that I know and I respect that shit. Now, I'm asking you if you wanna do business with me. You got a nice setup. I just wanna be a silent partner in the thing. We can combine forces and whatever you need, just ask. We'll split all profits in half, ya dig? So, what you think, cuz?" Hoffa asked.

"It sounds good. Let me know what you want me to do and we'll do it," Sunami agreed.

"That's whass cracking! We can talk later. I see you chillin' with ya peoples and shit. I don't want to interrupt that too much more than I have. And as a token of my appreciation, anything you need taken care of before we start our movement, say the word and it's done, cuz."

The first thing that popped into Sunami's mind was the person Bird answered to. The person behind the scenes, pulling the strings. Surely, he wouldn't let Bird's death go unanswered. It would be a dent in his pocket that couldn't be ignored!

"Well, there is one lil' problem, Hoffa. Something that has the potential to cause a major problem in the future," Sunami said.

"Name the problem, cuz, and that's word, on my hood it won't exist," Hoffa vowed.

To Be Continued...
Hood Consigliere 3
Coming Soon!!!

Lock Down Publications and Ca$h Presents assisted
publishing packages.

BASIC PACKAGE $499
Editing
Cover Design
Formatting

UPGRADED PACKAGE $800
Typing
Editing
Cover Design
Formatting

ADVANCE PACKAGE $1,200
Typing
Editing
Cover Design
Formatting
Copyright registration
Proofreading
Upload book to Amazon

LDP SUPREME PACKAGE $1,500
Typing
Editing
Cover Design
Formatting
Copyright registration
Proofreading
Set up Amazon account

Upload book to Amazon
Advertise on LDP Amazon and Facebook page

***Other services available upon request. Additional
charges may apply
Lock Down Publications
P.O. Box 944
Stockbridge, GA 30281-9998
Phone # 470 303-9761

Submission Guideline

Submit the first three chapters of your completed manuscript to ldpsubmissions@gmail.com, subject line: Your book's title. The manuscript must be in a .doc file and sent as an attachment. Document should be in Times New Roman, double spaced and in size 12 font. Also, provide your synopsis and full contact information. If sending multiple submissions, they must each be in a separate email.

Have a story but no way to send it electronically? You can still submit to LDP/Ca$h Presents. Send in the first three chapters, written or typed, of your completed manuscript to:

LDP: Submissions Dept
Po Box 944
Stockbridge, Ga 30281

DO NOT send original manuscript. Must be a duplicate.

Provide your synopsis and a cover letter containing your full contact information.

Thanks for considering LDP and Ca$h Presents.

<u>NEW RELEASES</u>

TORN BETWEEN A GANGSTER AND A GENTLEMAN by
J-BLUNT & MISS KIM
BABY, I'M WINTERTIME COLD by MEESHA
ANGEL 4 by ANTHONY FIELDS
HOOD CONSIGLIERE 2 by KEESE

By **T.J. Edwards**
GORILLAZ IN THE BAY V
3X KRAZY III
STRAIGHT BEAST MODE III
De'Kari
KINGPIN KILLAZ IV
STREET KINGS III
PAID IN BLOOD III
CARTEL KILLAZ IV
DOPE GODS III
Hood Rich
SINS OF A HUSTLA II
ASAD
RICH $AVAGE III
By **Martell Troublesome Bolden**
YAYO V
Bred In The Game 2
S. Allen
THE STREETS WILL TALK II
By **Yolanda Moore**
SON OF A DOPE FIEND III
HEAVEN GOT A GHETTO II
SKI MASK MONEY II
By **Renta**
LOYALTY AIN'T PROMISED III
By **Keith Williams**
I'M NOTHING WITHOUT HIS LOVE II

SINS OF A THUG II

TO THE THUG I LOVED BEFORE II

IN A HUSTLER I TRUST II

By Monet Dragun

QUIET MONEY IV

EXTENDED CLIP III

THUG LIFE IV

By **Trai'Quan**

THE STREETS MADE ME IV

By **Larry D. Wright**

IF YOU CROSS ME ONCE II

ANGEL V

By **Anthony Fields**

THE STREETS WILL NEVER CLOSE IV

By K'ajji

HARD AND RUTHLESS III

KILLA KOUNTY III

By Khufu

MONEY GAME III

By Smoove Dolla

JACK BOYS VS DOPE BOYS IV

A GANGSTA'S QUR'AN V

COKE GIRLZ II

COKE BOYS II

LIFE OF A SAVAGE V

CHI'RAQ GANGSTAS V

By Romell Tukes

MURDA WAS THE CASE III

Elijah R. Freeman

THE STREETS NEVER LET GO III

By Robert Baptiste

AN UNFORESEEN LOVE IV

BABY, I'M WINTERTIME COLD II

By **Meesha**

MONEY MAFIA II

By **Jibril Williams**

QUEEN OF THE ZOO III

By **Black Migo**

VICIOUS LOYALTY III

By Kingpen

A GANGSTA'S PAIN III

By J-Blunt

CONFESSIONS OF A JACKBOY III

By Nicholas Lock

GRIMEY WAYS III

By Ray Vinci

KING KILLA II

By Vincent "Vitto" Holloway

BETRAYAL OF A THUG II

By Fre$h

THE MURDER QUEENS III

By Michael Gallon

THE BIRTH OF A GANGSTER III

By Delmont Player

TREAL LOVE II

By Le'Monica Jackson

FOR THE LOVE OF BLOOD II

By Jamel Mitchell

RAN OFF ON DA PLUG II

By Paper Boi Rari

HOOD CONSIGLIERE III

By Keese

PRETTY GIRLS DO NASTY THINGS II

By Nicole Goosby

PROTÉGÉ OF A LEGEND II

By Corey Robinson

IT'S JUST ME AND YOU II

By Ah'Million

BORN IN THE GRAVE II

By Self Made Tay

FOREVER GANGSTA III

By Adrian Dulan

GORILLAZ IN THE TRENCHES II

By SayNoMore

Available Now

RESTRAINING ORDER **I & II**
By **CA$H & Coffee**
LOVE KNOWS NO BOUNDARIES **I II & III**
By **Coffee**
RAISED AS A GOON I, II, III & IV
BRED BY THE SLUMS I, II, III
BLAST FOR ME I & II
ROTTEN TO THE CORE I II III
A BRONX TALE I, II, III
DUFFLE BAG CARTEL I II III IV V VI
HEARTLESS GOON I II III IV V
A SAVAGE DOPEBOY I II
DRUG LORDS I II III
CUTTHROAT MAFIA I II
KING OF THE TRENCHES
By **Ghost**
LAY IT DOWN **I & II**
LAST OF A DYING BREED I II
BLOOD STAINS OF A SHOTTA I & II III
By **Jamaica**
LOYAL TO THE GAME I II III
LIFE OF SIN I, II III
By **TJ & Jelissa**
BLOODY COMMAS I & II

SKI MASK CARTEL I II & III

KING OF NEW YORK I II,III IV V

RISE TO POWER I II III

COKE KINGS I II III IV V

BORN HEARTLESS I II III IV

KING OF THE TRAP I II

By **T.J. Edwards**

IF LOVING HIM IS WRONG...I & II

LOVE ME EVEN WHEN IT HURTS I II III

By **Jelissa**

WHEN THE STREETS CLAP BACK I & II III

THE HEART OF A SAVAGE I II III IV

MONEY MAFIA

LOYAL TO THE SOIL I II III

By **Jibril Williams**

A DISTINGUISHED THUG STOLE MY HEART I II & III

LOVE SHOULDN'T HURT I II III IV

RENEGADE BOYS I II III IV

PAID IN KARMA I II III

SAVAGE STORMS I II III

AN UNFORESEEN LOVE I II III

BABY, I'M WINTERTIME COLD

By **Meesha**

A GANGSTER'S CODE I &, II III

A GANGSTER'S SYN I II III

THE SAVAGE LIFE I II III

CHAINED TO THE STREETS I II III

BLOOD ON THE MONEY I II III

A GANGSTA'S PAIN I II

By J-Blunt

PUSH IT TO THE LIMIT

By **Bre' Hayes**

BLOOD OF A BOSS **I, II, III, IV, V**

SHADOWS OF THE GAME

TRAP BASTARD

By **Askari**

THE STREETS BLEED MURDER **I, II & III**

THE HEART OF A GANGSTA I II& III

By **Jerry Jackson**

CUM FOR ME I II III IV V VI VII VIII

An **LDP Erotica Collaboration**

BRIDE OF A HUSTLA **I II & II**

THE FETTI GIRLS **I, II& III**

CORRUPTED BY A GANGSTA I, II III, IV

BLINDED BY HIS LOVE

THE PRICE YOU PAY FOR LOVE I, II ,III

DOPE GIRL MAGIC I II III

By **Destiny Skai**

WHEN A GOOD GIRL GOES BAD

By **Adrienne**

THE COST OF LOYALTY I II III

By Kweli

A GANGSTER'S REVENGE **I II III & IV**

THE BOSS MAN'S DAUGHTERS I II III IV V

Keese

A SAVAGE LOVE **I & II**

BAE BELONGS TO ME I II

A HUSTLER'S DECEIT I, II, III

WHAT BAD BITCHES DO I, II, III

SOUL OF A MONSTER I II III

KILL ZONE

A DOPE BOY'S QUEEN I II III

TIL DEATH

By **Aryanna**

A KINGPIN'S AMBITON

A KINGPIN'S AMBITION **II**

I MURDER FOR THE DOUGH

By **Ambitious**

TRUE SAVAGE I II III IV V VI VII

DOPE BOY MAGIC I, II, III

MIDNIGHT CARTEL I II III

CITY OF KINGZ I II

NIGHTMARE ON SILENT AVE

THE PLUG OF LIL MEXICO II

CLASSIC CITY

By **Chris Green**

A DOPEBOY'S PRAYER

By **Eddie "Wolf" Lee**

THE KING CARTEL **I, II & III**

By **Frank Gresham**

THESE NIGGAS AIN'T LOYAL **I, II & III**

By **Nikki Tee**

GANGSTA SHYT **I II &III**

By **CATO**

THE ULTIMATE BETRAYAL

By **Phoenix**

BOSS'N UP **I , II & III**

By **Royal Nicole**

I LOVE YOU TO DEATH

By **Destiny J**

I RIDE FOR MY HITTA

I STILL RIDE FOR MY HITTA

By **Misty Holt**

LOVE & CHASIN' PAPER

By **Qay Crockett**

TO DIE IN VAIN

SINS OF A HUSTLA

By **ASAD**

BROOKLYN HUSTLAZ

By **Boogsy Morina**

BROOKLYN ON LOCK I & II

By **Sonovia**

GANGSTA CITY

By **Teddy Duke**

A DRUG KING AND HIS DIAMOND I & II III

A DOPEMAN'S RICHES

HER MAN, MINE'S TOO I, II

CASH MONEY HO'S

THE WIFEY I USED TO BE I II

Keese

PRETTY GIRLS DO NASTY THINGS
By Nicole Goosby
TRAPHOUSE KING **I II & III**
KINGPIN KILLAZ I II III
STREET KINGS I II
PAID IN BLOOD **I II**
CARTEL KILLAZ I II III
DOPE GODS I II
By **Hood Rich**
LIPSTICK KILLAH **I, II, III**
CRIME OF PASSION I II & III
FRIEND OR FOE I II III
By **Mimi**
STEADY MOBBN' **I, II, III**
THE STREETS STAINED MY SOUL I II III
By **Marcellus Allen**
WHO SHOT YA **I, II, III**
SON OF A DOPE FIEND I II
HEAVEN GOT A GHETTO
SKI MASK MONEY
Renta
GORILLAZ IN THE BAY **I II III IV**
TEARS OF A GANGSTA I II
3X KRAZY I II
STRAIGHT BEAST MODE I II
DE'KARI
TRIGGADALE I II III

240

MURDAROBER WAS THE CASE I II

Elijah R. Freeman

GOD BLESS THE TRAPPERS I, II, III

THESE SCANDALOUS STREETS I, II, III

FEAR MY GANGSTA I, II, III IV, V

THESE STREETS DON'T LOVE NOBODY I, II

BURY ME A G I, II, III, IV, V

A GANGSTA'S EMPIRE I, II, III, IV

THE DOPEMAN'S BODYGAURD I II

THE REALEST KILLAZ I II III

THE LAST OF THE OGS I II III

Tranay Adams

THE STREETS ARE CALLING

Duquie Wilson

MARRIED TO A BOSS I II III

By Destiny Skai & Chris Green

KINGZ OF THE GAME I II III IV V VI

Playa Ray

SLAUGHTER GANG I II III

RUTHLESS HEART I II III

By Willie Slaughter

FUK SHYT

By Blakk Diamond

DON'T F#CK WITH MY HEART I II

By Linnea

ADDICTED TO THE DRAMA I II III

IN THE ARM OF HIS BOSS II

By Jamila
YAYO I II III IV
A SHOOTER'S AMBITION I II
BRED IN THE GAME
By S. Allen
TRAP GOD I II III
RICH $AVAGE I II
MONEY IN THE GRAVE I II III
By Martell Troublesome Bolden
FOREVER GANGSTA I II
GLOCKS ON SATIN SHEETS I II
By Adrian Dulan
TOE TAGZ I II III IV
LEVELS TO THIS SHYT I II
IT'S JUST ME AND YOU
By Ah'Million
KINGPIN DREAMS I II III
RAN OFF ON DA PLUG
By Paper Boi Rari
CONFESSIONS OF A GANGSTA I II III IV
CONFESSIONS OF A JACKBOY I II
By Nicholas Lock
I'M NOTHING WITHOUT HIS LOVE
SINS OF A THUG
TO THE THUG I LOVED BEFORE
A GANGSTA SAVED XMAS
IN A HUSTLER I TRUST

By Monet Dragun

CAUGHT UP IN THE LIFE I II III

THE STREETS NEVER LET GO I II

By Robert Baptiste

NEW TO THE GAME I II III

MONEY, MURDER & MEMORIES I II III

By **Malik D. Rice**

LIFE OF A SAVAGE I II III IV

A GANGSTA'S QUR'AN I II III IV

MURDA SEASON I II III

GANGLAND CARTEL I II III

CHI'RAQ GANGSTAS I II III IV

KILLERS ON ELM STREET I II III

JACK BOYZ N DA BRONX I II III

A DOPEBOY'S DREAM I II III

JACK BOYS VS DOPE BOYS I II III

COKE GIRLZ

COKE BOYS

By Romell Tukes

LOYALTY AIN'T PROMISED I II

By Keith Williams

QUIET MONEY I II III

THUG LIFE I II III

EXTENDED CLIP I II

A GANGSTA'S PARADISE

By **Trai'Quan**

THE STREETS MADE ME I II III

Keese

By **Larry D. Wright**

THE ULTIMATE SACRIFICE I, II, III, IV, V, VI

KHADIFI

IF YOU CROSS ME ONCE

ANGEL I II III IV

IN THE BLINK OF AN EYE

By **Anthony Fields**

THE LIFE OF A HOOD STAR

By **Ca$h & Rashia Wilson**

THE STREETS WILL NEVER CLOSE I II III

By **K'ajji**

CREAM I II III

THE STREETS WILL TALK

By **Yolanda Moore**

NIGHTMARES OF A HUSTLA I II III

By **King Dream**

CONCRETE KILLA I II III

VICIOUS LOYALTY I II

By **Kingpen**

HARD AND RUTHLESS I II

MOB TOWN 251

THE BILLIONAIRE BENTLEYS I II III

By **Von Diesel**

GHOST MOB

Stilloan Robinson

MOB TIES I II III IV V VI

SOUL OF A HUSTLER, HEART OF A KILLER

GORILLAZ IN THE TRENCHES

By SayNoMore

BODYMORE MURDERLAND I II III

THE BIRTH OF A GANGSTER I II

By Delmont Player

FOR THE LOVE OF A BOSS

By C. D. Blue

MOBBED UP I II III IV

THE BRICK MAN I II III IV

THE COCAINE PRINCESS I II III IV V

By King Rio

KILLA KOUNTY I II III

By Khufu

MONEY GAME I II

By Smoove Dolla

A GANGSTA'S KARMA I II

By FLAME

KING OF THE TRENCHES I II III

by **GHOST & TRANAY ADAMS**

QUEEN OF THE ZOO I II

By **Black Migo**

GRIMEY WAYS I II

By Ray Vinci

XMAS WITH AN ATL SHOOTER

By Ca$h & Destiny Skai

KING KILLA

By Vincent "Vitto" Holloway

BETRAYAL OF A THUG

By Fre$h

THE MURDER QUEENS I II

By Michael Gallon

TREAL LOVE

By Le'Monica Jackson

FOR THE LOVE OF BLOOD

By Jamel Mitchell

HOOD CONSIGLIERE I II

By Keese

PROTÉGÉ OF A LEGEND

By Corey Robinson

BORN IN THE GRAVE

By Self Made Tay

MOAN IN MY MOUTH

By XTASY

TORN BETWEEN A GANGSTER AND A GENTLEMAN

By J-BLUNT & Miss Kim

<u>BOOKS BY LDP'S CEO, CA$H</u>

TRUST IN NO MAN

TRUST IN NO MAN 2

TRUST IN NO MAN 3

BONDED BY BLOOD

SHORTY GOT A THUG

THUGS CRY

THUGS CRY 2

THUGS CRY 3

TRUST NO BITCH

TRUST NO BITCH 2

TRUST NO BITCH 3

TIL MY CASKET DROPS

RESTRAINING ORDER

RESTRAINING ORDER 2

IN LOVE WITH A CONVICT

LIFE OF A HOOD STAR

XMAS WITH AN ATL SHOOTER

Keese